A Man Who Starts

Stefani Wilder

Tipped Z: Book 2

Stefani Wilder is a pen name for Robin Stephen

text copyright © 2015 by Robin Theodora Stephen Deutschendorf

stefaniwilder.com
robinstephen.com

PRINT ISBN: 978-0692517727
E-BOOK ISBN: 978-0-9844912-8-5

Brown Wing Press
Iowa City, IA
brownwingpress.com

First Brown Wing Press Edition

BOOKS BY STEFANI WILDER

A Man Who Rides
A Man Who Starts
A Man Who Heals

Vaquera's Haven
Vaquera's Bronc

For Brian—the only cowboy for me.

Chapter 1

I barreled through the swinging doors of the saloon. They clacked as I hit them, swinging crazily with the force of my exit. Outside, I drew the hot air into my lungs and oriented myself towards a knot of people gathered in the dusty street below. "Get back, everyone." I bellowed the words at the top of my voice, straining to reach as many ears as possible. "She's gonna blow!"

With no greater explanation, I ran across the wooden porch and leapt off the edge. My horse, tied to the nearby hitching post, shied away from my leap. I didn't have time to reassure him. I crammed my hat lower on my head, untied the rope that held him in place, and flung myself into the saddle. I collected my reins and wheeled the horse. He needed no encouragement. He spun away from the fence with a squeal, tossing his head against the tie-down he wore.

An explosion sounded as we sped into the street,. The booms and rumbles reverberated throughout the town. Clouds of gray smoke billowed from the swinging door I'd exited moments before. A man blew out with the smoke, staggering backwards and slamming against the porch railing with a dramatic crash. He fell onto his back and lay prone.

I barely gave the man a second glance. The horse was a coil of nervous energy beneath me. I opened him up. We galloped away, careening past the wooden buildings and heading for the outskirts of town.

Around us, people milled in groups among the weather-beaten buildings. Sunburned tourists in floppy hats, family groups with ice-cream smeared children, and random clusters of sullen teenagers drifted from one attraction to another in the time-honored shuffle of the theme-park goer. Many of them stopped as I thundered by. They stared at me, then turned to gape towards the rising smoke.

"They've blown the safe." I shouted this warning several times as I rode, pointing back towards town. My last task as I fled the scene was to attract as many people to the drama that was about to unfold as possible.

Finally, the galloping horse passed the last of the worn buildings. We continued into the less cultivated land beyond. Soon we were on a deserted road surrounded by scrub desert. We'd left all the spectators behind.

I checked the horse to a more sedate pace. He was excited and not inclined to slow. He had no feel for my seat. I had to haul him down with the reins. He snorted but slowed a little with each check. Behind me, I could hear the amplified voices of the main actors ringing over the rooftops as the familiar safe robbery skit played out.

As the town and all associated noise fell away behind us, the horse began to relax. I was able to ease him from a canter to a lope to a trot to a prance. At last, he made one final downshift. He dropped to a walk and released a huge sigh. The feeling of frantic nerves and energy drained out of him. I patted his sweat-soaked neck and let him walk up the slow rise to the stable complex, rewarding his quiet eagerness with a loose rein.

He wasn't a bad horse. None of them were. They were just used hard, with too much running around getting their heads hauled off by people who barely knew how to ride. The horses weren't the priority around here. Entertainment was.

Behind me, I heard a cheer rise from spectators I could no longer see. The thunder of hooves drifted up from the set and the pop of distant gunshots filled the air. My horse stiffened again and strained towards the sound. I let him stop a few feet away from the stable and swung out of the saddle. "They're blanks, Twitchy." I smoothed his forelock and organized the reins. We were almost through the season and he still spooked at all the same things.

I tipped his nose back in my direction and pulled off his bridle. He gave another sigh as I loosened his cinch a few notches. I led him to the pen where the two other horses that made up my performance string stood dozing in the shade of a ramada. Turning Twitchy out with the others, I hung his bridle up and undid the top button of the wool vest I wore, glancing at the empty path to the stable to reassure myself no wayward tourist would see me. Then I checked the clock on the lock screen of my phone and swore under my breath. Cody was always starting this skit late. Though my part was minimal, it was my part. I often had to wait around as his team tinkered with the strange mass of materials that produced the smoke for the explosion.

Now, as usual, I was pressed for time. I hustled into the barn and down the aisle, hurrying past pens where more horses stood. I removed my hat and removed the pins that held my long braid to the top of my head. I launched myself into the dressing room, barely waiting for the curtain to drop shut behind me before I started to paw at the buttons and laces that held my garb in place. Most of my clothing was authentic, which meant it took for-freaking ever to get on and off. Before zippers, apparently, the way to create form-fitting garments was the employment of endless rows of tiny buttons.

I listened as I hurried through my costume change. Other riders were returning from the skit now. I heard Chuck and Paul trot up, laughing at some joke. They dismounted, spurs jingling.

I disrobed down to my underclothes. The main problem was the sports bra. In the skit I'd briefly starred in, I was a young man. I wore slacks and a vest over a blousy shirt, my hair concealed beneath my hat. While I was not the most well-endowed woman on the face of the earth, I couldn't pass as a man without taking certain steps. I was wearing two sports bras, the one on top a good deal tighter than the other.

I began the process of shimmying out of the ultra-tight bra as more riders returned. What had been a quiet, secluded building a moment before now filled with the rise and fall of conversation and the thump and thuds of horse hooves.

It was late in the season, which meant it was hot. And since it was hot, I was sweaty. This made getting in and out of clothing more difficult than usual. With a grunt and a final heave, I pried myself free of the damp, clinging bra. I tossed it into my hamper.

"Bandit Queen stage call in fifteen." Cara's crisp voice cut through the general din. I sighed and pulled on a blouse and split skirts. Finally, I crammed my feet into the knee-high packers I would wear for my next roll.

As I fumbled with more laces, there was a tap on my doorjamb. Cara's voice sounded through the curtain. "Nora, need help with anything?"

I resisted the urge to complain about the late start of the previous skit. After all, it wasn't Cara's fault any more than it was mine. I tied off my cuffs and smoothed my hair, trying to decide if I should redo the braid. "I'm good," I said. "One bandit queen coming right up."

○

I left work hot, exhausted, and later than expected. Which is to say it was a normal day around *Old Pueblo: the Authentic Western Experience*. My bandit queen duties discharged once again, I found myself piloting my old Dodge Power Wagon out of a parking lot that was nearly empty, though it had been packed to the gills a mere hour before. I had rinsed off the worst of the dust and sweat and make-up and changed into user-friendly, modern clothing. I was no longer an accessory to a robbery or a bandit queen. I was an unremarkable young woman in her mid-twenties.

I hummed as I drove. The Power Wagon's radio had gone out at some point. I'd removed it, planning to find a replacement. But the hole in the dash had been there for over six months now, gaping at me with mild resentment and sometimes letting inexplicable puffs of dust into the cab.

The truck was something of an indulgence. The thing was ancient—older than me. It spouted black exhaust when started on cold mornings, rattled over washboard so hard it made your teeth shake, and the gas mileage was abysmal. But when I'd turned sixteen my father had said (somewhat cruelly, in retrospect) he'd give me the old truck if I could make it run. It had been sitting on blocks for years and I'd known nothing about working on cars at the time. I'm pretty sure he'd tossed the offer out there as a way to put an end to my constant applications for my own car without actually giving in.

My father should have known better. When I want something, I go after it. At 16, I wanted freedom enough to take up the life of an amateur mechanic.

I don't think my dad counted on the internet. It only took a few Google searches before I landed on the right forum. There I found an entire posse of enthusiastic Power Wagon owners willing to guide me. Nearly a decade later, I suppose I continued to drive the grizzled thing partially out of spite, partially out of affection.

Fortunately, I didn't drive much. My regular circuit included the short trip from my apartment to Old Pueblo and the even shorter trip from my apartment to the ranch where I'd grown up: the Tipped Z.

I was still humming when I reached the electronic gate that marked the ranch's property line. I punched in the gate code and sat looking at the dusty landscape as the entry unbarred, ignoring the cluster of signs that promised dire consequences for trespassers. When the gate was open, I continued up the long, gently curving drive and rumbled past the low-slung barn and ranch house. I continued down a narrower branch of the driveway. It descended, wrapping around a little ridge. There, nestled up against the hillside, was my brother's house.

I parked out front and stepped from my cab into the silence left when I killed the truck's engine. I gathered my things and headed for the door, which Erin pushed open for me before I could knock. Her eyes took in the state of my face. "You look exhausted. How was work?"

I grimaced, unable to overlook the contrast. Erin, as ever, looked calm and composed.

I laughed as she turned and led me to the kitchen, some of the tension from the day draining away. The Power Wagon had an AC and that AC did even produce an infinitesimal amount of cool air. But my brother's house had been built with maximum attention paid to details like energy efficiency. It was deliciously cool inside. I went to the sink and poured myself a glass of water while Erin grabbed two beers from the fridge and popped them open.

I stood by the counter for a moment, sipping the water. "It's the same old thing. I'm supposed to be everywhere at once, playing every role, resolving every issue that might crop up with any horse, all while using and wearing only clothing and equipment society abandoned a century ago."

Erin laughed, handing me a beer. She was barefoot and her hair was tied back in a ponytail. "They rely on you because you're the only good hand they've ever had around that place."

I gave a shrug. The house was clean and quiet, copper countertops gleaming in the light that spilled through the large windows. Outside lay a view of the empty desert with the mountains shouldering towards the sky. I felt myself relax another few notches. I took a sip of beer and drifted towards the living room. "I've got two hands, like everyone else. I can only work so many miracles at a time."

Erin, who was my soon-to-be-sister-in-law, followed me with a mildly amused expression. Erin was often mildly amused. Or mildly annoyed. Or mildly some other thing. It was one of the things that made her a good friend. She was the steady type.

I reached the living room and flopped into the armchair that had once belonged to my grandfather. Erin settled onto the couch. Though she lived here now, there was still something cautious about how she treated the furniture. It was as if she wasn't convinced it would be seemly for her to appear too comfortable.

We sat in the quiet for a moment. My eyes settled on the large photograph that hung on the wall behind Erin's head. It was a beautiful shot, all whites and blacks and high contrast. Silhouettes of horses and riders stood out against a field of dust. I was one of those riders, flanked by my brother and father and mother. Clint's first wife had been behind the lens. She'd died years ago. While I was glad my brother had finally moved on, I still sometimes felt an odd little lurch when I remembered the way she used to watch us, always smiling and snapping photos.

I slid my eyes to the side, hoping Erin hadn't noticed me giving the photo any more attention than usual. Outside, the light was fading. The mountains stood out against a pink and orange sky, brilliant in the late light. "Anyway, work is work. There are more important things to talk about. Are you ready?"

I meant the question to be playful, but it came out sounding serious. I was no stranger to attending almost-brides. Many of my high school friends were now married. I'd inhabited the position of maid-of-honor more than once. In most cases, this kind of question would have elicited a few gushy giggles and a heart-felt confession about a broken nail or an annoying relative who insisted on including something embarrassing in the ceremony or the party favors.

Erin, however, was not like most of my girlfriends. Beyond being decidedly more down-to-earth, she had approached her own wedding with an air that was almost cautious. "I'm not going to turn into a bridezilla," she'd sworn to me the day my brother had proposed. "I swear it."

Now, she picked at the label on her beer bottle. It was something she did when she was nervous. By the time she was done drinking the beverage, she'd have the whole thing off in one piece. "I'm ready to be married." Her tone was low and thoughtful. "I'm just not sure I'm ready for the wedding."

I rotated my chair so I faced her. The AC kicked on, blowing more cool air into the room. Erin curled her legs up beneath her on the couch. She had a way of shrinking when she felt she'd become the center of attention.

"That's no way to think about it." I spoke in a hearty tone, as if she was a child refusing a favorite treat. "You're going to blow everyone away in that dress, you're going to rock the daddy-daughter dance, and you and my brother are going to radiate love like a nuclear power plant radiates energy. Everyone is going to go home saying you're the perfect couple, and then you're going to live happily ever after. You might as well enjoy the spectacle since I don't think anyone sees divorce and a second marriage in your future."

A small smile touched Erin's lips. But even as I stopped speaking I could practically hear her unspoken thought.

Clint's first marriage hadn't ended in divorce, either.

"Come on." I stood abruptly, launching myself out of my chair with too much energy. "If that wayward brother of mine is going to stay out late chasing cattle around, we should go play with the puppies. Puppies are the best cure for pre-wedding jitters I know."

○

We walked the short distance from my brother's house to the barn. Erin followed without protest, too polite to point out I was the one with the jitters. As we walked together through the warm evening, I wondered where my restless energy was coming from. I wasn't worried about losing my brother to Erin. If anything, he'd been far more present since her arrival on the scene. He smiled more these days, laughed more, and sometimes even willingly entered into a conversation without being prodded.

No, that wasn't the problem at all.

"Is Wyatt in yet?" The question popped out of my mouth as we walked through the warm, dusky evening. It was what I'd been struggling not to ask, or even think, since the moment my old truck had trundled through the Tipped Z's gate.

It was a stupid question. If Wyatt had arrived, his battered Dodge Ram would be parked outside the barn. The Ram wasn't there, so Wyatt wasn't here. It was simple. And yet, I couldn't keep from asking.

Erin answered as she hurried to keep pace with my unnecessarily fast walk. "Clint said he's driving in from Colorado. I don't know if he's hauling a trailer or not. He might show up pretty late."

I nodded, feigning disinterest. Wyatt was my brother's best friend. And by best friend, I mean only friend. He was the sole male member of the human species my brother seemed able to exchange more than three consecutive words with at a time.

He was also the person I'd been in love with since approximately the age of zero.

Not that Wyatt knew this. Or cared. Not that I cared, either. I had been determined not to care about Wyatt for almost as long as I'd been lovesick over him.

We reached the end of the narrow path that led from Clint's house to the back of the barn. My father's two cattle dogs, Fuzzface and Chet, looked up as we walked into the hay room through the open bay doors. But we were old news around here. They wagged their tails but neither deigned to rise. "What about Ted?" Erin said. "Is he back yet?"

Erin didn't mean the question as a rebuke, but it felt like one. Ted was my almost-certainly-on-the-verge-of-proposing boyfriend. Due to his job, he spent a lot of time on the road.

"He flies in tomorrow morning." I continued around the dogs and past the massive stack of hay bales that hulked in the corner, heading for the dark aisle that opened off the hay room.

The aisle led to the lower-ceiling portion of the barn, which was lined in stalls. The tack room opened off one side. There was another horse-sized door at the far end, but I'd never seen it open. We seldom kept horses in stalls. The large double stall had been given over for use as a kennel.

Erin and I peered over the half door. Peach looked up at us with a plaintive expression. Her six puppies were sleeping. I could read the plea in her eyes. *Don't wake them up. Please, please don't wake them up.*

I glanced at the food and water dishes in the corner. Both full. As I stood deliberating whether I needed puppy love more urgently than Peach needed a break from the demands of motherhood, the low growl of a diesel engine dawned in the quiet evening. As we stood and listened, tires crunched on the hard dirt of the driveway.

Erin gave me a quick smile. "Maybe that's Wyatt now."

I hadn't turned on a light. It was dim in the stall barn. As I turned, I felt my heart begin to dance some sort of spasmodic can-can in my chest. It was so stupid for this guy to have such an effect on me. It was beyond stupid. It was pathetic. I had a life. I had a man. I had a *good* man. And if Wyatt had demonstrated one fact over the years we'd known each other, it was that he had a list of things he wanted out of life and I was not on it.

Erin and I started back the way we'd come. The two dogs were on their feet now, curious about this new arrival. I was re-entering the hay room when Wyatt strode through the door that led in from the parking area.

He looked like he always looked—lean, a little scruffy, a little tired. And so handsome he nearly seared your eyes out.

He cast a quick glance around the room. "Oh, hey Nora." He spoke in a tone of mild surprise, as if I was the one who'd shown up at his ranch. But his manner was casual, as if we'd last seen each other a few days ago at the local gas station instead of over two years before when he'd climbed into his truck, said, "See you," and driven off. I'd been thinking I'd see him again the next day. It wasn't until later I learned he'd once more declined my brother's offer to take a more permanent position at the Tipped Z and hit the road on his colt-starting circuit.

Wyatt walked into the hay room. He took his hat off and held it in both hands. He walked with the faintest hint of a limp. He had for years. But I could remember when he hadn't. I could also remember when he'd been too young to grow the stubble that now peppered his cheeks. "Clint still out?" He jabbed his chin at the open bay door at the other end of the hay room, indicating the horizon and the sunset.

"Yep." I forced myself not to stare, trying to match his blasé tone. This was difficult, as my entire body had gone on high alert at the sight of him. My heart was racing and the air felt charged, as if he radiated a mild electric force field "And Wyatt, this is my brother's fiancé, Erin. Erin, this is my brother's best man, Wyatt."

Wyatt turned, looking fully at us for the first time. "Erin." He took one long step forward to shake her hand. She smiled. He smiled back. And when he smiled, I felt the same swooning infatuation I always felt when he smiled. Even when he wasn't smiling at me.

He removed his hand from Erin's and returned it to the brim of his hat. He glanced again towards the open door, perhaps wishing he could summon Clint through sheer force of will. "Guess I'll take my bag on up to the house and get a shower, then."

My father stood, tapping his spoon on the side of his glass. Around the long room, conversations quieted and died out. Heads turned. My father set the spoon down.

It was Friday evening, nearly 24 hours after Wyatt's arrival at the Tipped Z. It had been a busy 24 hours. The wedding was to take place at Erin's parents' house. Her parents lived quite near my parents. After Clint had finally reappeared the evening before, riding in just before full dark, I had absconded with the bride. We'd gone over to her parents' house, where we'd done a test run on hair and make-up. Hilariously, it was Erin's father who collaborated with us in our efforts to make Erin even more beautiful than usual, her mother only peeking in once or twice to make dry comments and drift off again, carrying her glass of wine.

Today had been consumed with the rehearsal. It never ceased to amaze me how complicated even simple weddings managed to be. Erin was laid back about everything, but there were still questions about where to place the chairs and from which direction to approach the gazebo, not to mention contingencies in the unlikely event of rain.

Now, we were almost there. It was the wedding eve. The rehearsal had gone well. All that was left was the rehearsal dinner.

Ted had made it back to town. He occupied the seat next to mine. As my father welcomed the two dozen or so guests that lined the several long tables, thanking them for coming to support and honor his son, I took a good, long look at my boyfriend. He was an attractive man, with a well-defined jaw and deep, kind eyes. He wore a light wool blazer and his rimless glasses. He listened to my father with earnest attention until the brief speech concluded, then participated in the quiet applause as my father sat down.

He noticed me looking and smiled. Conversation resumed around us. "Things went well today?" He looked up towards the top of our long table as he spoke, where Erin and Clint sat side by side.

Things had gone well. In some cases, the fact it was the groom's second wedding but the bride's first might have been a source of tension. In this case, it didn't seem to matter. Erin wanted a simple wedding. Clint wanted Erin to be happy.

"Yeah." I twirled the stem of my wine glass between my fingers. "If we can all remember our instructions until tomorrow, everything will be fine."

I glanced up the table too, pretending to look at Erin and Clint but allowing my eyes to stray to Wyatt. Wyatt sat next to my brother. He was shorter than Clint but broader. He had the same well-tanned, well-used look to his face and hands. He'd shaved since the day before and wore what passed for a nice shirt in the world of roving colt starters. He also wore a dark gray vest and well-heeled boots.

"Is that the best man?" Ted had followed my gaze. Ted was not in the wedding, so hadn't been present at the rehearsal.

"That's good old Wyatt." As the words tumbled out, I resisted the urge to wince, aware I was trying too hard to sound casual. "He got in last night."

A server came by and took our plates. It was late in the dinner, the meal almost over. I forced myself to look away from Wyatt and pay attention to Ted. It was hard not to compare the two of them. Ted worked in marketing. He was kind of a big deal in marketing. He was a big deal in marketing in a very particular niche. He worked mostly for companies that made products for performance horse trainers and competitors. His current biggest client was TruGlide, a firm that produced a particularly fancy version of the shoes reining horses wore. The shoes were smooth and flat on the bottom, allowing horses to slide through sand when coming to a sudden stop from the gallop. They were also embellished somehow to make as much sand spray out from beneath the horse as possible.

Although Ted was constantly on the fringes of the horse world, he was no cowboy. He was even less a cowboy than a reining competitor whose horse was trained by a high-dollar trainer, tacked and groomed by a stable hand, qualifying points collected by an assistant rider, and finally ridden by the actual owner only in the most high profile events of the year.

Ted's not being a cowboy was one of the things that had attracted me to him, I reminded myself as the server came around again and handed me a dessert menu. My father was a cowboy. My brother was a cowboy. My grandfather had been a cowboy. Most of my friends growing up had been cowboys. One of the primary goals of my young life had been to avoid dating cowboys.

I pushed thoughts of Wyatt to the back of my mind and forced my eyes to the menu. "You thinking dessert?"

Ted considered for a moment. Around us, the sounds of quiet conversation continued. We were at the end of one table. Erin's ancient and deaf aunt sat to my right. My attempts to speak with her earlier had produced confusion and discomfort for both of us, so I'd given up. To Ted's left sat the minister who would be performing the ceremony. He'd been engaged in a long and earnest conversation with his seat-mate on his other side for the whole dinner, leaving Ted and me to our own devices.

At the top of the table, several people burst into sudden peals of laughter. I looked up to see even Clint chuckling a little. I felt that wistful sense of not being in on the joke. My brother murmured something I couldn't hear. Erin and Wyatt laughed even harder.

"The apple crumble looks good." Ted was gazing at the menu, unaware of what we were missing out on. I tried not to feel excluded, reminding myself I saw Erin and Clint all the time. It made sense they'd spend this evening socializing with people they did not get to spend time with all that often.

Still, there was a bitter little twist in my stomach as I set my menu aside. "I don't think I'm in the mood for dessert."

Ted looked up with a benevolent shrug as he set his small menu on top of mine. "If you change your mind, I'll share."

The wedding day dawned clear and bright. I woke up in my apartment. Brilliant sunlight was spilling through the full-length balcony doors, reflecting off the pale carpet into my face.

I rolled over, muttering, and bumped into Ted. He was sleeping on his back with one forearm thrown across his eyes. It was a position I couldn't imagine finding comfortable. He didn't stir as I readjusted myself and tried to decide whether or not I'd be able to get back to sleep. I lay back on my pillows and felt my mind come alive.

My brother was getting married today. The thought came suddenly, pushing all others aside. Instantly, I began to compile a list of things I would need to do before the ceremony.

I knew then there would be no going back to sleep. My brain, once activated, did not spin down easily. So I gave up on the pretense, slipped from underneath the covers, and left the bedroom.

I padded into the dim, cool kitchen. Ted had given me a single cup coffee maker after he'd begun staying the night regularly. He'd done it because we had different taste in coffee. At first, I refused to use the thing. Something about it made me feel indolent. Over time, however, my attitude towards the single-cup brew strategy had softened. It was so darn easy to use, I'd slipped into doing so daily.

This morning, I fished one of my dark roast canisters out of the cupboard and popped it into the machine. I checked my phone to the clicking and sighing of the water beginning to heat. I found no panicky texts from the bride. So that was a good thing.

I wandered around the kitchen and living area, tidying while I waited for the coffee, stirred to restlessness by the feeling that it was a big day but I there was nothing I could do to prepare yet. The ceremony was at 4:00. I needed to show up at Erin's house in plenty of time to do the bride's hair and make-up and put on my own dress. Which meant the many hours before me were devoid of anything I needed to do except try not to think about Wyatt.

My brother's best man was staying at the ranch. Wyatt always stayed at the ranch when he came back to Tucson for short spells. He did this because he was one step short of estranged from his own family. His family and mine had once owned adjoining ranches. His family and mine had once ridden and worked cattle together, sharing equipment and labor and horses. There had once been the kind of unquantifiable bond that develops when families work together for generations between his people and my people.

That was how it had been until Wyatt's father had defected. He'd turned his nose up at cowboying and gone into finance. Everything that eventually went bad in Wyatt's family spun out from that decision.

In the kitchen, the coffee maker clicked and beeped. I left the stack of mail I'd been sorting. My mug sat steaming on the platform, ready for my attention. I stirred in cream and sugar and headed back across my small floorplan to peek around the bedroom door at Ted. He was still sprawled on his back in my bed, arm over his eyes. Without his shirt, he was not at all unpleasant to look at. Ted had a physique that was just shy of impressive. He liked to run. He also did things like pull-ups, push-ups, and sit-ups. His arms and torso had good definition, even if he didn't quite look like some of the ripped rodeo models that appeared in his ads.

I turned away from the door and paced back into my living room. There were reasons—lots of them—that I was with Ted and not Wyatt. Unfortunately, those reasons seemed to melt away every time the thought of Wyatt crossed my mind. Sipping my coffee and staring out the window, I thought of the way he'd looked last night, sitting next to Clint, wearing his vaquero's vest, laughing at something my brother had said.

Good. He'd looked really, really good.

I looked at the red numbers of the stove clock. 8:37. Wyatt and Clint were doubtless on horseback at this very moment, riding out on the pretense of checking the herd so my brother could show Wyatt the young stud colt we were considering keeping back to strengthen and diversify our line.

"Don't be late, you idiots." I muttered this warning under my breath. The picture of them riding across the dusty ranchland was as clear in my mind as if I could actually see them.

There was a soft sound behind me. I turned to see Ted standing in the bedroom doorway. He'd pulled on a shirt and his hair was adorably rumpled. He smiled as he adjusted his glasses. "Hey gorgeous," he said. "Guess I'm still worn out from the travel. You been up long?"

I lifted my mug to indicate its near-fullness. Ted walked across the room, stopping to give me a peck on the cheek. He smelled of sheets and morning and sleeping male human. I could feel the warmth of his palm through my thin tank-top when his hand lingered for a moment on my side.

Ted moved past me into the kitchen. As he selected a K-Cup flavor for his morning brew, he glanced back over his shoulder. "Shall I make us some eggs?"

This, I reminded myself as he set the brewer going again, was one of the many, many reasons I was with this guy and not a cowboy. Cowboys never made you eggs in the morning. Not because they were unwilling, but because by 8:30 in Arizona, even a lazy cowboy has already been on horseback for at least two hours.

Chapter 2

◉

"There." I fastened the little eye-hook at the top of the dress's zipper. "You're all hooked in."

Trace, Erin's best friend and matron of honor, straightened from making some adjustment to the hem of Erin's skirts. "Oh, Erin." Her voice was breathy. "You look amazing."

Erin turned to regard herself in the full-length mirror that had been added to the room for the occasion. We'd taken over Erin's mother's studio for bridal party preparations. The room was lined in shelves that bristled with pens and inks, not to mention several narrow rows of cork that ran the length of one wall. Erin had explained her mother pinned photographs to these strips when she was working. Erin's mother was a medical illustrator, which meant the subject-matter on display in this room was typically on the biological and possibly gross side.

All such imagery had been removed for the day, however. A plain white sheet had been thrown over the drafting table where Erin's mother usually worked. All other surfaces were cluttered with the accoutrements of a bride-to-be.

The ghost of a smile flitted across Erin's face as she surveyed herself in the mirror. She did look good. The dress was perfect. It was white with a flared skirt and some tasteful embroidery. "I can't believe it's me." Her tone was solemn.

Trace took one of Erin's hands. "You're going to be great." Her eyes were misty, her voice rich with feeling.

I drifted away from the pair of them to rustle around on the hangers for my own dress. I was useless in these sorts of moments. Most forms of intimacy made me uncomfortable, so I tended to trivialize everything by making off-color comments intended to lighten the mood.

There was a tap on the door. Erin's mother peeked in, a thin, pale girl hovering behind her. The girl was Adele, one of three cousins from the same family who'd been roped into filling out the ranks of Clint and Erin's wedding party. "Almost time," Erin's mother said, taking in my jeans and t-shirt with a look indicating unease.

"She's ready." I opened the door a little wider. "You should come in."

As her mother entered, Erin turned around. The two looked at each other, some silent sentiment passing between them. Erin's relationship with her parents was strong, if a little atypical. I got the feeling I was intruding on a private moment. I snatched my dress off its hanger and fled into the makeshift changing area. I made a point not to listen to the low-voiced, heartfelt conversation taking place on the other side of the screen.

By the time I emerged in my silvery gray bridesmaid dress, the rest of the female side of the bridal party was assembled. Erin's mother moved among the girls, straightening and securing flowers and ribbons like a designer before a runway show. She looked at me and nodded. "Okay." Her eyes were serious but satisfied. "We're ready."

We bridesmaids, clad in matching dresses and shoes, filed our way out of the house. We found the three groomsmen on the side patio under the supervision of Erin's father, who looked handsome in his trim suit. The groomsmen were not speaking as we approached. Wyatt stood a little apart from Erin's two cousins, staring down towards the bottom of the yard, his expression somewhat grim.

My partner in the wedding line-up was one of the cousins—a serious young man who lived in New York and designed the little plastic pieces companies like IKEA use to make their furniture go together easily and stay in one piece forever after. His name was Drew. Before speaking with him at the rehearsal, I'd never once put any thought into where those little plastic pieces come from. He was an easy partner. Not overly talkative, but not painfully quiet either.

He and Erin were not close, but finding people to stand up on my brother's side had been a challenge. My brother did not have friends the way normal people have friends and my family was small. Erin hadn't wanted a large wedding party but everyone had agreed three was the minimum.

Erin did not come with us out onto the side patio. She hung back as her mother sent her father off to his appointed place with a jerk of her chin.

Drew turned as we joined the groomsmen, smiling easily. Trace approached Wyatt, who turned from his contemplation of the scenery to take her hand and set it on his arm.

I tried not to listen to the mean voice in my head that said Trace and Wyatt were not a good aesthetic match. Trace was the kind of person who possessed effortless beauty, then ruined it with too much make-up. Wyatt was the opposite—good looking despite a seemingly concerted effort not to be.

Drew offered me his arm. Tearing my eyes off Wyatt, I set my hand in the proper position. Behind us, his little brother and sister likewise paired off. Erin's mother disappeared to occupy her place with other important family members in the front row of the grid of temporary chairs arranged all around the festooned gazebo in the low part of the yard.

We waited. A ripple of tension passed through us as the music piping over the scene fell silent. I stared at the back of Wyatt's head as the song changed, cueing us for entry.

It was close to midnight by the time I had the opportunity to congratulate my brother. The ceremony was beautiful, the dinner lovely, and the opening of the dance floor was greeted with universal enthusiasm. As the DJ began spinning catchy tunes with thumping beats, ties were loosened or shed. Shoes were kicked aside. Once tidy hairstyles, painstakingly constructed, fell to dishevelment as the dancing spread like a contagion among the guests.

One of the things that endeared Ted to me was his enthusiastic and tireless attitude about dancing. We'd joined the dancing early and kept at it for hours. Now, however, the late hour was taking its toll. Things were beginning to wind down. The older guests had left and the energetic dance tunes were now regularly interrupted by slower, less danceable music.

During one of these numbers, Ted got into a conversation with Drew, the plastic thingie designer. I slipped away to the restroom. Returning from the house to the back porch, I stopped to rest on a bench set into a quiet alcove against the side of the house. My feet were tired. My ears were ringing. I was very happy.

It was a perfect night. The breeze carried the hint of a cool edge. The party music played around the corner. I'd long since removed my shoes but my feet throbbed. I sighed at the relief of having my weight off them.

The side door opened behind me. I turned to see my brother emerge from the house, face lit by the ropes of tiny lightbulbs woven along the railing.

Clint paused, looking out into the dark of the night. He saw me and started in my direction. He was wearing a pair of dress boots. His heels made sharp thuds on the floor as he walked.

I sat back and looked up at my brother. He said nothing, only lowered his long body onto the bench next to mine.

Some people find my brother's silences off-putting. Maybe it's harder when you're not a person who was raised in a house where understanding the body-language of animals was more important than getting good grades. Nevertheless, I never had trouble reading Clint. Right now, he was tired but pleased. He was feeling satisfied. He was glad to have a quiet moment to sit with me. I knew all this because it was written in his relaxed hands, his soft brow, the quiet way he let out a breath as he sat down. He didn't have to explain himself to me.

We sat for a while, listening to the thud of the music, the chatter of the dancers, and the distant call of the night birds. "We're going to head out soon." He spoke quietly enough his words were hard to pick out of the ambient noise.

I leaned down and massaged the ball of my left foot, where someone had stepped on me during the electric slide. "You two are going to be happy."

Clint turned a little. The bench was tucked into a dim corner. Only the high planes of his face caught the light. I could make out the corner of his mouth, twitched up into a smile. "We already are."

He was right, of course. Clint didn't waste breath on saying things that weren't true. I abandoned my foot so I could punch him lightly in the arm. "You know what I mean."

His smile faded. He gave a slow nod. He gazed into the darkness beyond the patio. He looked like he might have said something more.

Before he could speak, Erin appeared. She walked around the corner from the dance area. She'd lost her shoes too, and held her long skirts gathered in one hand. Her hair was now more wild than perfect but she glowed with an overflowing sense of happiness that made these details unable to detract from her beauty. She stopped when she saw Clint and me sitting together, eyes full of emotion. "Thank you so much, Nora. For everything."

A shadow drifted up behind Erin. As Clint rose, Wyatt resolved out of the darkness. He looked even more rumpled than she did. He hadn't lost his boots, but he'd stripped down to his undershirt. I could make out the definition of his biceps in the low light.

"Erin says you guys are heading out?" Not looking at me, as usual, Wyatt addressed my brother.

Abruptly, the music cut off. There was a collective groan from the remaining dancers, a burst of static, and the music boomed back to life.

"Yes. Soon." Clint stepped over to wrap an arm around Erin's shoulders. She leaned against him, closing her eyes.

"I'll say goodbye then. And congratulations. Erin, it was a pleasure to meet you. I've got to leave first thing in the morning."

It was hard to read faces in the darkness, but I saw my brother stiffen. He spoke in a voice that was quiet but a little strained. "We could use an extra hand if you wanted to stay on for a bit."

Wyatt looked off into the night. I wasn't as used to reading him, but I thought I saw tension in his shoulders as well. "I'm signed on to start twenty racehorses near Santa Anita. Some exciting prospects." Wyatt sounded pleased and proud, but there was a hint of something stubborn in his words.

Clint's expression didn't change. My brother had never been impressed by fame or large-scale recognition. I shifted my rubbing to the other foot, which hadn't been stepped on but was feeling abused nevertheless. I knew variations of this same conversation had played out dozens of times between my brother and his best friend. The end result never varied. Wyatt would go when Wyatt would go.

Clint knew this. He extended his hand. "Thank you for coming." He and Wyatt shook. Then the newly minted married couple turned and walked away.

Wyatt and I watched them go, me from my vantage point of the bench, Wyatt from his position near the corner of the house. The song shifted from something fast and poppy to something slow and romantic, a sure sign the DJ was wrapping things up.

I waited, certain Wyatt would walk away. But he didn't. He stayed where he was, standing in his t-shirt and staring after Clint as if there was something more he wanted to say.

I became aware that Wyatt and I were alone. Or, as close to alone as one can be at a wedding reception. I shifted on my bench.

Wyatt turned as my dress rustled. He blinked a few times, as if returning from a long and complex line of thought. Then he strolled towards over as casually as you please to sit down on the bench next to me.

When my brother had sat there, it had felt natural and easy. Now the bench seemed very small. A giddy sense of Wyatt's closeness sent a warm thrill through my entire body.

I sat as still as a startled rabbit. Wyatt turned again to consider the darkness into which Clint and Erin had disappeared. His voice, when he spoke, carried a wistful quality. "He always wants me to stay."

I contemplated this remark. Wyatt's tone was confidential, as if I was his friend rather than just his best friend's little sister, as if we had spoken about personal matters before, as if I was more than someone who never quite registered on his radar. It was a strange shock to find myself thrown into the role of confidant.

Trying to act natural, I considered possible responses. "I want you to stay, too," seemed both too honest and too pushy. I settled on a variation of what Erin had said to me about my role at Old Pueblo. "Good hands are hard to find."

Wyatt released a short, sharp laugh. He turned from his contemplation of the night to stare down at his lap. He rubbed at his short hair and sighed. "He told me yesterday I'm not realizing my full potential. He told me a good cowboy should finish what he starts, at least some of the time."

I shifted on the bench again, sitting up and smoothing my skirt. "He says the same thing to me."

Wyatt glanced at me out of the corner of his eye, grinning in a way that made my heart dip and stutter. It was a familiar grin. I'd often seen it on his face when we were all much younger, usually just before he and Clint rode off to do something stupid. "I hear you're working with some real fine horseflesh over Old Pueblo way."

I felt a slow flush creep up my neck. I wasn't sure whether to feel pleased Wyatt was aware of the details of my life or embarrassed he knew I had what he must consider a pretty lame job. I thought of the horse I called Twitchy, who grew more agitated and spooky by the week. If I was the only one who rode him, I might have been able to make progress. But I worked four days a week. My horses were used by other people when I wasn't there. Most of the performers at Old Pueblo thought the highest level of horsemanship could be summed up with, "Kick to go, pull to stop."

The silence grew and became heavy. "I'm teasing, Nora," Wyatt shifted so we were closer on the bench than we'd been before. Quite a lot closer. I could feel the warmth rising off his bare arm. "I think it's great you're doing your own thing."

The music faded from one slow song to another. I thought of poor Ted, standing at the edge of the dance floor wondering where his partner had gone. I would go find him, I promised myself, in just a minute.

I stared down at the unusual sight of nail polish on my toes. "It's not great," I said. "Not really. Not for the ranch. Not for Clint. Dad's not getting any younger and my brother works all the damn time. I should be around more. I just ..." I stopped, the words sticking in my throat.

Wyatt didn't say anything. He didn't have to. If there was anyone who knew what it felt like to be pressured by your family, it was him.

We were quiet for a moment longer. There was a break in the music. The DJ's voice drifted out, informing everyone it was the last dance. Wyatt stirred next to me as I heard the ring of approaching footsteps. He started to speak, started to say something that sounded a good deal like, "Do you want to ..."

He was interrupted by Ted sweeping around the corner. My boyfriend saw me and grinned. "Last dance, honey. Come on."

Dots paced back and forth in front of the closed front door, every now and then stopping to release a low, nervous whine. Her nails made a persistent clicking on the smooth tile, interrupting the peaceful sounds of the desert evening. I looked up from the magazine I was pretending to read. "You need to settle down."

The dog turned to regard me with her bright, piercing eyes. She whined again, in critique of my remark.

I glanced at the clock. It was just after 7:00 PM and I ached all over. This morning I'd helped my father dig out and repair a cattle guard. This afternoon I'd started breaking several colts to lead. They were long yearlings and had never been touched by a human or a rope in their lives. Dad had given them over to me, commenting he and Clint were, "A bit behind on the horses this year." Which meant this group was all but wild.

Fortunately, there were only five of them. Still, by the time I'd gotten a rope on each and the very basic concept of "yield to pressure" instilled, the sun was falling, the yearlings and my saddle horse were all thoroughly drenched in sweat, and I was beyond exhausted.

Now, I sat in my brother's house sipping a beer and trying to relax. My brother's dog, Dots, had tailed me all day with an aura of suspicion. As the afternoon had worn into evening, she seemed to have concluded her worst fears were confirmed. "This is not a permanent arrangement," I told her, trying to ease her anxiety. "Clint is on his honeymoon. He'll be back tomorrow."

The dog cocked her head, her wiry coat curling around her muzzle and eyes. She had a gray and white brindle coat, with the smattering of brown dots of color across her face that had given her the name. She was my brother's constant companion and even more of a workaholic than he was. He wasn't often away from her overnight.

I lowered my eyes back to the magazine but did not read. It's unsettling, being stared at, even when it's a dog doing the staring.

We sat like that for what seemed a long time. Dots staring, me pretending to read. I felt a disproportionate surge of relief when I heard Ted's car pull up out front. I had to force myself not to bounce up and greet him with an unseemly show of enthusiasm.

Ted tapped on the front door and let himself in. As he stepped inside, Dots clicked across the floor to sniff at his legs. But she knew Ted. While she did turn to give me one more long, plaintive look, she didn't make a fuss.

I rose and stretched, feeling the muscles in my shoulders knot and bunch. My eyes felt gritty with fatigue but I was glad to see Ted.

Already, Wyatt's strange influence on me was fading. Knowing my brother's best friend was halfway to California by now relieved some strange pressure that had been riding in the back of my mind for days. I was able to look at Ted and see him just as Ted, my lovely boyfriend, who had come over with a bottle of wine and Chinese takeout and was going to rescue me from the resounding silence my brother's house seemed to produce, then magnify.

"Hard day?" Ted watched my theatrics with a raised eyebrow as he set his burdens on the gleaming copper counter.

"Just a little. My father and I dug a hole halfway to China this morning. This afternoon I had to wrangle a whole herd of wild youngsters and get them ready to accept a halter."

Ted pulled the bottle of wine out of its brown paper sleeve and looked at me with a scrunched brow. Ted did ride horses sometimes. He'd been one of those unfortunate boys who'd wanted to barrel race, only to discover when he reached his teens that his center of gravity was against him. He'd given up horses then and now only returned to the saddle on rare occasions. He certainly had never been anywhere near a horse that wasn't entirely broke. His idea of haltering was walking up to a sleepy horse in a stall and slipping a bit of nylon webbing over its face.

Ted began hunting through drawers in search of a bottle opener. "How about a glass of wine? I have something to tell you."

Curious, I downed the last of my beer, rose from my place on the couch, and went to a cabinet. I took down two wine glasses and carried them to Ted. He poured and we adjourned to the living room, Dots trailing behind us like a resentful chaperone.

"So tell me." I settled into my grandfather's chair and tucked my feet up, taking a sip of wine. It was good—something red that was somehow both light and rich at the same time. I hadn't thought to read the label before we'd left the kitchen. But then, wine wasn't my deal. It was one of Ted's areas of expertise.

Ted lowered himself onto the couch where Erin had sat a scant few days ago, before she'd been my sister-in-law. He set his wine on the coffee table and looked at me with a bright, hopeful expression. "I may have the opportunity of a lifetime." His tone was serious. "For you, I mean."

Inexplicably, the pace of my heart ticked up a few notches. I took another sip of the wine and waited for him to go on. Dots, convinced at last we were not going back outside to do more things with horses and cattle, collapsed onto the tile floor with an aggrieved sigh.

Ted leaned back into his seat, glasses winking in the sheen of the overhead lights. "You know how I was gone for a few days?"

I said nothing. Of course I knew he'd been gone for a few days. He'd been in Texas, called over at the last minute because of some marketing disaster that had gone down with his biggest client, TruGlide.

I nodded, quelling the impatient desire to hurry him along. Ted, unlike all male members of my family, had a bit of a tendency to embellish the telling of stories, drawing out the suspense and even providing more detail than strictly necessary.

Ted looked at me a moment longer, his expression suggesting I was a five-year-old girl and he'd booked pony rides for my birthday party. "The TruGlide Girl broke contract," he said. "She walked out in the middle of a huge shoot. She's refusing to do anything more for the company."

I blinked, trying to decipher what this had to do with me. Ted waited, expression expectant. "So?" I said.

Ted leaned forward and shuffled through the magazines on the coffee table in front of him. He came up with a recent issue of *Western Rider*. He flipped it over.

I knew the ad that occupied the back cover. I'd seen it all over the place. Ted had produced it. It featured the TruGlide Girl beaming from the back of a massive sorrel horse that was all but doubled over in its effort to stop from a gallop. A huge spray of sand blasted up from around the horse's haunches. The copy read, "He gives you his best effort. Give him the best glide. TruGlide® patented SureSlide™ shoeing technology offers superior support and slide. Bring home a winner." The TruGlide logo occupied the lower right-hand corner.

A queasy feeling began to form in the pit of my stomach. This was not an entirely new subject between us. Ted had once or twice indicated he thought I had the looks and the skills to ride for some of his clients.

I looked at the girl on the back cover. Her long blonde hair flew out behind her glittery Texas style hat. Her clothing was festooned in sparkles. She and the horse were both airbrushed within an inch of their lives.

Ted tapped the back cover as if it corroborated some part of his story. "I've talked to Jay." Jay was the authority in all things marketing at TruGlide. He and Ted had gotten friendly over the years. "He says they'll audition you before putting out a general call. They're in a tight spot because they've got a big appearance coming up. They need to get someone back in the roll ASAP and they don't have time to deal with incompetence."

The last TruGlide Girl, I knew from Ted's stories, had been a pain from the start. She'd turned out not to be as proficient on horseback as she'd represented herself. This truth had emerged in a series of embarrassing gaffs over the first year of her contract. Things had seemed to settle down, at least to the point that I stopped hearing TruGlide Girl horror stories from Ted. Clearly, things hadn't been as good as they'd seemed.

Slowly, Ted's words penetrated past my own thoughts. A feeling of disbelief settled over me as I absorbed his meaning. "Wait." Confusion mingled with fatigue and the wine to create an unpleasant lifting sensation in my forehead. "Audition? What are you talking about?"

Ted gave me a long, serious look. He picked up his wine glass, took a quick sip, and set it down again. "Think about it for a minute. This could be your lucky break. You wouldn't be some obscure performer at Old Pueblo anymore. The TruGlide Girl is big. You don't want to stay in a seasonal role at a western theme park forever, do you?"

The queasy feeling intensified. It was another variation on the question my brother and father seemed to ask me every other day. "Is this what you want to do you with your life? Really? Flail around on some half-broke horse, acting out the same overblown dramas day after day?"

When they asked, they were always trying to convince me to commit more time to the ranch. Now, Ted was asking the same question but the implication was quite different.

I thought of my brief conversation with Wyatt at the wedding. He would understand the confused blend of reasons that kept me from wanting to immerse myself totally in the Tipped Z. Ted didn't. He couldn't grasp my reasons for working at Old Pueblo. He thought it had something to do with wanting to be in the limelight. In reality, it was something that gave me an escape, preserving a part of my life without forcing me to turn my back on the ranch entirely.

I stared at the photo behind Ted's head. I found myself, reduced to a silhouette, riding a cloud of dust. "I'll think about it." I wasn't looking straight at Ted but I could see a flicker of disappointment move across his face.

"Of course." Ted's voice was kind and carried no hint of reproach. "Just don't think too long. They need you in Texas by the end of the week."

The hot breeze snapped the old Arizona flag that hung above the wooden town hall. Dust blew in little devils along the hard dirt streets. The sun was low and orange on the horizon. I leaned against the antiqued post office railing, wearing plain old jeans and a t-shirt. A scant hour before, I'd packed away my bandit queen ensemble for the last time.

"... been an unbelievable season and we've seen so much growth from all of you." Cara stood only a few feet away but her voice reverberated throughout the town, blasting out of speakers hidden all up and down the streets. It was the end-of-season we're-all-so-fabulous talk, after which we would all tell each how great we'd all been and get a little misty-eyed before going our separate ways.

"Thanks for all your hard work. I hope to see you all in fall auditions!"

Cara finished her speech. Everyone clapped. The quiet, attentive group broke into clusters.

I tipped my phone out of my pocket and glanced at the screen, releasing a small curse when I saw the time. Although traditionally the last Thursday of the season resulted in the entire weekday cast descending on downtown Tucson for a night of revelry, this year I would not be able to stay and participate in the socializing. With a somewhat regretful look at the swirling groups of people who had started as strangers and become coworkers over the course of the season, I turned to walk away. I had a flight to catch.

I strode up the dusty street, looking around at the weathered wooden buildings. If Ted had his way, this would be the last time I left here as anything other than a member of the public. If I ever returned to

Old Pueblo, I would do so as a spectator. All the secret life of the cast, the inner workings of the day-to-day show, the individual quirks of the horses, would be closed to me.

I felt a pang at the thought. Although it was far from a dream job, Old Pueblo had wormed its way into my heart.

I was nearly to the parking lot when a panting Cara caught up with me. She'd removed her microphone but still clutched a clipboard to her chest. She was puffing as if she'd sprinted all the way from the stables. "Nora," she said, coming up beside me. "I'm glad I caught you. I want to talk to you before you go."

I stopped beside the wooden turnstile that filtered visitors into the park. A strange mixture of impatience and regret flowed through me. I had to have this conversation with the manager every year. Cara was new, so she and I had never done this before. But I knew what was coming.

"Sorry to rush off." I tried to make my voice light. "I have a flight to catch."

Cara nodded, smiling hugely. It was her habitual expression. She was shorter than me and, as far as I could tell, had converted her metabolism to run on nothing but high fructose corn syrup and caffeine. "I'll be quick, then. I wanted to let you know we'd like you to stay on for the summer season."

I sighed, placing my hand on the "no exit" portion of the gate used to admit people in wheelchairs. The staff regularly did use it as an exit to avoid the round-about route visitors took through the gift shop in order to escape the park's clutches. "I can't, Cara. I'm sorry. I have obligations at the family ranch."

Cara's brow furrowed. Although Old Pueblo was not open to the public during the most brutal months of the Arizona summer, a skeleton crew of workers was employed year-round. They cared for the horses and assisted where needed when the park was rented out for filming movies or private parties. I'd been offered the summer shift at Old Pueblo for four years running. It was well paid: an opportunity coveted among the seasonal staffers. But I never accepted the position.

"I know." Cara tried to make eye contact but I gazed back towards the town. "I mean, I see in your records we've tried to keep you on before." Her smile got, impossibly, even wider. She squinted down at her clipboard, as if it could offer up a more persuasive argument. "That's why we're prepared to offer you a long-term, full-time position, with retirement and benefits and health care. All the bells and whistles."

I watched a discarded Kit Kat wrapper blow towards the authentic schoolhouse replica. Very, very few people at Old Pueblo had the kind of job that came with benefits. It was one of the ways the place stayed afloat. Temp workers were the foundation of the entire system.

I didn't know what to say. Sensing my unease, Cara took a step back. She made a casual, waving gesture with her hand as if I was the one who had been perpetuating the conversation. "But that's enough for now," she said. "I know you've got your flight. Call me when you get back, okay? We'll keep the spot for you for a week."

I could have told her right then I wouldn't take the position. Even if the TruGlide madness didn't amount to anything, a full-time job wasn't in the cards for me unless I intended to donate most of my wages to the Tipped Z so they could hire someone to carry out all the work I wouldn't be able to do over the summer.

But I didn't say anything. I thanked her one last time, turned, and pushed through the fence.

My old truck was a hulking presence in the back row of the parking lot. I strode across the hot blacktop. As I heaved the old door open and looked back towards the distant tableau of the replica town, I somehow knew I wouldn't be coming back here for a long, long time.

In retrospect, I'm not sure what I expected the TruGlide audition to be like. I only knew I looked up with surprise as Ted turned off the wide, flat street we'd been following since leaving our hotel. I grew even more surprised when he turned again to park in front of an unremarkable-looking strip mall.

I blinked out the window, glancing from the low building in front of us back to Ted. He gave me an encouraging smile. "Here we are."

I returned my gaze to the building. It presented a uniform exterior of reddish brick. Though I could make out several logos screened onto glass doors, they were too small to be seen from a distance

I blinked, trying not to show my confusion. "Oh," I said, unable to come up with anything more expressive. I pulled down the sun flap of the car we'd rented for our time in Dallas and obsessively checked my makeup in the mirror. I wasn't typically one for doing this, but I was finding it unnerving to know I was about to walk into a room and be judged against the TruGlide Girl.

Ted paused in the act of opening his car door. He leaned over to give me a peck on the cheek. "You look great."

I managed a wan smile.

Ted led me from the empty parking lot to a nondescript glass door that bore the TruGlide logo. Still, there was something very uninviting about this strip mall. The buildings around us were warehousy. In spite of all the doors and parking spaces, there was nary a human to be seen. A hot, heavy breeze washed over us.

The door opened into a small reception area. A desk stood facing us but there was no one behind it. A handful of chairs were arranged around a coffee table bearing a selection of magazines. It was hot inside the building. In my experience, most businesses in warm climates ran ACs ragged. Not so the TruGlide offices. I felt perspiration bead on my forehead.

Ted, looking as unflustered as if we'd walked into a McDonalds, approached the front desk and rang a small bell. We waited. The room was hot but dim. A clock ticked on the wall.

A moment passed. I stared at a large plant in the corner, trying to decide whether it was fake or just unhealthy. As more seconds dragged by, I began to wonder what I'd let myself in for. Ted remained near the desk, a sort of pre-smile expression on his face. We continued to wait.

Just as Ted was looking at the bell as if he was considering ringing it again, a thin, middle-aged man swept into the room. He was wearing an expensive shirt but the sleeves were rolled up in a disorderly way. The throat was unbuttoned a bit beyond what struck me as standard. He had dark hair and striking blue eyes set in a pale complexion that was currently flushed. He flapped a hand towards his face and said to Ted without preamble, "Oh my god. I'm so sorry. The AC is out. It's been a nightmare all morning. We have called a million repair places but the soonest anyone can come is in half an hour. We sent Claire out for fans but she's not back yet." He paused and let out a long breath through flared nostrils. "I think I'm going to die of heat exhaustion."

Ted laughed as if this was the most entertaining turn of events he could have imagined. "Jay, this is my girlfriend, Nora. Nora, this is Jay, head of marketing at TruGlide Enterprises."

I felt a strange and not entirely pleasant shifting sensation in my brain as my preconceived notion of what Jay would be like was snuffed out of existence by the reality. Jay took one step in my direction and extended a hand. The way he offered it confused me, as if I might be as likely to kiss it as shake it. I awkwardly put my hand in his. He gave me a limp squeeze before stepping back, looking at me with heartfelt regret in his eyes. "I'm so sorry we have to audition you in these conditions."

I looked around the drab front room, trying to come to a better understanding of the situation. The TruGlide Girl rode horses. Or at least, she posed with them. Every single TruGlide advertisement I'd ever seen featured a horse. But unless I was very much mistaken, we were leagues from the nearest place a horse might be expected to exist.

I forced a smile. "It's okay."

Jay sighed and turned on one heel. "You may as well come on back." He walked off, leading us up the hall he'd entered through. Following, we passed into a dimmer space, walked around a bend in the corridor, and then the room opened up. What had seemed an all but abandoned building was suddenly a large, open space full of desks and light and people.

Jay, one step ahead of us, gestured about the room to indicate clusters of desks separated by transparent walls. "So here's the guts of the TruGlide operation. Phone support over there, social media department there, general marketing and design here. Our engineers are in their own space, in the back. My office is this way."

"Engineers?" I echoed, staring around at the dozen or so people who sat in varying degrees of obvious physical discomfort in front of computer screens. Some of them were using sheets of paper or rolled up magazines as fans. All of them looked miserable. If it had been warm in the reception area, it was crushingly hot back here.

Jay turned around to face us, walking backwards as he answered my question. "The TruGlide shoe was created by the son of a reiner who went into engineering. The patented shape is designed for maximum slide while still lending stability to the horse during the pattern. But we're not resting on our laurels. We're continuously working to improve our product."

I nodded to show my perfect understanding of this explanation. Jay turned back around and led us through an open door into a large office with windows that overlooked a tableau of warehouses and parking lots. Jay walked around to settle himself behind a cluttered desk. A massive photograph of the TruGlide Girl dominated the wall behind him. I was no expert on the various iterations of said girl, but I suspected this girl who held court in Jay's office was not the one who'd blown her contract and split on short notice.

Muttering something I couldn't make out, Jay opened a mini-fridge that stood humming next to the desk. He handed Ted and me each a cool bottle of water, indicated we should sit, and settled himself behind the desk. His bright eyes came to rest on me, seeming to take me in for the first time. He pressed one finger to the bridge of his nose. "I was going to do the photography session first," he said. "But I think we'll wait and start with the verbal portion. Maybe at least we'll have some fans by the time we're ready to shoot."

I gave a wan nod. I glanced at Ted. He'd opened his water and now took a sip, not seeming discomfited in the least.

Jay settled back in his chair. His eyes flicked over my outfit. I'd worn nice jeans, a western shirt, and my dress boots. He seemed to take my clothing choices in. Then his gaze settled on my face. "So, Nora," he said. "Tell me why you want to be the TruGlide Girl."

The server set a basket of chips down next to the bowl of salsa. I grabbed a chip convulsively, noting it was still warm. Across from me, Ted sipped his water. He had a wary look that meant he knew I was not happy.

I was more than not happy. I was angry. I wasn't angry at Ted. I was angry because I'd gone blind into a situation that had turned out to be totally different from what I'd expected.

I dipped the chip and crunched down on it with unnecessary force. It was busy and festive inside the little Mexican restaurant we'd seen on our way to the TruGlide offices. Back then, before I knew what was in store for me, I'd cheerily agreed to Ted's suggestion we stop here for lunch before returning to our hotel.

"I think it went fine," Ted said. He said it as if this were the continuation of a conversation rather than the first words that had passed between us since Jay had led us back into the front room, now manned by both a receptionist and a fan, and seen us out the door. "Jay's like that. You never know what he thinks about something until later."

I pulled the wrapper off my straw and stabbed the lemon slice deeper into my glass. I closed my eyes, remembering Jay's sardonic, disinterested manner that grew more sardonic and disinterested the further we got into the interview process. I thought I had a very clear idea of what Jay had been thinking.

"I thought it was going to be riding," I burst out. My tone came out loud and harsh, but I couldn't help it. "An interview? A photoshoot? What about horses? You told me the last TruGlide Girl was incompetent with horses. Wouldn't they test for that before hiring someone new? Geez, Ted, why didn't you warn me?"

Ted flushed. We were both still cooling down. The AC repairman had arrived partway through my supremely awkward interview with Jay, but it had taken him until nearly the end of my photoshoot to fix whatever was wrong with the AC. When cool air had begun blasting from the vents, the entire overheated staff that occupied the large room had raised a feeble cheer.

"I didn't realize you thought there would be riding." Ted unwrapped his straw and stuck it in his ice water. "I'm sorry."

I crunched another chip and made a conscious effort to let go of the embarrassment and frustration. "Whatever." Maybe it was better this way. "It doesn't matter. I won't get the job. I hope this doesn't hurt things between you and Jay."

Ted considered me for a moment. He reached for a chip. "I don't know why you think you did poorly, Nora. I think you were great."

I stared at him with genuine mystification. Had he been in the same room I'd been in? Had he heard my stammering and insufficient answers to all the bizarre questions Jay had thrown at me? *What was the first advertisement that ever made an impression on you? What image do you see when you think of TruGlide? How would you like to adapt the TruGlide Girl's role to be unique to you?*

He hadn't asked a single question I'd been prepared to answer. And that was all *before* the photoshoot. The memory of that farce made me want to lower my forehead onto the table with a groan of embarrassed desolation. I was sure the entire fiasco had produced nothing but a series of images of me radiating varying degrees of confusion as the photographers told me to position my chin this way or that way, raise my lower eyelids (but not actually narrow my eyes) look towards the camera (but not at it) and all other manner of incomprehensible instructions I'd been scarcely able to carry out.

The sweat was drying on my forehead and Ted was looking at me with a fond expression. He opened his mouth to say something but closed it again as I shook my head. "I never should have agreed to do this," I said. "I'm needed at the ranch. Erin helps as much as she can, but she's still not that handy with a rope and she doesn't have any confidence around the young horses. It's like I told Cara when she tried to keep me on for the summer at Old Pueblo. I can't work full time without screwing over my dad and my brother."

Ted listened to my tirade but a strange expression crossed his face partway through. He let me finish, then shifted in his chair so he could pry his cell phone out of his pocket. "Text."

I ate another chip as Ted entered his pin and stared down at his screen. Without a word, he slid the phone across the table to me.

The screen was open to a text conversation. Most of the messages were old, leftovers from past correspondence. But the most recent message, contained in a blue bubble next to a tiny photo of Jay wearing a massive pink sparkly sombrero, was as clear as it was brief.

"She's hired."

Chapter 3

I tossed my keys into their basket on the counter and flopped my duffle bag onto the floor next to the couch, pausing to stretch my cramped back. Ted had suggested I invest in a rolling carry-on size suitcase, saying a duffle bag was fine for traveling now and then but a suitcase made moving around airports a lot easier. This was relevant to me because I was going to be spending a lot of time in airports in the near future.

I was officially the new TruGlide Girl. After the shocking text from Jay, Ted had explained 1) Jay was never outwardly impressed by anything and 2) TruGlide was desperate. They were desperate because they had an event less than one week away in which the TruGlide Girl positively must appear and ride a horse.

I wandered into my kitchen, gazing blearily at the clock on the stove. It was 11:33 PM on Monday. Sunday had been full of contract negotiations, followed by a whirlwind experience that involved a man, a tape measure, and more glittery clothing than I'd ever seen in one room in my life. Monday had involved a speech coach, a posture coach, a haircut, and a hat fitting.

Now, I was home. My quiet apartment was cool and dark. I let out a slow sigh and walked into the kitchen to pour myself a glass of water.

It was surreal. It was so surreal, the surrealness seemed to have extended past the TruGlide craziness and into my real life. I sipped my water and stood blinking and staring around my apartment as if I'd never seen it before.

I was exhausted. Ted had dropped hints he'd like to stay the night but I had pretended not to pick up on that. Despite being the most sociable member of my family, even I could reach capacity. I needed to be alone. I needed to think. I needed to process.

I carried my water into the living room and sat down on my couch. I caught a glimpse of a catalogue that had arrived in Friday's mail. I grabbed it and thumbed through, flipping through a selection of western wear, tack, and kitsch until I found what I'd been expecting. There was a full-page TruGlide ad separating the kitsch from the horse supplements. It was different from the one I'd seen on the back of *Western Rider*. It was a different horse, but this one was no less energetic in his attempt to stop from a gallop. I thought I detected a hint of stiffness in the girl's smile.

I stared at the girl I was supposed to metamorphosize into. Despite spending almost every moment of my waking hours over the weekend with TruGlide people, I had yet to garner any more specific details as to why the previous girl had left so abruptly. I'd asked Ted but he'd said he didn't know and not to worry about it.

I tossed the catalogue back onto the pile and flopped onto my couch. It was late and I was tired, but I felt a strange reluctance to go to bed. The problem was, I couldn't decide whether or not I was happy. This had come on so fast. Mere days ago, I'd been telling Cara why I couldn't stay on at Old Pueblo. Now, here I was, committing, at minimum, three months of my life to advertising a product I had only the haziest understanding of.

Ted supported me when I requested my initial contract be short-term. Jay seemed to think this a good idea as well. As things stood, I was only signed on for this wild scheme for a short while.

The problem was, it was precisely the same short while I was most needed around the Tipped Z. Which meant I was going to have to tell my brother something he did not want to hear.

Scowling around my sitting area, I leaned forward and pried at my boots until I'd hauled them free of my feet. Removing these particular boots while sitting down was quite an effort. But somehow heaving at them and cursing seemed easier than leaving the couch and walking back across the room to the boot jack.

Boots removed, I settled onto the couch cushions and stared up at the ceiling. Outside, I heard a coyote raise its voice in a thin howl. The single voice rose alone for a time, then the rest of the pack joined in. The high yips rose and fell into the night. For my part, I could never quite decide if the sound of coyotes was more eerie or nostalgic.

They did, however, remind me of home. Their yipping was a nightly serenade at the ranch. I thought again of my tall, somber brother and my still-very-healthy-but-getting-older father. I thought of the expression that would cross my brother's face when I told him about my new job.

My brother was not a gifted communicator. His primary method of conveying his innermost thoughts boiled down to different methods of staring. I could well imagine the stare he would direct at me when I broke my news. It made me squirm to think of it.

Which made me reconsider my previous thought. Perhaps my brother was a gifted communicator after all. Just not a verbal one.

And, just like that, an idea popped into my head. I didn't have to *tell* Clint about my new job. I could text him. Texting would take him out of his comfort zone (the ranch, staring) and into mine (the modern world, the English language). Suddenly energized, I bounced off my couch, realizing my phone was still off and stowed in the inner pocket of my purse.

I fished it free and turned it on. Unlike the rest of my technologically impaired family, I'd embraced the smartphone era without hesitation. My Nexus 5 was a brilliant, pleasing cherry red.

I held down the side button to call the device back to life, wandering into my bedroom as it sang its little ditty and swirled its lights at me. I let it finish its startup process as I changed from my travel clothes into the tank top and shorts I slept in. Then I brushed my teeth.

When I returned to my bedroom, my phone was fully on. I woke the screen to see I had a text. It was not from my brother but Erin.

I tapped the preview bubble and the message opened. "You coming out tomorrow? Because your brother gave me a filly to start and I have no idea what to do."

The round pen at the Tipped Z had solid sides. They were made of wooden panels snugged together and reinforced on the top and bottom. This design was quite deliberate. When young horses got panicky, they were liable to try to go over or through anything they could see beyond.

I approached the pen. It was Tuesday morning and I held a paper cup of coffee in my hand. The sun was still not quite intensified to baking status. As I walked, I looked around the ranch for any signs of life.

Off in the distance, a herd of horses grazed on the horizon. Chet and Fuzzface lay in the shade of the barn, sniffing in my direction but not bestirring themselves to come say hello. No other life was to be seen.

The round pen, however, was occupied. I knew this due to the conversation Erin and I have been conducting via text all morning. As a sort of late wedding present, my genius brother had given Erin a horse. And it was not the sort of horse you might expect a seasoned rancher to give his greenhorn wife. Had I been choosing a horse for Erin, it would have at least been broke to ride.

But not my brother. Oh no. He had given Erin an unstarted filly. She was three years old. And other than basic leading, she knew nothing.

This move baffled me. Although I didn't put a lot of stock in plenty of the conventional wisdom that governed how many people kept their horses, there was one well-known formula that was all too likely to be accurate. It was a simple, easy to remember principle. Green horse + green rider = black and blue. Hell, green horse + seasoned trainer still had a chance to = black and blue. This seemed like an accident waiting to happen.

In short, as I approached the round pen and climbed up one of the short ladders to reach the viewing platform, I couldn't guess at my brother's reasoning.

The filly stood near the panels of the round pen with one hip cocked. Looks-wise, she didn't immediately grab your attention. She was a plain bay, with a snip and a star and two hind socks. But it didn't take an expert to see her conformation was exceptional. She was as Tipped Z as they come. Her father was from our stud whose line went back to the very beginning of this ranch. Her mother was one of my father's most accomplished bridle horses. We'd kept her, I knew, both because she was not flashy to look at so wouldn't fetch as good a price as a youngster, and because if her temperament turned out to be what it should, we'd like her to have babies.

I recognized her because she was a horse my brother had asked me to start earlier this season. I'd said I would, but hadn't gotten around to following through.

My phone chimed. I looked away from the filly and down at the incoming text. Erin had responded to my, "I'm here," message with, "Be right out." I put the phone back in my pocket and stared down at the filly. I sipped my coffee, feeling an unpleasant blend of nerves and confusion.

I'd followed through on my plan to inform my brother of my abrupt career change via text rather than in person. What I hadn't considered when I'd composed and sent my brief explanation before getting into bed the night before was the potential for delay. If I was somewhat lackadaisical about keeping my phone with me and on, my brother was positively careless. Since his marriage, he'd at least agreed to make sure he carried a cell phone with him when he was out on horseback. That didn't mean he'd agreed to leave it on or to check it with any regularity though. Erin wanted him to have one so he would have some means of calling for help other than sending Dots in search of rescue in the event of an accident.

Now I didn't know if Clint had seen my message and declined to respond, or if he hadn't seen it and therefore did not yet know my news. It was maddening to wonder.

I heard a step behind me. Erin walked around the corner. I had to smile when I saw her. I could still recall the first time she'd appeared at the ranch, the day she'd rolled up in her little car, wearing designer jeans and running shoes, staring at the cluster of warning signs my father had erected to keep unwelcome visitors at bay as if they would bite her.

Now, she looked like a rancher's wife. She had a flat-brimmed hat on her head, positioned to keep the sun out of her eyes. A pair of chinks covered her jeans, their fringe swinging around the tops of her well-healed, well-worn boots. She saw me looking over the pen. "What do you think?"

I waited until she'd climbed up beside me, looking down at the filly and trying to think of something to say that would not betray the fact I suspected the stress had driven my brother mad. "She's a beauty." This was not a lie. If I hadn't been so strapped for time, I'd have enjoyed starting this horse myself.

Erin's face lit up. She stared down at the young horse with a kind of awe. "Clint showed me her papers. He's got her registered in my name and everything."

I suppressed a groan. I wondered if my brother had come up with this solution as an indirect means of forcing me to take on a task I'd been neglecting.

"He said he's going to help me," Erin went on. "We already did one session with her this morning. Then your dad needed something. Clint said he'd come back, but then he came to the fence and said he had to go out somewhere and it might a while. He said to put her in the saddle pen. But then I tried to get her halter on and I couldn't get near her. So I thought I'd maybe wait for you." Erin's voice took on a wistful quality as she regarded the horse. It reminded me of how a mother might look at a wayward teenager who has broken her heart by getting caught up in drugs or crime or atheism.

"Well," I said, straightening and trying to inject my tone with some enthusiasm, "let's get her caught, then."

About an hour later, a beaming Erin untied the filly's halter and watched as the sweat-soaked young animal hurried away to roll in the gritty sand of the saddle pen. The saddle pen was a smallish dry lot where we kept horses we didn't want to have to hike a mile (or several) to get our hands on. The exact horses we kept near the ranch rotated.

Clint often had a youngster penned here, whose job it would be first thing in the morning to ride out, find the horse or horses Clint wanted to work that day, and pony them back in. My dad often kept a project horse here as well. When I was coming in for an afternoon, they'd often put Sally here so I would more quickly be able to do something other than getting my own horse caught and saddled.

Now, Erin's filly stood up hurriedly as the small herd noted her presence and came trotting over from the gigantic old tire full of hay that served as a feeder. Erin and I waited by the gate and watched as the various horses snorted and postured a bit, then pranced around the space to show off and establish dominance. While Erin seemed content to watch, I was sweaty, thirsty, and annoyed. My brother still hadn't texted back but I had received several emails from my stylist at TruGlide asking unintelligible questions about my hair's personality. As ridiculous as they seemed, they weren't the sort of questions I could ignore.

I moved slowly but steadily towards the gate as Erin drifted after me, only turning away from her filly when the herd cantered down a low hill and the lay of the land concealed them from view.

It had been a productive morning, all told. It hadn't, of course, taken us an hour to catch the filly. But I'd had Erin work at catching her and letting her go, driving her and asking her to come in, until the filly demonstrated a reasonable understanding of the idea that humans were to be approached rather than avoided. Then we'd worked on leading. Now I was ready to get out of the sun.

Erin, for her part, had spent the morning vacillating between studied confidence and stymied awe. Up until this point, Erin's hands-on experience with horses extended to animals that were not only broke, but BROKE. The horse that had become hers by default, Duke, was a quiet giant who invested a considerable amount of mental energy in finding ways to do what he was asked while moving as little as possible.

This mare was young, athletic, and did not know much about people. She overreacted to some things and underreacted to others.

In short, she was a normal youngster. Which meant she was a handful.

As Erin and I walked the short distance from the saddle pen to the hay room and stepped off the baked sand through the bay doors, Erin spoke. "I hope I don't ruin her."

Coming from Clint's wife, this was not a surprising statement. Clint was the sort of person who believed horses only reached their full potential if everyone who so much as looked at them in passing did everything precisely right, all the time. It was one of the reasons he usually refused to take riding students. It was physically painful for him to watch someone pull a little too hard on a rein or release pressure a little too late.

I had more faith in the intelligence and flexibility of animals. I laughed. "You won't."

Erin turned to me, expression doubtful.

I stopped to wipe my forehead and fan my face with my hat. "Oh, you'll make mistakes. But horses are more resilient than certain people may have led you to believe."

Erin smiled the gentle smile that meant she was thinking romantic things about my brother. "Thank you, Nora." She sank onto the stacked bales behind her and said in a wondering tone, "I'm exhausted."

Before I could answer, Fuzzface looked towards the small door that led in from the parking area. A moment later, Chet looked up as well. A moment after that, I heard the engine. Both the dogs went stiff and stood, walking towards the open door in alert "we are not familiar with this vehicle" mode. Curious, I trailed after them and peeped out the door.

I saw the bumper at approximately the same moment the driver's door opened and a boot stepped out onto the packed dirt parking area. Heart suddenly pounding, I retreated from the door to stare at Erin in consternation. She looked up at me, confused by my reaction. "Who is it?"

Before I could answer, Wyatt stepped around the door with Chet and Fuzzface at his heels. He stopped inside the room, letting his eyes adjust to the shadows. I saw him see us.

"Wyatt." The word jerking out of me in an unplanned spasm, like a stuck horse turning loose.

Wyatt took his hat off and held it against his chest like he'd entered a church. He glanced over at me and Erin. "Ladies."

I became very aware of my sticky shirt and all the wispy stray hairs that had made their way out of my braid to cling in a damp, unattractive way to my forehead. My hair's personality, I decided I would tell my TruGlide stylist, was backstabbing.

Wyatt came a few steps further into the barn and glanced down the aisle that led to the stalls. Then he walked to the open bay door to look out over the scrubby pastures. "Heard you got a new job, Nora." He spoke without looking at me.

I stared at his back, dumbfounded. Erin's face took on a puzzled look that told me she'd not heard my news. What was it with my brother and this guy? Did they share some sort of arcane telepathic connection?

"Kind of landed on me out of the blue, more like." I tried to make my voice sound casual.

Wyatt turned from his contemplation of the landscape. Backlit, he made a fine outline. His shoulders were broad, hips narrow. Before he could speak again, I rallied my wits. "I thought you were starting racehorses in California."

A pained look crossed Wyatt's face. His jaw bore that perfect amount of stubble that indicated a certain scruffiness without going so far as to be sloppy. "Had a disagreement with the boss over my methods," he said. "Decided to move on." He glanced out the doors again, as if he might see something on the landscape that hadn't been there before. "I got your brother's text at the crack of dawn, just before I would have hit I-17 and headed north. I'd planned to drop in at the Babbitt ranch. They've always got colts to start this time of year. I thought they might give me some rides. But then Clint's offer popped up. Seemed too much a chance to turn aside from, you know?"

There was a moment of silence as I parsed this. Wyatt had lost his job in California. He'd been in his truck, having apparently driven through the night. He'd been in Phoenix, about to go north, several hours ago. He'd gotten a text from my brother probably right when Clint woke up and saw my text letting him know about my employment plan for the summer.

It all clicked together. I felt a strange dip in my chest, as if my heart had taken on an entirely different relationship with gravity than the rest of my body. "How long will you be staying?"

Wyatt shrugged. His eyes flicked to me and then darted away again. "Hard to say."

⚙

"No, look *up*." My stylist's tone was filled with frustration. "Lift your eyebrows. I can't work with a frown."

I tried again to look up. But I found this difficult on account of the fact that my eyes were closed. My efforts must have produced some improved effect, however, because I felt the feathery touches of a makeup brush on my eyelids. My stylist's silence indicated I'd perhaps gotten it right this time.

I sat in the sort of rotating chair usually reserved for people getting their hair cut. I wore one of those black sheets that was supposed to prevent shorn hair from falling into your clothes. But my hair was already done and was not to be touched, at all, by my own hand or any other, on pain of death. My outfit was also assembled and on my person. I could hardly breathe due to the crusty bling adhered to the fabrics. I was finding out bling was heavy and nonflexible and had a tendency to gouge you when you sat down.

The last step was the makeup. When that was done, I would be released from this chair. I would then proceed to the dress rehearsal for my first TruGlide event. Normally, I was informed, the dress rehearsal would be less elaborate. I wouldn't be done up in full costume and my full staff wouldn't attend me. But since tomorrow was going to be my first time out in public as the TruGlide Girl, I needed a trial run. So here we were in a makeshift dressing room at the back of the giant, empty arena that would be full of spectators tomorrow.

As I looked up into the red darkness of the interior of my eyelids, my thoughts wandered back to Wyatt and his surprise appearance at the

Tipped Z. More of the story had emerged over the course of the last few days and been relayed to me via Erin.

According to Clint, Wyatt had been let go from his job at the track because his boss felt he'd been "babying" the colts. This was surprising information. I'd seen Wyatt start plenty of horses. He usually had them out of a round pen and doing a job within a few rides. Therefore, I guessed in this case "babying" was a code for "doing groundwork."

In some areas of the horse world there seemed to be this stoic resistance to any method that might lead a horse to take to riding more easily. I supposed it was because gentle horses were perceived by the ignorant to be less spirited. Anyone who'd seen my brother's dog quiet bridle horses run down a bull or cut a calf out of herd would know this wasn't true. But some racehorse owners felt a colt that didn't balk and buck and come undone his first ride was not being started properly.

"Okay, now I need you to pout." I pulled my mind back to the present and attempted to comply. The brushing sensation left my eyelids and transferred to my lips. My stylist had not specified whether or not I could open my eyes. I played it safe and kept them shut.

I was not a stranger to stage makeup. Every day at Old Pueblo the stylist had swept through to put finishing touches on the cast. But most of us had done the bulk of our application ourselves. It appeared, in the TruGlide world, I was not to be trusted with my own appearance.

My stylist was named Maggie. She was a middle-aged African American woman with a slim, well-clad figure and an intimidating set of false nails that clacked against each implement she picked up. She made little noises of displeasure and concern as she worked, often swiveling me a bit back and forth in the chair, apparently to better assess the impact of her handiwork on my unsatisfactory features. "Okay," she said at last. "Considering I don't have a feel for your skin yet and your custom bases have not arrived, I guess that's the best I can do." Her tone was aggrieved, as if I had constructed this situation just to challenge her skills.

I took this as leave to open my eyes. It took a moment for them to adjust to the bright light. Then, I stared into the mirror.

The TruGlide Girl stared back. I felt a strange shock—a shifting tilt in my head. This was me? I raised a hand to the elaborate coloring of my lips but Maggie swatted it away with the same efficiency a cook might block a child from a rack of cooling cookies. "Na ah. Do not touch. Try not to lick them, either."

As I wondered how I could get through a reining demo without licking my lips, Maggie stooped to remove the black sheet. She swung it aside and my bling-infested outfit sprang to life, sparkling. I had to squint at myself in the mirror.

I wore a brilliant red top festooned with swirls of fake gemstones. My jeans had blingified rear pockets. They were plain enough on the front, but this was because I was going to strap on a pair of fawn white chinks with red fringe and accents. My boots were also red with white toe stitching.

No matter what kind of performance I managed to put on, I was going to shine in at least one sense of the word.

I was enduring some last-minute adjustments to the arrangement of my hair when Jay found me. He came striding into the makeup area, his narrow face grim. I'd begun to grow at least somewhat used to Jay since the fiasco that had been my audition but he was still difficult to read.

He stopped in front of me and looked me up and down for a long, long time. My stylist melted into the background. I stood alone, feeling brittle and overly made up, enduring the scrutiny.

Jay's look was direct but not rude. It was not at all the sort of look I was used to receiving from tipsy frat boys when I went out to hit the downtown scene with my girlfriends. This was the look of an artist stepping back to get perspective on his painting or a car enthusiast who had just hand applied a fresh coat of wax.

In short, Jay was no longer looking at me. He was looking at the TruGlide Girl. I found this knowledge comforting. I endured the blue stare until, at last, Jay said, "The red is good on you. But it's not going to work with this horse."

It was something about the way he said "this horse" that got my attention. I considered the phrasing. But before I could say anything, Jay added, "Nora, don't frown. The TruGlide Girl always looks friendly."

I did not have a mirror handy. Nevertheless, I was reasonably aware of what my mouth was doing. "I'm not..." I started.

Jay tapped his forehead. "A frown starts here." He indicated the place between his eyebrows. Then he gripped my elbow and steered me out of my staging area and through a door into a massive space full of echoes and shadows.

Annoyed, I moved with him, forcing myself to release the tension in my brow. The area around us was full of nothing. "There's no one around, anyway."

Jay's stern expression grew frosty. Apparently he was not prohibited from wearing unfriendly facial expressions. His response was quick and predictable.

"When you're in costume, you are in character, no matter who is or is not present. I would think you'd know that." He gave me an assessing look, as if he was wondering if he'd made a mistake hiring me.

I let out a slow breath and tried to look contrite without wrinkling my forehead. We continued to walk, our footsteps ringing on the bare concrete floor. "I'm sorry. I'm a little nervous. I don't have a feel for my character yet." I paused, watching as a maintenance worker appeared in the distance and began to sweep the floor.

We were in a rodeo arena in Phoenix where a reining competition would take place tomorrow. The place was resounding in its emptiness now, but I knew the next day would be a different story.

Jay didn't answer. He led me unerringly across the large space. I tried not to think about how many people could fit in a place like this and the fact that all of them would see me in my ridiculous costume. I glanced at Jay. "What did you say about my horse?"

We reached the end of the space. Jay pushed open a set of metal doors. They led into a warm-up arena, which was occupied by one drowsy horse and one bored-looking boy of about twelve or thirteen. "They said the horse would be light gray." Jay's tone was aggrieved. "We planned your outfit accordingly."

We stopped walking. The metal door boomed shut behind us. I considered the horse. It was, indeed, not gray. It was a deep sorrel with four tall white socks and a broad blaze that went crooked where it met the nose, giving the horse an off-kilter look. I stared at the animal as the horse's boy stared at me. "You didn't know what color my horse was?" I tried to sound more confused than accusatory.

Jay flicked a cool glance in my direction. "The gray one injured a leg or something." He paced around the arena, frowning. "This isn't going to work. Red and red. It's not enough contrast. We could do you in purple but I don't think we have a purple outfit assembled."

I felt there was something here I was not understanding. It niggled at the edge of my awareness, some small but crucial piece that had not yet clicked into place. I watched Jay as he paced. "How many horses does the TruGlide Girl have?"

Jay waved an airy hand at the horse and the boy. "We have regional partners who provide mounts. This horse is qualified to do what you need to do out there, I'm sure." His tone was dismissive and uninterested. I blinked several times and I tried not to grow discomfited by the fact the boy was still staring at me. I knew I sparkled like a disco ball but I was ready for him to get over it.

At that moment, another man came striding out of a different door that led into the warm-up arena. He wore a curled Stetson and square-toed boots with short heels. He was middle-aged and he walked as if the oversized gold and silver buckle on his belt provided the impulsion that allowed him to move. He strode across the arena, smiling at Jay and me in turns. I, remembering my character, smiled back. But I did not smile directly at the man. I employed one of my Old Pueblo tricks, which was to smile at an area rather than a single person.

"Jay," the man said expansively, coming to stop near the boy's shoulder. The horse, who had been dozing, came awake as the man drew near. Its ears tipped back in a way I recognized as defensive.

My opinion of the man took a considerable hit. Jay, who had not bothered to smile, gave the man one of his long, cool looks. "We were told the horse would be gray." His tone was frosty. "Light gray," he added with a glance at my glittering red and white outfit. "This color scheme will not cut it. We've had a recent change in the roll. What normally would be a last-minute scramble is ..." He trailed off, as if the impossibility of the situation exceeded his vocabulary.

The man's smile grew stiff. "We had a little accident getting the gray one in the trailer. I assure you this horse is capable of putting on a fine show." The man had a vague Texas accent. His tone managed to be obsequious, condescending, and self-satisfied all at once. It began to dawn on me I had not been introduced. I couldn't decide whether or not I should be offended.

As if these words were the last straw, Jay turned on the man, pale face livid as two bright spots of color lit his high cheekbones. "Mr. Simmons." He pronounced the name like a rebuke. "This is not some common competition for points, or time, or whatever. This is a performance. We coordinated the TruGlide Girl's entire outfit around the belief the horse would be gray." His voice, which had risen to a sort of crescendo on the last few words, now softened and took on a tone of unmistakable threat. "Now. Can you get me a gray horse—light gray— within an hour? Or am I going to need to find a new regional vendor?"

Mr. Simmons' face had drained of color as Jay spoke his piece. Now, it flushed red. He stepped towards his horse, snatching the reins from the boy so abruptly the horse flung its head, popped itself in the mouth with whatever massive bit it was wearing, squealed at the shock of it, and hopped into a mini rear. Mr. Simmons strode forward, whacking the horse on the shoulder with the ends of the reins. The animal shied away. Mr. Simmons gave the bit a jerk and the poor horse slung its head one last time before it lapsed into a sort of catatonic stillness.

Mr. Simmons turned blazing eyes on Jay. "This is bullshit," he said. "I don't need to take this kind of crap from the likes of you." There was something sneering and unpleasant in his face that made my cheeks flush red with embarrassment, as if his words had been directed at me.

He stormed away, dragging the horse after him. The boy, forced to wrench his eyes away from me, followed at a nervous jog. I watched in bemused confusion as the three of them exited through the large bay door that led into a parking lot.

I looked at Jay. He stood with two long, slender fingers pressed to the bridge of his nose, as if he had a migraine.

Having now seen what it looked like when Jay's wrath was invoked, I decided to save my questions for later. Clearly, we were now lacking a horse, of any color, both for today's dress rehearsal and tomorrow's event. I was certain, however, Jay did not need me to point this out to him.

We stood in silence for a long time. Outside, the motor of a truck roared to life. The arena was silent except for a few sparrows fluttering and chirping in the rafters.

I waited. When Jay spoke, he did so without looking at me. The voice coming from behind his hand was free of the ire it had carried a moment before. "Nora." His tone was low. "Would you happen to know of somewhere nearby where one might find a gray horse on short notice?"

I stared at him. Presumably, he meant a gray horse that could execute a reining pattern and some impressive sliding stops. While we did have several gray horses at the ranch and all of them could stop on a dime, they were trained to move in a way that was designed to maximize their soundness and longevity, not blow their hocks before they were fully grown. They wouldn't work for this show.

I was about to shake my head, but Jay looked up with an expression of pleading supplication. I caved. I reached for my phone. "I'll call my brother."

Only when my fingers found my empty pocket did I remember the TruGlide Girl did not carry electronics on her person. Jay's mouth quirked into some semblance of a smile as he handed me his iPhone. I dialed the Tipped Z.

Chapter 4

Jay passed me the bag of Skittles. I accepted it, tipping the red crinkly bag so several small bits of compressed sugar fell into my palm. I held my hand towards Jay, who plucked the purple Skittle free from the cluster of its yellow, green, orange, and red peers. Jay, I had discovered recently, adored purple Skittles. I hated them.

Jay and I were sitting side by side in foldable black chairs with the TruGlide logo embroidered on their backs. Jay was in full-on lounge mode, one of his thin legs cocked over the chair's arm, the other propped on an ice chest that stood before us.

It was still the day of the ill-fated dress rehearsal, but I was no longer dressed. That is to say, Maggie and my other stylists had long since departed, taking my outfit with them for the night. I'd reverted to my serviceable jeans and t-shirt.

Jay and I were waiting. We'd been waiting for a long, long time. This was the third bag of Skittles Jay had purchased from a vending machine. We'd also ordered sandwiches.

Jay had spent much of the day on the phone, pacing around the echoing expanse of the under-bleacher area, gesticulating and talking in ringing tones that reverberated around the strange space. I, having resolved to bring several books with me to every event from now forward, passed the time by watching Jay and trying very hard not to think about certain key aspects of the way this day was panning out.

When I'd dialed the Tipped Z after Mr. Simmons the reining trainer had disappeared with his horse and his boy, I hadn't expected anyone to answer. More than anything, I'd made the call to mollify Jay. There was a phone in my parents' house and also one in the barn, but rarely were there actual people near enough to hear either one ring. My plan had been to call Clint's house next, fully believing Erin would answer and tell us Clint was out doing something somewhere and she didn't know when he'd be back.

So I'd been quite surprised with the Tipped Z phone had been picked up on the second ring. "Tipped Z." It was Wyatt's voice. There had been a humorous tone to it, as if he was smiling at some private joke.

The surprise kept me from making any noise at all until Jay made a hurrying gesture with his hand. "Wyatt?" I said.

"Nora?" he said back.

After the warm bloom of surprise he would recognize my voice so quickly had worn off, I'd asked for my brother.

"Not here, señorita," Wyatt said. I heard something clink in the background, followed by the thud of a hoof. "He and your father had to go to some land-owners association meeting. They left me with a bunch of trims to take care of."

This comment deepened my feeling of surprise. My brother was very particular about who he let touch the feet of our ranch horses.

Then the words sank in. It was what I'd expected. If Clint wasn't around the ranch, it was unlikely I'd be able to reach him.

Before I could say anything else, Wyatt said, "Why? What's up? Aren't you supposed to be at that thing for work?"

I glanced over at Jay. He was watching me from under his hand like a hawk watches a frolicking rabbit.

I hurried to explain. "Yes, I'm at work now. That's why I'm calling. We have a bit of a problem." Then, because I couldn't think of a way to get off the phone without telling him, I explained the situation.

Now, I handed the bag of Skittles back to Jay, placing a green one on my tongue and feeling the bite of the sugar and the fake lime flavor. I hadn't eaten Skittles in years. If I wasn't very much mistaken, the inside of my mouth was now blotched with a riot of colorful stains.

Jay, who had his phone set in the drink holder of the chair arm and kept looking at it as if he hoped it would ring, tipped more Skittles into his own hand. "I just hope it's not too dark of a brown."

Jay had said this at least four or five times in the last several hours. I suppressed the urge to sigh. I'd explained what a palomino was and shown him photos on my phone. However, since I'd been unable to show him a photo of the exact horse that would be arriving at any moment now, he remained unconvinced we'd dodged a bullet.

When I made no reply, Jay continued. "I wouldn't have thought a gray horse was such a difficult thing to get ahold of."

I'd spent much of the afternoon vacillating between various extreme emotions and had now settled in a nervy sort of fatigue. I found myself answering Jay with a touch of asperity. "Most reining prospects are very young. Gray horses are all born black or some other dark color. They fade with time. All the grays Wyatt's guy had around were still on the dark end of the spectrum."

Jay gave a nonlinguistic grunt. I was still trying to wrap my mind around the bizarre fact Wyatt had not only answered my phone call, but he'd also solved our problem. I hadn't even known what kind of help I'd been hoping for when I placed the call. But as soon as I'd explained, Wyatt had spoken up. "I know a guy in Scottsdale. I've been starting colts for him for years. Let me see if he's got anything that might work. Call you back."

Wyatt had hung up. Jay and I had waited in tense silence until Jay's phone rang again a few minutes later. Jay had looked at the screen and handed it to me without answering.

"No grays," Wyatt said. "At least, no light grays." My heart started to plummet before he added, "But he's got a super nice palomino mare. She's been earning points in regionals."

"Oh." I looked at Jay with trepidation. "This sounds promising."

It had proven to be complicated. Since I'd driven up to Phoenix without a trailer, I could not go pick up the horse myself. According to Wyatt, the guy who owned this fortuitous palomino would let us use her for the weekend but could not deliver her. And so, Wyatt simply said he'd bring her over for us. Before I'd been able to consider the inconvenience this would cause him or wonder if there could be a simpler way, he hung up.

I didn't have Wyatt's cell number. So we waited. It was a couple hours from the Tipped Z to Scottsdale and at least another hour from Scottsdale to the arena where Jay and I sat and ate Skittles for what felt like the longest afternoon of my life.

As Jay fretted over the precise shade of this palomino's coat, I wondered about Wyatt. Why was he doing this for me? And more importantly, how angry was Clint going to be? First, I'd abandoned him for the summer. Second, I'd commandeered the hand he'd found to replace me on a day he was needed around the ranch.

But most of all: Wyatt. Wyatt, who never seemed to be able to say more than three words to me without asking where Clint was, was driving all over the state of Arizona to bring me a horse.

Jay crumpled the empty Skittles bag in his hand. He was gazing with a speculative expression towards the dark cranny where the vending machines crouched when we heard the rumble of a truck engine in the arena. We'd propped one of the metal doors open so we could sit in the cooler area under the bleachers but still know the moment Wyatt arrived. I surged out of my chair as Jay rose with a languid, unhurried manner that suggested he'd just woken from a nap rather than spent the bulk of the day sitting around with his newest employee.

We walked towards the door as the nose of Wyatt's familiar Dodge rolled to a stop in the arena. The driver's door opened. The same boot I'd watched step down to earth at the Tipped Z a few days before descended again. Then Jay and I were through the doors and Wyatt was standing there adjusting his hat and smiling at me around a bemused expression. "Nora," he said after Jay introduced himself and they shook hands. "I've never seen you so ..." He stopped, as if experiencing a sudden change of heart about what he'd been going to say. He went very still, apparently confused by the fact that I was wearing makeup. I wondered what kind of reaction he would have had if he'd seen me in full TruGlide Girl regalia.

We stood like that, me waiting, Wyatt staring, until a thump sounded in the trailer. Wyatt seemed to shake himself back to life. Turning, he said, "Best get this girl unloaded."

The horse Wyatt stepped out of the trailer was a magnificent animal—tall and round with a downy white mane and tail. She had the short, shiny coat of a horse that has never been allowed to experience seasonal variations in temperature. Her nose and ears were clipped, her hooves oiled. But she backed out of the trailer softly and then stood with Wyatt, head raised, brown eyes wide, showing no signs of stress.

Jay, who'd been watching Wyatt, shifted his gaze to the horse. He pursed his lips as he took in her creamy coat and perfectly white mane and tail. "Well," he said, sounding pleased. "I think this one will do just fine."

I stood staring at the sunset, listening to the hiss of the pump as I filled Wyatt's truck with gas. Around me, the hot air smelled of dust and gas and creosote. Overhead, the voices of the Dixie Chicks drifted out of the tinny station speakers. On the nearby roadway, cars and trucks whizzed by in the warm evening.

I stared at the scene with bleary eyes. I was almost intolerably tired. The events of the past 48 hours seemed little more than a colorful blur in my memory.

The horse had worked out. Wyatt had given me a crash course on how to ask for a sliding stop, left me his truck and the trailer he'd borrowed from the ranch, and taken my truck back down to Tucson. I'd been left with the palomino, Wyatt's keys, and directions back to the place Wyatt had picked the horse up.

Compared to the fiasco of the dress rehearsal, the event itself had seemed unbelievably straightforward. After spending an uncomfortable night in a hotel and enduring the process of being turned into the TruGlide Girl again, the horse and I had waited together until it was our turn to perform. Since we were a living, breathing, sliding advertisement rather than performers or competitors, there was a great deal of leeway in what I could do when I put on my show. "Do the slides," Jay directed me. "And make the horse run around. Don't forget to smile."

For all the care and attention that went into the simplest details of my outfit, I found it bizarre that things like the horse I rode and what I did, precisely, while hundreds of people were watching was left more or less to chance.

I did the slides. I made the horse run around. I smiled. It went off without a hitch. The horse knew her job. The crowd cheered. While I was riding, a smooth-voiced man boomed over the PA system, extolling the virtues of the TruGlide patented shoeing system.

It was the part that came after I got off the horse I found difficult. With the palomino safely returned to her stall, it became my job to "work the crowd." This involved walking around with little TruGlide gift bags and forcing them into the hands of anyone who made eye contact with me. Sometimes the exchange culminated in posing for photos.

I escaped as soon as Jay found me and said we'd "reached our target saturation." This, I gathered, meant I was done for the day. I all but sprinted for the dressing area, stripped off my costume, washed off as much of my makeup as I could. Then I loaded up the horse, declined Jay's repeated offers to put me up for another night at the hotel, and drove off.

Now I was on my way home. The trailer was light and empty, the horse having been safely returned to her rightful owner. My nails were thick with polish, my hair crusty with product. More than anything, I needed a shower and a good night's sleep.

The pump clicked off. Being extra careful to screw down the cap and close the compartment on this truck that wasn't mine, I realized it would have been nice for me to have cleaned the windshield. Too tired to delay my return home by even a minute or two, I collected my receipt and stepped up into the cab of Wyatt's truck.

It was impossible not to think about Wyatt as I put his truck in gear and rolled forward. I still couldn't believe the way he'd dropped everything to solve my problem. Which hadn't, strictly speaking, even been my problem. Jay was the one who'd rejected the red horse.

Once, when Ted and I first started dating, he told me a work story in which he'd described Jay as "high-maintenance." At the time, I hadn't computed what he meant. Now, I was beginning to understand.

Still, I felt a certain closeness had been forged this weekend between Jay and me. We'd had a problem. We'd worked it out. Jay had thanked Wyatt, even if he hadn't seemed to grasp what a remarkable feat Wyatt had pulled off in providing us with an extremely well-trained reining horse of a suitable color at the 11th hour. Wyatt himself had not seemed to think it a big deal. The night he'd arrived with the horse and I'd saddled up for a test ride, he'd said as I settled onto her back, "I started this one. She was a doll. I imagine she's a pretty nice ride these days."

Back on the highway, I felt myself fighting heavy eyelids as the sunset faded and the night grew thick around me. It was very important I not wreck Wyatt's truck and my father's trailer. Doing so would amount to the worst sort of ingratitude. Not to mention, it would delay the warm shower and soft bed I'd been fantasizing about for half the day.

On the seat next to me, my phone lit up and began to ring. I answered, relieved to have something to think about other than how tired I was.

Ted's voice was warm and concerned when he responded to my hello. "How you holding up?"

Ted had been on Jay's side on the question of the hotel room. I was the only one of the TruGlide staff not staying in Phoenix another night. But then, I was the only one of the TruGlide staff who lived in Tucson.

I gazed at the road. Traffic was light. I was on the narrow, two-lane highway that connected the small town of Florence to the greater Tucson area. "I think my hair weighs three times as much as usual. Whole sections have lost the ability to bend."

Ted laughed. A truck roared by in the other lane, its high, bright lights temporarily blinding me. "Jay says you were great today."

The remark surprised me—not only because it revealed my boss had been speaking to my boyfriend while I'd been returning borrowed horses and driving across the state of Arizona, but because the feedback was so unequivocally positive. "He says you saved his bacon."

It wasn't easy to hear Ted over the growl of the engine and the highway noise. "It was all Wyatt." I thought again of how Wyatt had looked when he'd unloaded the palomino, smiling in a way that had made me remember him as a ten-year-old kid, the day he and my brother noticed the bull had gotten out. They'd taken their old saddle horses and a couple of dogs and managed, remarkably, to get the animal back into its pasture. My father had been incensed but he could hardly punish them for doing something so helpful. I'd watched from the sidelines as my father had lectured them on how dangerous bulls could be. Wyatt stood there, pretending to listen, smiling that smile that indicated he was awfully pleased with himself.

There was a beat of silence. Ted spoke. "That was nice of him." Another beat. A small car with a tapered hood and a loud engine whipped out of the lane behind me and passed with an unnecessary revving of its engine. I ignored the look the driver cast at me and kept my eyes on the road. "I thought he went to California," Ted added.

Around me, the night was all silver and black. The shapes of saguaros and mesquites loomed briefly into three dimensions as my headlights hit them, then faded into flat cutout shapes. I hadn't told Ted I was driving Wyatt's truck home. It seemed an unnecessary detail. Next to me on the bench seat lay a random selection of Wyatt's belongings. A flattened baseball cap, a battered paperback without a cover, a soft-sided cooler. There was a bootjack in the footwell and three folding camp chairs stowed behind the seat.

It was strange I could feel I knew Wyatt so well despite the fact we'd never had an adult style "let's talk about life" conversation. It was strange Ted and I had had loads of those conversations and yet I'd never be able to see his smile and recall his face at ten years old. "My brother asked him to come back to the ranch."

In front of me, the road did a sharp bend. I let off the gas for a moment as a coyote, thin and slinking, made its way from the shadows at one side of the highway to the other. "I should go," I added. "I need to be alert on this highway."

There was something a little unhappy in Ted's silence. But whatever he might have been thinking, he didn't give it voice. I listened to the rumble of the truck's engine until he said, "Remember, pull over if you get tired. There's nothing wrong with stopping if you realize you're too worn out to keep going."

I adjusted the brim of my hat, pulling it down a little lower to keep the sun out of my eyes as it rose over the mountains.

"And she's stepping under nicely on both sides." Erin's voice carried a pleased tone. I listened, standing on the observation platform overlooking the round pen, watching Erin and her filly do their thing. "I've been working with her every day," Erin added, stopping to rub the filly's neck.

What she'd shown me was pretty good, especially when you considered Erin's inexperience with green horses and the filly's absolute lack of prior education. Erin had the filly leading well and yielding to pressure. The filly, for her part, seemed to be taking to these new tasks with equanimity. If she came into Erin's space a little more than I would have liked and sometimes stared off into the distance instead of responding to something Erin was asking—well, those were little details we could iron out with time.

"Good work," I said. Sleeping in my own bed the past two nights had nearly restored me. I was already finding myself inclined to look back on my first TruGlide experience with good humor. My nails were back to their natural, unpainted state. Although the smell of all that crazy product still lingered in my hair, I was sure it was only a matter of another shower or two. "Have you had a saddle on her?"

Erin turned to look up at me, an expression of consternation on her face. "No." Her voice was quick and worried. "Should I have? Clint keeps saying he'll check in with me on how she's doing but ..." She trailed off, turning for a moment to regard the filly's profile. "Things keep coming up."

A little twist of guilt worked in my stomach. If I hadn't commandeered Wyatt for half the weekend, my brother might have had a little more spare time. Judging from the stiff set of Clint's shoulders when he'd seen me arrive that morning and the way he'd stalked off without speaking to me, he was aware of this fact as well.

"It's no big deal." Perhaps spurred farther than I might have otherwise gone due to feelings of guilt, I added, "We can go ahead and do it now if you want."

Erin agreed without hesitation. She removed her filly's halter and left her in the pen. We adjourned to the barn to gather the required equipment. I glanced at my watch as we walked. I had a video call with Jay a little later today. We were going to "discuss outcomes" and "modify our game plan" now that I had survived my first event as the TruGlide Girl. I wanted to be home in plenty of time to prepare to speak to him. Because I had a plan.

Still, I had enough time to help Erin with this. Clint and Wyatt were off repairing a fence somewhere and my dad was delivering a horse we'd sold. Now was as good a time as any.

"How was your thing this weekend?" Erin asked as we made our way passed the sprawled forms of Chet and Fuzzface and into the tack room. "Wyatt said the arena you were going to perform in was huge."

Unaccountably, my face went warm and prickly when Erin said this. In the interest of keeping my back to her, I strode into the room with unnecessary speed, flipping on the light as I passed the switch. "You should have seen my outfit. I could hardly see for the way all that bling reflected the overhead lights."

Erin veered across the room to where her saddle sat on its rack. Hers was by far the newest rig in the room. Though the seat was starting to look respectably broken in, its pommel and cantle and skirts still shone buttery smooth and unblemished in the dim light.

I, however, walked to a different corner of the room. As Erin set her hand on her horn, preparing to lift her saddle off its rack, I said, "Hold your horses there, girl. You don't want to put that beauty on a colt."

Erin's saddle was on the extravagant side. Clint had given it to her a few months after their engagement. He'd had it custom made by a guy who specialized in crafting good using saddles with a stout horn and solid tree built with lighter rigging, skirts trimmed back to a bare minimum. Erin liked it because it was easy for her to get on and off the towering Duke. Clint liked it because it was sturdy enough to rope off of.

Erin turned to look at me, hand still on the horn. I handed her a stack of old pads of varying thicknesses. "Bring these." Then I lifted what had been beneath the pads.

The saddle I carried back to the round pen was as old and used as Erin's was new. I didn't know its full story but there was no question as to its place on the ranch. It had been old even when I was a kid. My grandfather, father, and brother all preferred it for starting colts because it had a snug seat and a narrower tree that fitted well on most Quarter Horses still in the process of filling out.

Erin, carrying the pads, trailed after me as I made my way back to the round pen. She looked at the saddle with an air of dubious curiosity. "What's wrong with mine?"

We reached the round pen. I worked the latch on the gate with one hand, propping the saddle on my hip. "This one is already good and scuffed up and the tree is as sturdy as they come. If a horse flips over or goes down on it, it'll be fine. And even if the tree did break," I gave the worn skirts a pat, "it would be a fitting end to a long life."

I walked through the gate and looked back. Erin seemed to have frozen in place, her face a little pale in the bright sun. When she caught my eyes, she seemed to snap back to life. "Flip over?" She hurried through the gate and latched it behind her. "Do they do that?"

In our absence, the filly had rolled. She was now nosing along the edge of the pen, investigating interesting smells. As we walked in, she lifted her head and looked at us.

I carried the saddle to the center of the pen and set it down in the sand. I tried to make my tone reassuring. "Only sometimes. I mean, it's not what they normally do. Not very often."

Erin, setting the pads on top of the saddle, stared at the filly with new-dawning skepticism. I thought she might change her mind about going ahead with the saddling. But she straightened her shoulders and turned to look at me. "Okay. Let's do it."

"Well, it sounds like we're pretty much in agreement," Jay said. "Is there anything else you wanted to talk about?"

I perked up. I was sitting at my kitchen table, laptop open in front of me, still trying to get the trick of looking at the camera instead of my own face so it would seem like we were making eye contact. Jay was seated in his office in Texas. I could see the side of the horse and the top of the TruGlide Girl's boot behind him in a section of the massive photo behind his desk.

Jay himself was back to normal. Any sense of comradery we'd achieved over the weekend seemed to have faded away. His bright eyes were sharp and direct as he asked me quite a few questions about how I thought I'd done in my first appearance as the TruGlide Girl. These had been difficult to answer since he asked them before telling me how *he* thought I'd done. In fact, if I hadn't had the positive feedback via Ted, I would have spent the bulk of the meeting convinced the entire event had been a massive failure.

The areas Jay identified as my weak points were "accessibility" during my time working the crowd, and my "unity" with my character. He said I hadn't seemed very at home in my roll. Which was true. But then, it's hard to relax when breathing at the wrong angle causes the sharp edge of a fake plastic star adhered to your shirt to stab you under the ribs.

My strong points, according to Jay, were "flexibility" and "resourcefulness." Which, to my ear, translated to mean, "Wyatt."

I had spent the bulk of the discussion trying to look attentive while also resisting the urge to point out it was natural I didn't look natural in my role yet as I'd only been the TruGlide Girl this once.

I also spent the meeting feeling a little self-conscious. I'd thought Erin and I would be able to get the saddle on the filly with plenty of time for me to get home for a shower and change before my meeting. Unfortunately, things hadn't gone as planned. Erin, although she was smooth and comfortable around steadier horses, was a tad jumpy around the filly. She'd been doing up the girth when the filly stamped at a fly.

Erin had jumped back. The filly, who'd been doing fine up until then, suddenly was not fine anymore. She leapt away from Erin's startled jerk. The saddle lurched with her. The young horse, terrified, bucked off the half-cinched saddle and then galloped around the pen in a wild panic until we got her caught and calmed back down.

I didn't spell this out to Erin, but it was the worst thing that could have happened during a first saddling. The filly had learned a) saddles are scary and b) scary things can be gotten rid of by bucking.

Though I didn't make an issue of it, Erin seemed to understand the severity of the mistake. After her first scare, the filly wouldn't stand still when the saddle came anywhere near her. We had to backtrack to teaching her to accept the touch of the saddle pad and slowly build up to being able to get the saddle on her back again.

We'd stopped without trying the cinch again, mainly because I ran out of time. I barely made it back to my apartment to receive Jay's call at all. As he started our discussion, I sat at my kitchen table, listening to him talk and feeling the sweat dry out of my shirt.

Now we'd arrived at the moment I'd been waiting for. I sat up, judging from Jay's expression he didn't expect me to have anything more to say. I hurried, lest he say goodbye before I had time to speak up. "Actually, Jay, I did have one idea."

Jay had reached for his mouse in anticipation of closing our conversation. Now he paused, looking back at the camera with a mingled expression of mild surprise and mild annoyance. But his tone was receptive when he said, "What's that, Nora?"

I took a quick breath. I'd considered all sorts of ways to pitch my plan to Jay, including vague thoughts of Powerpoint presentations. Now, however, all my planned arguments deserted me. The words tumbled out in a hurried, breathless, heap. "I want my own horse."

Jay went very still. Even across a webcam, his eyes were piercing in their brightness. "Your own horse?" He sounded like a weary father who was now going to have to explain for the hundredth time why his daughter couldn't have a pony.

This wasn't starting the way I'd planned. I scrambled for words, trying to find the persuasive arguments that had seemed so clear to me earlier. "Remember my interview? You asked me how I wanted to make the roll of the TruGlide Girl my own."

Jay's head on my screen gave one quick, short nod.

I was gaining momentum. "My strength is my horsemanship. I'm a fifth-generation rancher. The training methods used at my family's ranch have been passed down and refined for decades."

"I take it," Jay said, his face slipping into that sardonic, unamused smile of his, "you already have your own horse, then?"

I resisted the urge to make a sharp reply. Ignoring his comment, I continued. "There's only so much I can get done climbing onto a horse I don't know and charging out into an arena with nothing but instructions to slide and run. If we invested in a good horse, like the one we borrowed from Wyatt's contact, and I could ride it at every event, I could work out a routine that was a lot more impressive than a few gallops across the arena and some sliding stops."

The expression on Jay's face seemed to indicate a bad smell had made its way into his office. "Ugh, Nora." He pressed his fingers to the bridge of his nose. "The logistics. We make appearances all over the Southwest."

"So what?" I was determined not to be cowed. "Horses aren't hard to move. We buy a truck and a trailer and hire a guy to drive the horse around and take care of it on the road. You can slap your logo all over the trailer and people will get interested and curious when they see the famous TruGlide horse on the highway." I could tell Jay wanted to say something more, but I hurried on, leaning towards the camera and speaking faster. "Think about it, Jay. Animal stories sell. Right now, we've only got me and my character. By nature, the TruGlide Girl is perfect and untouchable. But a horse is warm and fuzzy and friendly. We can get a horse and tell its story. People will eat it up."

I ran out of breath. Jay was looking at the camera with a flat stare. "Boobs and butts," he said.

I blinked and turned up the volume on my laptop, certain I'd misheard. "Excuse me?"

Jay released a quick, frustrated breath. "Boobs and butts are what sells in my demographic, Nora. I'm targeting professionals in the high-end of the reining industry. These are middle-aged men who buy, train, and sell horses for a living. They are motivated by pretty women." He held up a hand as he saw me gathering myself to protest. "It's a fact, Nora, born out by study after marketing study. I didn't make the world the way it is but I have to recognize realities if I'm going to move product."

All the excitement and momentum drained out of me. I remembered with sudden discomfort the tightness of my jeans and the padded bra that had been provided for me to wear under my blingified shirt. "Fine." Abruptly, I was done with the conversation. "But next time when a horse that's the wrong color shows up, I might not be able to help."

Jay's gaze had shifted to something behind the camera. He wasn't even looking at me when he said, "Next time a horse that's the wrong color shows up, we'll have your whole wardrobe assembled and with us, so it simply won't matter."

I stared down at my plate, poking at the remains of my seafood pasta with a disinterested fork. Ted, halfway through his ravioli, was looking content. The restaurant was quiet. It was one of the reasons Ted liked coming here during the week.

Thursdays were our date night. We always either ate out or cooked in at one of our apartments, spending the evening together and talking about the week so far. Usually, I enjoyed our dates. Tonight, I'd found myself having difficultly putting effort into our conversation.

If Ted had noticed, he'd decided on some explanation for my withdrawn behavior—such as being tired or worried about my roll or some such thing. He was wrong though. Since my talk with Jay on Monday, I couldn't seem to get over being irritated about that conversation. Whether it was fair or not, I couldn't help but associate Ted with Jay. Ted, after all, was the sole reason I'd ever met Jay in the first place.

We'd made it most of the way through dinner, Ted chatting about the food and the weather and the service and work. But all night, the memory of what Jay had said festered under the tide of my thoughts.

The conversation had lapsed into what Ted seemed to think was a comfortable silence when I couldn't contain myself any longer. "Is it true?" I spoke with abrupt impatience, setting down my fork and looking at Ted, unable to keep a slight tone of accusation out of my voice. "What Jay said about boobs and butts? Those things being the only way to sell to a man?"

Ted looked startled. His expression tightened, as if the food in his mouth had lost all flavor. He took a moment before attempting an answer, sipping some wine and clearing his throat.

When he spoke, his tone was apologetic. "It's an oversimplification, Nora. A major oversimplification. Look at Apple, for instance. They've never had a female model in any of their ads."

I considered this, pushing my plate to the side and pulling my glass of wine closer. Soft Italian music piped into the room through invisible speakers as servers in striped waist aprons moved from table to table, taking orders and delivering food.

"But Apple targets young people, hip people. I don't think many reining trainers have iPhones and iMacs."

Ted took another bite of ravioli, shrugging as if the point was both academic and irrelevant. I watched him, noting the way he kept his eyes on his plate.

"It doesn't bother you?" I said, affecting a conversational tone as I swirled my wine in my glass. "This job was your idea. Now my boss, your friend, has explained the assets that got me hired are not at all the ones I thought were required for the job."

Ted released a short, tired sigh. The server came by to refill our glasses and ask if I needed a box. When we were alone again, Ted said, "Jay isn't my friend, exactly. Colleague would be a better word."

I considered my boyfriend. It was not, of course, news to me that pretty women appeared in lots and lots of ads. I'd known from the start

Ted spent time with models. I'd seen sketches of his ad concepts, which usually included stylized, faceless women posing with one product or another. How many times had I flipped through magazines, gazing down at one airbrushed model after another, hardly registering the fact a beautiful woman leaning against a bright green tractor didn't tell you anything about how well that tractor did its job?

I thought again of my TruGlide outfit—the overdone makeup, the tight clothes, my instructions from Jay. *Run the horse around. Do the slides. Don't forget to smile.* More and more, it was evident what I did out there, what the horse did, didn't matter.

What mattered was how I looked doing it.

"I thought this job was going to be about riding." Despite my efforts to sound mature and thoughtful, this comment came out sounding whiney.

Ted looked at me, setting his fork down and reaching across the table to pat the back of my hand in a strange little gesture that seemed more suited to a grandfather than a boyfriend. "Right now," he said, "Jay doesn't know you very well. You're just getting started. It's a time of high stress for the company. What's most obvious about you at a glance is that you're beautiful. But that's not all there is to you. Jay is all about adapting. Be patient. I'm sure the position will evolve over time."

Having delivered this speech, Ted looked pleased with himself. He picked up his fork again to attack the final pile of ravioli. I watched, trying to decide whether or not to tell him about how Jay had summarily rejected my idea of getting a horse I could work with consistently, the better to employ my background in horse training.

"At least," Ted said, still eating, "you don't have another performance for a while. Jay tells me you have some big shoots coming up. That should be a nice change of pace."

I looked away from Ted. Our table was by the window. The Italian restaurant was in the same complex as a supermarket and a bike shop. The bike shop was closed. But a steady stream of people drifted in and out of the Safeway, pushing carts or lugging bags or trying to keep children from dashing in front of moving vehicles. The idea of having to spend an entire day doing nothing but changing into different outfits and attempting to follow the instructions of various photographers did not strike me as a nice change of pace. I was going to have to fly back to Dallas, without Ted this time.

With a sudden sense of longing, I thought of the ranch. Erin and I had done another session with her filly this morning. The saddling had gone better after more groundwork. I was hopeful the mistake would amount to only a minor setback.

While we were working, I'd looked up at one point to see Wyatt standing on the viewing platform watching us. Now I felt a strange regret I wouldn't be able to keep helping Erin with her filly while I was away. Considering the fact I'd been putting off starting this horse for nearly six months, it didn't make much sense I was so keen to work with her now.

My newfound motivation, I assured myself, had nothing to do with the fact that being around the Tipped Z these days meant running into Wyatt quite frequently. It meant catching his eye and smiling when we passed on our way from one chore to the next, or exchanging banter as we worked together on some little job.

As if reading my thoughts, Ted continued. "I'll miss you when you're gone this week, though. I'm used to being the one doing the traveling." He said this with a sort of mystified laugh, as if the fact of my sudden autonomy was confusing to him.

I decided I was being uncharitable. Ted, after all, had helped me get this job because he thought it was a great opportunity. He was doubtless right. And the deposit I'd discovered in my checking account earlier in the week, which included "event pay," had cast my earnings at Old Pueblo in a very unflattering light.

I reached across the table to take one of Ted's hands. His palms were smooth and cool to the touch. "I'll miss you too."

The server came with the check. Ted smiled and handed over his credit card before I could offer to split.

I walked out of the Tucson airport, suitcase rolling behind me. I felt a strange sense of relief as the sliding doors parted and a blast of hot air hit my face.

It was Wednesday, and I was back from my multi-day shoot in Dallas. I'd been a little surprised, after my plane touched down and I'd taken a hired car to the TruGlide offices, to find myself a little bit glad to see my squad of stylists. Under all Jay's sardonic reserve, I even thought I sensed the teeniest hint of friendly ease.

The days in Dallas were a blur. We shot on multiple locations, which meant driving around in a van full of stylists and photographers headed to some destination that provided horses or scenery or both. In spite of myself, I fell into the rhythm.

Over the course of several days, the requests of the photographers to tilt my chin this way or that, to tighten this muscle or relax another, started to seem less bizarre. I got used to the hovering way the horse handlers watched me, always staying just outside the camera frame, ready to intervene if their charge did anything unexpected.

Returning to Tucson was reemerging into a different kind of reality—a reality where no one cared what my hair looked like or what angle the sun was at behind me.

I made it clear of the airport doors and stepped out of the flow of people heading for the parking lots. I veered to the curb and stopped to pull my phone out of my pocket. Ted was out of town, on location at a different job, and wouldn't be back for several days. Erin had said she'd pick me up from the airport.

Now I saw with a little sinking feeling Erin hadn't responded to the text I'd sent her when the plane touched down. I pushed my phone back into my pocket and squinted into the glare. I moved down the sidewalk that ran the length of the pick-up area, turning with hope every time a new car nosed into view.

Erin was reliable. It would be very unlike her to forget something like picking me up from the airport. So I told myself to relax, checked my phone again, and began to wander down the sidewalk towards a clear space on the curb.

I'd been looking for Erin's little car, so the sight of Wyatt's truck didn't immediately register on me as significant. When it did, I did a double-take. His Dodge, by now, was intimately familiar. For a moment, I stared in a kind of stunned disbelief as my heart jolted in a hammering spasm and began to beat harder and faster than necessary.

Ever since the TruGlide event in Phoenix, thoughts of Wyatt had stalked me like a persistent pack of coyotes. I would think of him at the most random moments, such as every time I heard the Dixie Chicks or saw a palomino.

Now, I told myself, this wasn't what it seemed. Maybe Erin had borrowed Wyatt's truck. Maybe we were going to pick up something large on the way home, something her little car wouldn't have been able to carry.

There was a glare on the truck's windshield. I couldn't see who was behind the wheel. I waved and could tell by the truck's trajectory the driver had seen me. The Dodge popped forward, snugged up to the curve in a fluid swoop, and rocked to a quick stop.

Not Erin behind the wheel, then.

Before I could prepare myself, Wyatt was there, stepping out of the driver's side door and striding past the truck's hood. He looked as good as ever. But something niggled at me the moment I saw him.

Unlike my brother, Wyatt was aware there was more than one brand of jeans in the world. He wore Wranglers to ride, but when he wasn't planning to be on horseback during the day, he wore more versatile clothing.

It was his outfit that tipped me off. He was wearing a pair of relaxed-fit jeans, a t-shirt, and tennis shoes. No hat. No boots. No belt.

"Nora." Something in his voice made my heart constrict in a completely different way. There was also something wrong with his face. He wasn't smiling. Not even a little.

Wyatt stepped onto the curb, looking at me with serious eyes. "It happened in the middle of the night. We didn't want to tell you over the phone."

Panic coursed through me like a poison. A million possible disasters bloomed in my mind. Clint, dead. Erin, dead. Dad, dead. Mom, dead.

Wyatt seemed aware of the turn my thoughts had taken. He was quick to deliver the news. "It's your father. They think it was a stroke. He's in the hospital now. Clint and Erin and your mother are with him. Erin was going to come get you but the doctor was expecting to have some test results back very soon. She wanted to be there."

His words settled like frozen stones in my stomach. I stared at the scuffed toes of his tennis shoes, understanding but not ready to accept.

Stroke. The word was such a double-edged thing. My father used it a lot, actually. I could remember him yelling at me the very first time I started a colt. "Pet him. Pet him. He needs some comfort. No, don't whack him like he's a piñata. Stroke him. Long, firm strokes. All the way up and down his neck. You know this, Nora. That's right. Good girl."

I thought of what I knew about stroke victims. Most of my knowledge came from movies. I thought with horror of Anthony Hopkins in *Legends of the Fall*, muttering and sighing as he tried to assemble a rifle his son brought as a gift from his travels, not knowing his father was half paralyzed.

My eyes went hot and prickly. Wyatt stepped forward and put an arm around my shoulders. I was too stunned to react to the physical contact. Wyatt continued to speak in his low, serious tone. "They think he's going to be okay. He's sleeping now, but they don't think it was a big one. We'll know more soon."

I hardly noticed as Wyatt collapsed the handle on my suitcase, which Ted had given me as a surprise gift that night after our dinner at the Italian restaurant. Wyatt set the bag in the back of his truck and opened the passenger door for me. All around, the hum of the airport continued unaffected. People streamed out of the automatic doors, cars drifted up to the curb, people laughed and hugged and greeted one another.

I stepped up into the cab of Wyatt's Dodge, noting the absence of the flattened cap and paperback. Wyatt closed the door and walked around to his side. The cab rocked as he climbed in.

We didn't speak as he put the truck in gear. My mind seemed to have frozen. I could not imagine my father in the hospital. The very thought of it filled me with horror. My father was not made for hospitals. He was made for horses and ropes, for dust and mountains and cactus. He belonged at the Tipped Z. It wasn't right for him to be somewhere else, stuck in a situation he wasn't in charge of.

Wyatt navigated out of the lanes of slow traffic, shifting and speeding up as we exited the airport. As we merged onto the main road, I felt a strange urge to go back to the airport, leave the truck, go back inside, and come out again. I wanted to reset this moment and do it over, as if I could erase what I'd been told.

I looked at Wyatt. He was staring out the windshield with a fixed expression that made me think he hadn't gotten much sleep. "Thank you," I said, realizing I hadn't spoken since he'd arrived.

He cast a quick glance in my direction. "For what?" He seemed confused.

I made a gesture at the dusty dash of his truck. "For picking me up."

He looked ahead, easing the truck to a stop at a light and taking it out of gear. His voice was low and sad. "It was the least I could do."

Chapter 5

My father, it turned out, was well on his way to being discharged by the time Wyatt and I made it to the hospital. The doctors had returned with the results of whatever tests they'd run. They confirmed the stroke had been minor. Nothing about my father's blood or physiology explained why he'd had it at all. My father was lean and fit, a man who'd used his body for his entire life. While he'd smoked when he was younger, he'd given that up when he became a father.

And he was not a good patient. He insisted from the moment he woke up that he was fine and wanted to go home. He was brusque and irritable with the doctors, impatient with tests and questions.

It was hard for me to see him this way. It was amazing, I thought as I stood with Wyatt in the corner of the hospital room, watching my mother handle my father's crabby outbursts and childish protestations with a mix of pleas, threats, and failure to acknowledge him. Never in my life had I realized what a fragile thing independence was. My father was a man who'd worked his whole life to preserve and expand what his father had made, and his father before that. My grandfather had died in the saddle, suffering a cardiac arrest and falling to the ground, dead as a doornail, at the age of 78. My father, when he told this story, emphasized this happened when they were on the way home from a day's work, the implication being my grandfather would not have died in the morning, thus shirking the day's duties.

My father was transformed by the accoutrements of the hospital. On the ranch, he was lean in a solid way. He was tall, always towering over other men in his boots. But in a hospital bed, he was skinny. His skin had an unhealthy pallor beneath the tan of his face.

The stroke had happened in the night. My mother had woken to find my father on the floor on his side of the bed. She hadn't been able to wake him up. The doctors didn't seem to have any kind of satisfactory answer as to why it had happened. They shrugged and agreed he didn't have any real risk factors. But he was over age 55. Sometimes these things happen.

Finally, the doctors let my father out of bed. As soon as he was allowed to stand, he turned to the cluster of us in the corner of his room and asked if we would give him a little privacy so he could get dressed. This had prompted a whispered conference between me, Clint, and my mother, wherein it was decided Wyatt would take me home. Clint and Erin would wait in the hall until my father was ready to leave.

So it was I found myself once more sitting in the passenger seat of Wyatt's truck, staring out the windshield at the bright shapes of moving cars and noting with surprise the light on the mountains was going orange with sunset. I glanced at the clock in the dash and blinked with surprise. "How is it 6:00 already?" My plane had touched down at 1:35.

Wyatt, who'd been silent since we'd walked together into the hospital, answered me with his eyes on the road. "I believe hospitals create a sort of time warp effect. When my grandmother was dying, my sister and I agreed it must be the result of all that misery and pain concentrated in the same place. It does something. Messes with the space/time continuum."

Wyatt's tone was serious as he pronounced this theory. I remembered his grandmother's long illness. She'd died when we were in high school. "How's your grandfather doing?" I asked.

A small grin cracked the corner of Wyatt's mouth. Although Wyatt refused to see most of his family, it was on his grandfather's behalf he'd all but disowned his own parents. "He hasn't changed."

I didn't know the full story about the breach in Wyatt's family but I did know it all revolved around the ranch. Wyatt's great-grandfather and my great-grandfather had come to Arizona together, leaving behind histories they never fully revealed, eager for a fresh start. They'd established the Tipped Z and the Rocking J ranches adjacent to each other. Their families had worked side-by-side for many years.

It was Wyatt's father who'd changed everything. He'd revolted against the idea of becoming a rancher. Being an only child, his defection changed the game for the Rocking J. Wyatt's grandfather and grandmother had stayed on, stubborn in their insistence they could make a go of it. That had worked for a long time. But as Tucson grew and they got older, gradually, the ranch had failed. They'd had to let go of grazing leases and sell off land to developers. Although the young Wyatt had latched onto his grandparents' lifestyle with a tenacity his father always disapproved of, Wyatt's interest in the family ranch had been too little, too late.

The Rocking J was now a housing development. Where the sprawling adobe ranch house once stood, rows and rows of cookie-cutter houses had sprouted. Wyatt's grandfather, heartbroken, had left Tucson. From what I understood, he now lived in Prescott where he had a small house and a few horses he rode every day. His income came from the hand-braided bosals and reatas he made and sold to a local tack shop—which, in turn, sold them on eBay.

I'd never spoken to Wyatt about the loss of the Rocking J. But I knew the death of his grandmother had started the slow slide that had eventually led the situation to where it was now: the ranch lost, Wyatt and his grandfather on one side of a rift, the rest of his family on the other.

All this unspoken past seemed to hang in the air as Wyatt navigated the streets to my apartment. The idea so much heritage and history, could hinge on a single person was alarming. All my life, the Tipped Z had seemed like the most solid thing in existence. But seeing my father lying in a hospital bed, knowing what had happened to the Rocking J— it all sat like a horrible secret in the pit of my stomach.

"He's going to be all right." Wyatt said this out of the silence, as if reading my thoughts. "He's a tough old dog. He won't go down without a fight."

I forced a smile at this. The Dodge's engine growled as Wyatt accelerated after a stoplight. "Without a fight," I echoed. The weight in my stomach grew heavier.

Because Wyatt was right. My father would be okay today. He would probably be back on a horse tomorrow, with or without the doctor's blessing.

But someday—not tomorrow, not next month, but someday—my father would die.

The knowledge bloomed through me, seeming to fill my body with a cold, seeping dread. Wyatt, watching me out of the corner of his eye, seemed to understand what I was thinking. "Nora." His voice was soft. I looked over. For a moment his eyes left the road and caught mine. "What we have is now. We can't let worries about tomorrow poison today."

I seemed to feel an electric shock as he spoke, and it had nothing to do with what he said. It was his eyes that did it to me, and not for the first time.

I had felt that sense of electricity between us so many times before, I'd almost gotten used to it. I'd felt it when we were kids. He and my brother would come clattering in from whatever exclusively-boy activity they'd been engaged in. I would be at the kitchen counter, helping my mother bake cookies or bone chicken thighs. Clint would dash in for two glasses of water. Sometimes I'd look up to see Wyatt looking at me—looking straight at me as if he'd never seen me before. I'd feel this shock. It was always like that. When we were kids, when we were teenagers, even now that we were adults.

I looked away from him, aware of the tightening in my jaw as I redirected my gaze out the passenger side window. Because there was another reality between me and Wyatt. For every time our eyes had met like that and held, there were a dozen, no, a hundred other times when he hadn't seen me, hadn't looked, hadn't noticed, hadn't bothered to say hi when he called to speak to my brother and I answered the phone.

Wyatt was an old wound, I reminded myself. He was a wound that seemed to fester instead of heal, one that always took me by surprise when it broke open and exhibited how little it had changed. So he was suddenly around the ranch all the time and he was being extra nice to me lately. It didn't—couldn't—mean anything.

I had Ted. I had my life. There was no place in it for a man who had proven, repeatedly, the single thing he was best at in life was leaving.

The blinker clicked its steady rhythm. Wyatt turned into my apartment complex. The truck lost momentum as we approached the upcoming fork. I said, "Left." He turned into the winding lane that forked several more times before reaching the ramada where my old Power Wagon squatted in all its massive, rust-splotched glory.

"Thanks for all the driving today," I said. "And for helping with my dad."

The words sounded hollow even to me. Wyatt was looking at me, brow furrowed. "Nora?" His tone made my name into a question.

Another frisson raced through my body, this one warmer. I felt my cheeks flush and my heart began to beat a staccato rhythm against my ribs. I wondered, not for the first time, if Wyatt also felt those shocks when our eyes met.

I said nothing. I waited. A movement outside the window drew my eye. I turned to see a figure straighten up from leaning against a familiar car.

"Ted." I spoke the name in a quiet voice. Confusion passed over Wyatt's face. Then he turned and saw my boyfriend.

Ted followed me up the concrete path to my apartment as Wyatt's truck pulled out of the parking lot. Ted was carrying my suitcase. Wyatt had taken it out of the back of the truck and handed it to him, as if I was too delicate to manage my own luggage.

After such a taxing day, I found myself annoyed with both of them. Wyatt had been a source of confusion in my life for as long as I could remember. Ted, now, was trailing behind me with an accusatory air.

It was not uncommon for Ted's trips to shift around. This wasn't the first time he'd gotten home early and come by to surprise me. Usually, I was happy to see him. Today, I was not.

"My father had a stroke." I spoke these words into the fading light as I fitted my key and turned the deadbolt. The lock had a little hitch in the turn, which I pushed through with practiced ease. "Wyatt picked me up and took me to the hospital. We stayed there with my family for most of the day. Then he brought me home."

I said these words not looking at Ted, partly because it was easier to say these impossible words—*father, stroke, hospital*—while looking at a blank door rather than a human face, and partly because I could not help but resent that Ted was so clearly waiting for an explanation.

I walked into the apartment and flipped on the light, setting my keys in their place and realizing I was ravenously hungry. Other than two 100 calorie snack packs on the airplane, I hadn't eaten all day.

Ted drifted in behind me, setting my suitcase to one side and closing the door. He watched me as I stalked into the kitchen. My fatigue and hunger and confusion were all uniting into a feeling of frustration that was focusing itself on Ted. He had, I told myself, no right to make assumptions and jump to conclusions. I was a free woman. Wyatt was a lifelong friend who happened to currently be working for my father. He'd given me a ride home from the hospital. The *hospital*. So why did I feel like I'd been caught out somehow?

"Is your dad okay?" Ted's tone was subdued. I could see that he, too, was struggling with a mix of emotions. As I pulled the fridge open and stared inside at my mostly empty shelves, he added, "I have Chinese food in the car, if you're hungry. I got in early." His tone went a little apologetic. "And you weren't answering your phone. I thought you'd be tired, so I brought dinner by."

I closed the refrigerator. My phone, I realized, was most likely at the bottom of my purse, on silent. I hadn't thought about it since Wyatt had shown up at the airport.

All the pent-up emotions I'd been feeling took a shift towards sadness. I stood in the kitchen, blinking at my apartment. There were little reminders of my family everywhere. Clint and Erin's "save the date" card was still on the refrigerator. The old cast-iron kettle on the stove had ostensibly been in my family for almost as long as the ranch. In the living room, three framed photos hung on the walls, all shots of my father and brother and mother and me on horseback, doing the things you do when you work on a ranch. They'd been a gift from Clint's first wife, given to me when I got my first apartment. She'd enclosed a note. "There's nothing like a blank wall to make a place feel empty."

The sadness inside me shifted and swelled. Ted walked into the kitchen and put his arms around me. My eyes were hot and my throat felt tight, but I didn't cry. Somehow, I never seemed to cry in situations that typically demanded it. Even at my sister-in-law's funeral, watching my brother try to speak, hands shaking, voice cracking, surrounded by other people who were sobbing, my eyes had stayed dry.

Now, Ted didn't say anything. He merely took me in his arms and hugged me. I was stiff at first but gradually I felt my muscles soften. The heat and emotion seemed to peak and fade to a more tolerable level of dull sadness. Finally, I leaned my head on his shoulder. "Dad's been discharged," I said. "They expect him to make a full recovery. But it's unclear why it happened."

Ted's parents didn't live in Tucson. He'd grown up in the Chicago area and he wasn't close to his family. I'd met them once the winter before when they'd come out for a brief visit. Ted's father was a round, balding man whose job had something to do with real estate and who talked a good deal. Ted's mother was a quiet, apologetic woman who worked as a nurse in a children's hospital. Neither Ted nor his parents had seemed to get any enjoyment out of the time they spent together.

Ted said nothing more until I extricated myself from his arms. Although I hadn't cried, my nose had started to run. I sniffled. "And I'm starving, actually."

Ted smiled. "Cashew chicken, coming right up."

As he turned for the apartment door, I thought again of that shock, that feeling of electricity that had seemed to pass between me and Wyatt in the truck.

I shook my head, pushed all thoughts of Wyatt into an empty room at the corner of my mind and headed for the bathroom to wash my face and my hands.

For once I parked at the house, pulling my rumbling Power Wagon up next to Dad's gleaming white diesel and stepping out into the already hot day.

After the Chinese food, Ted had stayed the night. I'd managed to tell him about the details of what had happened with my father. Gradually we'd moved on to talking of other things. I'd told him about my trip, he'd told me about his.

When we'd been almost done with dinner, his phone had given off a chime to indicate he had a text. He'd checked his screen as I was loading the dishwasher. He'd smiled, looked up, and handed me the phone.

It had taken me a moment to recognize myself. There I was, standing next to a horse. The background was a green blur behind me. I was looking over my shoulder, smiling back at the camera. My hair was blown softly back as if stirred by a breeze.

Everything about the photo was fake. The colors were too bright. My face was smooth and flawless. I swear my eyes looked bigger than they really were. The entire image glowed with the gimmicky perfection of unreality.

Ted had spoken, sounding pleased. "Jay says they got some nice shots."

I'd gone to my purse and unearthed my own phone from the bottom, expecting to have received the same communication from my boss. Instead, I found the three missed calls from Ted.

For some reason, Jay's text had reignited the uneasiness I'd first felt when Wyatt had told me what had happened with my father. It had stayed with me for the rest of the night.

Now, as I closed my truck door and walked across the tile patio to the front door of my parents' house, I felt a sudden swell of panic. I became abruptly convinced my father had taken a turn for the worse, that he was, right now, sitting in a chair drooling and mumbling, and my mother hadn't called anyone because she was refusing to accept the reality of the situation.

I opened the door and stepped into the house. "Mom?" There was a small quaver in my voice.

My parents' house was a long, low structure, with stucco walls and tile floors and huge, thick beams of old wood providing structural support. It was always clean and still inside. When I'd been a kid, the front rooms had been all but off-limits to us. As far as my parents were concerned, children were allowed to be children in their bedrooms. During meals, they were permitted in the dining area. After dinner, they were allowed in the kitchen to clean up. Otherwise, our place had been outside.

Looking back on my childhood, I could recognize my parents had been strict. There had always been a line between their kids and themselves. It wasn't that they hadn't made us feel loved or valued. It was that they'd had a lot to do and any child who made more work for them was going to learn a thing or two about being a responsible member of a family.

Perhaps because of this, I now didn't feel entirely at home in parts of my parents' house. My old bedroom was another story. I still stayed the night sometimes. That room made me feel comfortable and secure and happy. But there was something about the echoing entryway and quiet living room that made me hurry through them every time I came home.

I found my mother peeling potatoes in the kitchen. She had the radio on and hadn't heard me come in. She turned when she saw me, peeler in one hand, half-naked potato in the other. "Nora." She turned back to the sink. She rinsed her hands, put down the potato, dried off on a dishtowel, and came over to give me a hug.

My mother was a small woman. She and my father had married young. She'd spent many years pulling more than her own weight around the ranch. Now, when I hugged her, she seemed small and frail in my arms. I let her go. She returned to the sink, picking up her potato to continue peeling.

"How's Dad?" The kitchen table was empty, already cleaned of any evidence of breakfast. I'd half expected to see my father there, sipping coffee and reading the newspaper. (Yes, my father still read the newspaper.) But the house was silent around us.

"He and Clint and Wyatt rode out this morning." My mother spoke in her normal, placid tone but I thought I detected a small undernote of worry.

I sighed and glanced out the window at the hot, bright morning. It was going to be a scorcher. "I guess he didn't put much stock in the doctor's advice to rest a few days."

My mother finished with the one potato, placed it in a bowl, and selected a new one from a colander on the other side of the sink. "He promised to let the boys handle the heavy stuff. I don't know what we'd do if Wyatt wasn't here."

It was a simple observation, spoken in a reflective tone. It was not, I told myself, in any way directed at me. Still, my stomach knotted up again. I could think of nothing to say.

My mother and I were both silent for a moment. I listened to the scrape and plop of her peeling. The kitchen smelled of coffee and damp earth. I tried to imagine my mother living here alone. I couldn't do it.

"I think Erin's working with that filly of hers," my mother said after a while. "I wonder if you could maybe check in on things, make sure it's all going well between them?"

I felt a strange sense of relief at being given permission to go. "Sure. And let me know if I can do anything else."

My mother nodded. I turned and walked once more through the quiet house, thinking to myself how impossible my entire family was when it came to honest, forthright communication.

As I stepped back out into the building heat, my thoughts were diverted onto a new course. Two old wooden rocking chairs occupied the front porch, positioned for a view of the mountains. When I'd crossed the porch a moment before, these chairs had been empty.

Now one was occupied. Erin sat there, hunched forward in an unnatural curl.

I paused a moment before stepping all the way outside. Erin was sitting on the edge of the chair, not rocking, her arms clamped around her midsection, shoulders curled. A fine layer of sand clung to her shirt and jeans on one side of her body. When she looked up, there was a smudge along her cheek and tear tracks on her face.

I recognized the signs, but I made sure the door was snugged shut before I spoke. If Erin hadn't come into the ranch house, it meant she didn't want my mother to know what had happened.

And I understood. I loved my mother. But she was a bit confusing even when she was your biological parent. I could hardly imagine what it would be like to have her as a mother-in-law.

I moved softly, crossing the porch to look Erin up and down. I didn't see anything too alarming—no jagged bones poking through skin, no massive facial contusions. "Nothing broken, I hope?"

Erin swallowed, gave a hiccupping laugh, and used the sleeve of her shirt to wipe at the tears on her face. "I don't know what happened. One minute everything was fine. The next, she ..." Erin trailed off, looking at me for a moment before dropping her eyes to stare blankly at the porch floor. "She started bucking. I couldn't stay on. I fell off and she bucked and bucked and bucked for such a long time."

I felt a clench of guilt. I couldn't help but think if I'd gone straight to the round pen instead of stopping at the house, I might have been able to head this off. "Is she still in the round pen?"

Erin, biting her lip, shook her head. "I took her saddle off and turned her back out. I hope that wasn't the wrong thing. I didn't know what else to do. I didn't think anyone else was here. I don't think I'm injured or anything, but I didn't want to get back on. I was going to go home but I saw your truck."

"No, that's good." I tried to think. The barn and surrounding area were empty and quiet. Even Chet and Fuzzface were not in evidence, which meant my father had taken them when he'd ridden out today. This meant they were most likely moving cattle, which meant they might be gone for hours yet or might be back at any moment. "Come on," I said. "You can tell me all about it while we get you cleaned up."

Looking relieved, Erin stood. She limped a little as she followed me in silence. We made our way to the winding path that led from the barn to Clint's house.

Once inside, Erin changed into fresh clothing while I waited in the kitchen. When she returned, she showed me the rope burn on her fingers and a place on her elbow where she'd lost some skin. I watched as she washed out the grit. She winced but seemed otherwise steady. The tears, I thought, had been more to do with humiliation and frustration than pain.

Finally, Erin had finished cleaning up. Dabbing at the raw elbow with a paper towel, she turned to face me. I had busied myself with making coffee while she'd been out of the room. Now we took our warm mugs to the table. As we sat down together, Erin let out a shaky sigh. "I'm so afraid," she said.

I sipped the coffee. Clint and Erin had a thing for bitter flavors. I hadn't added enough sugar. "Afraid of the horse?"

Erin looked briefly amused. She shook her head. "Of disappointing everybody."

I thought again of my father, my mother, my brother, and now Erin, all working their tails off to keep this place alive. I thought of Wyatt driving to the airport to pick me up. I thought of the hole the loss of the Rocking J had left in his life.

Then I thought of my team of stylists. I thought of that photo on Ted's phone.

"It's not your fault." I spoke in as firm a tone as I could manage. "You shouldn't have been trying to do this alone." The truth of what I was saying seemed to echo inside me. We'd all been bucked off, of course. But it was a pretty rare event. As Clint liked to say, a horse only bucked when you failed him—when you'd already made a series of mistakes that led to him losing all faith in his rider.

Erin was simply too new to this. There would have been warning signs, indications the filly wasn't prepared. Clint would have seen them. Wyatt would have seen them. I would have seen them.

But none of us had, because we hadn't been there.

My eyes strayed to the photo on the wall—the black and white shot full of horses and dust and silhouettes. I felt a sudden wave of fear. Erin was fine. She was banged up. Most falls off horses were more painful to the ego than the body.

But not all falls. Things could happen. A head could hit a fence post or a solid arena wall. A horse could go down, rolling over the rider. This fall could have been worse.

It could have been deadly.

As my mind imagined the terrible sequence of events that would have unspooled if Erin had suffered a fatal accident this morning, a rock-hard resolution formed inside me. I was done. Contract be damned, Ted's friendship with Jay notwithstanding, I was going to call my boss. I was going to quit. I would say there was a family emergency. I was needed here. If I hadn't been away this week, hadn't been running around Dallas getting photographed, Erin would never have been in that saddle alone.

And who knows? Maybe if my father hadn't been over-exerting himself to cover the gap my absence left in the ranch, he wouldn't have had the stroke.

I began to talk, a plan and a sense of resolve forming inside me. "We don't need to tell anyone. Not," I hurried to say, "that there's any shame in getting bucked off. But I understand if you want to keep it to yourself. We'll fix this. The horse will be fine. I'll help you get her more ready before you climb on again. From now on, for a while at least, I'll be here every time you work with the filly, okay?"

The look Erin directed at me was so full of gratitude it made me feel a little squirmy. Unable to meet her eyes, I left my seat in search of the sugar.

I'd just reached the kitchen when my phone rang. I pulled it out of my purse, which I'd left on the counter. My stomach did a flip when I saw the screen taken up with the photo I'd snapped of Jay attempting to relax in one of the foldable TruGlide chairs at the Phoenix event, a bag of Skittles in one hand and one foot propped on the cooler.

"Jay." I picked up the sugar bowl to carry it with me back to the table. "I was about to …"

He cut me off, his voice so full of excitement it seemed likely he hadn't heard me start to speak. "Nora!" He spoke in as expansive a voice as I'd ever heard him use. "You'll never believe this, but I bought you a horse."

Jay's words left me as speechless as I had ever been. And so, when he paused for my reaction to his news, I found myself staring at Erin and no doubt making a face similar to how my pet Beta fish had once looked when it had flipped itself out of the bowl when I'd been trying to scoop him into a net for cleaning purposes.

"His name," Jay went on into my silence, "is Zippo. And he's a beautiful animal."

"Zippo?" I echoed, finding my voice by repeating what he'd said.

"Zippo." I could hear the buzz of the office in the background, which made me guess he was striding around the TruGlide headquarters as he spoke: a habit of his. "Like the lighter. Cute, right?"

I closed my eyes in a long, slow blink, my ability to speak deserting me again. Erin was watching me with a look of concern. I tipped the speaker away from my face and mouthed, "My boss," in an exaggerated whisper. Then I returned to the task of trying to think of something to say to Jay, who clearly didn't realize a considerable percentage of Quarter Horse names included some variation of the word Zippo.

"Is that his whole name?" I managed to ask after an awkward pause.

Jay's mood seemed to shift. Some of the elation left his tone. "Oh, there are some other words in there too. It's long and strange. But don't you want to know what color?" Some of the enthusiasm returned with the last sentence.

"Palomino?" I ventured. Jay had seemed pleased with the coloring of the mare Wyatt had acquired for us over the two days we'd had her.

Jay hardly gave me time to get the word out before he hurried on. "It's possible you haven't heard of it. I'm told it's quite unique."

I felt my heart go a little cold. What on earth had Jay purchased? My eyes drifted to the bright window as I waited for the axe to fall.

"Dunalino." Jay spoke the word like a benediction, then hurried to explain. "It's this amazing burnished gold with white accents and a stripe down its back. Seriously, Nora, this horse is beautiful. We could set you up in almost any color and it will look good."

"Awesome," I said with as much enthusiasm as I could muster, moving back to the table to stir a teaspoon of sugar into my coffee.

There was a slight pause. "Nora?" Jay's tone had changed again. This time he sounded like a mother about to ask a child if he'd cleaned his room when she knew he hadn't. "Tell me I didn't waste ten grand on this horse. Tell me you're excited."

My heart clenched further. I rushed ahead, stumbling to explain myself. "I'm sorry, Jay," I said quickly. "It's just my father had a stroke and I'm at my brother's house right now and I'm not ... I'm a little stressed."

"Oh, honey." Jay's mood took another complete shift. His voice was suddenly full of sympathy. "I'm so sorry. Why on earth didn't you say something? Call me back."

Then he was gone.

I stared at my phone for a moment before setting it back down on the counter. I felt stiff, as if my body had lost some of its ability to bend and flex.

I turned toward Erin. The thought process I'd been having as I'd walked into the kitchen, which had seemed so simple and right mere seconds ago now seemed utterly impossible.

Ten grand? Why hadn't Jay spoken to me first? Why hadn't he let me advise him on what kind of horse to look for? And how on earth was I going to quit now?

"Everything all right?" Erin spoke quietly as she took a sip of her coffee.

My mind was reeling. On top of everything else, I now felt guilty for using my father's stroke as an excuse to get off the phone. I'd made it sound like he was on his deathbed when really he was out on horseback against doctor's orders.

I collapsed into my chair. "There's a pretty decent chance my boss has made a huge mistake."

The horse, I eventually found out, was registered with AQHA as Chrome Zippo Whiz. In retrospect, I could understand how only the one word had stuck with Jay. The horse was a four-year-old gelding who'd been started on the reining circuit but hadn't progressed due to the "owner's lack of time and commitment."

Ted, it turned out, was not at all surprised when I told him about this turn of events. I told him how summarily and even rudely Jay had dismissed my suggestion of getting a TruGlide horse, and then how Jay had gone through with it without asking me a single question. "That's Jay," Ted said. "He likes to think everything is his idea."

He said this over the phone. I'd told him about what had happened, omitting my short-lived decision to quit my job. I'd called him because I was still at the ranch, still waiting for my brother and father and Wyatt to reappear. I'd been waiting for most of the day. Erin and I had done a groundwork session with her filly. I'd pointed out some of the indicators that would have warned me the horse was not ready to ride. Then Erin had to go grocery shopping and I found myself waiting in the hay room, sweating in the crushing heat and trying not to picture my father wilting under the baking sun. I had never, in all my life, worried about my father's health. Now I couldn't seem to stop.

I'd called Jay first, so he could finish talking to me about the horse. Then I called Ted to distract myself. My conversation with Jay had revealed I needed to speak to my brother, and soon. So I was waiting for Clint to come back and trying not to be nervous about it. I would not, I'd promised myself, leave the ranch until we'd had the necessary conversation.

"But don't worry," Ted said. "He will give you credit in the long run. He needs to be the one that provides the momentum, you know? He takes a while to absorb things, to assimilate them into his long-term plan." Ted's tone had taken on an affectionate quality as he spoke, as if Jay was his temperamental but totally-worth-the-effort lover.

My phone call with Ted didn't last long. He had work to do. So, I wound up sitting alone on the stack of bales in the silent barn, trying to process everything that had happened over the last few days.

The heat of the day had almost reached its zenith when my phone emitted a tone. I looked down at my screen to see Jay had sent me a photo of my new horse. I must admit I did a double-take. I'd Googled "dunalino" while I'd been waiting. The images the search returned were mixed in terms of their impressiveness.

This horse, however, was something to look at. He was long-backed and solid, bulky in that smooth way of horses that have been pumped up on rich feeds their whole life. The photo had been taken with the horse wearing a saddle. His muzzle and ears were trimmed and oiled, his tail silken and nearly long enough to touch the ground. He had that blank, lobotomized look of horses that were started young and shown hard.

But he was pretty. His coat was very pale and the sooty barring on his legs was quite visible. His mane and tail had a silvery cast to them.

I was trying to compose a suitably enthusiastic reply when I heard the distant clop of approaching hoof-beats. I sat up on my hay bales, stowing my phone. A moment later, Dots, Chet, and Fuzzface appeared. The dogs barely made it into the shade before they collapsed, panting, trying to achieve positions of maximum hot-belly-to-cool-concrete ratios.

I looked at the door with a lump in my throat. I hardly knew who I wanted to see more. My father, alive and well? My brother, looking to be in a good mood so our conversation had the highest possible chance of delivering the outcome I wanted? Or Wyatt, giving me another look like the one he'd directed at me in the car—the one that seemed to indicate there was more between us than the fact that he was friends with my brother?

As it happened, I got one of the three things I'd hoped to see. That was, happily, my father. He strode into the hay room, leading his horse to the wall so he could untack in the shade, looking entirely like he usually did. Which is to say stern, impassive, and silent.

Clint and Wyatt appeared a moment later. Clint looked hot and irritated, his rag damp and his face clotted in clinging dirt. Wyatt trailed after. Although he hardly could have missed me sitting there on the hay, he didn't so much as glance in my direction.

I waited, buzzing with too many emotions to try to sort out. When Wyatt approached my father's horse as if to unsaddle him, my dad treated him to a look so sharp it seemed in danger of causing physical harm. Wyatt turned aside, unconvincingly pretending to notice something about his boot that needed adjusting. By the time he straightened, my father was carrying his own saddle to the tack room.

Finally, the three men had their horses rubbed down. Wyatt took all three lead ropes and led the horses towards the door nearest the pastures. My father and brother walked together towards the door that opened into the parking area. "Clint," I said, jumping up off my bale and hoping I didn't sound as nervous as I felt. "I need to talk to you."

My brother stopped walking. For a moment, he didn't turn around. He stayed, back stiff and shoulders square, facing away from me. My father looked over his shoulder as he stepped out the door. Clint said, "I'll meet you at the house."

My father strode away without answering, his long steps unhurried but efficient, his spurs jingling and reflecting the sun. Clint turned around.

Through most of our lives, my brother and I had existed in relative harmony. Sure, we'd had our squabbles as children. Sure, we sometimes now didn't see eye-to-eye on certain details of our philosophy on horsemanship. Sure, we didn't talk a lot. But mostly, I thought, we understood each other.

So I was a bit unprepared for the look my brother now directed at me. His eyes, always sharp, looked out of his face with a sort of burning quality.

Angry, I registered. My brother was really, really angry.

I felt myself quail under that glare. A beat of silence passed. Clint said nothing, looking at me like a baited bull might look at a dog that was harassing him.

"Um, yeah. How was dad today?" This wasn't what I'd intended to ask but it seemed a safer starting place.

Clint said nothing. He turned his gaze from me and stared at the panting dogs still sprawled on the concrete floor. His jaw seemed to tighten, then release, then tighten again. I waited. For my brother, words had always been difficult.

"He rode with the reins in his right hand. All day."

I turned to stare at my father's retreating back. He'd made it across the parking area and was stepping into the shadow of the porch.

I felt my mouth go dry. I tried to understand what it might mean. My father, vaquero that he was, worked to get his horses straight up into the bridle so he could use the reins with his left hand and rope with his right.

The stroke, I remembered, had affected the left side of my father's body. The doctors had said he might experience reduced mobility.

A thousand questions swirled in mind. Was he having trouble using his left hand? Was he in pain? Were there any other symptoms?

But I knew there was no point in asking Clint these things. My father would not have told him.

"Weird."

My lame response seemed to hang between us. Clint's entire body was telling me he didn't want to be having this conversation. But I couldn't tell if his anger was directed at me or the helplessness of the situation with our father. He said nothing more so I hazarded on. "I was wondering," I said slowly, "if we could take on a boarder."

Clint, who had been standing not entirely facing me, eyes focused on the distant mountains out the bay doors, suddenly snapped his full attention onto me with a force that almost made me gasp. He glared. When he spoke, his voice came out in a hoarse, grating rasp that seemed to indicate he was nearly past his ability to speak at all. "If you're too selfish to help," Clint said, voice low, "the least you could do is stop making more work for the rest of us."

I wasn't sure I'd ever heard my brother speak in such a tone. I wasn't sure I'd ever seen his eyes flash like that. I remembered Erin's hunched form in the rocking chair, her comment. *I'm so scared.*

Surely, my brother hadn't become prone to losing his temper? Surely, her evident desire not to let him know the young filly had bucked her off had nothing to do with factors beyond wounded pride?

Looking at Clint, I found myself taking a small step back. He began to turn, swiveling on his boot heel in preparation for exiting the barn and leaving me and my ridiculous questions behind.

But I was not going to give up. I might be less inhibited than my brother, but our temperaments were not as different as they might seem at a glance. "Damn it, Clint. Hear me out." I spoke in a quick, sharp tone, feeling my temper stir as I thought about how irrational it was for him to dismiss the question before learning the details. "The TruGlide Corporation will pay us $2000 a month to keep a horse here. It will need to stay in a stall, but I'll do all the work."

Something in the set of Clint's shoulders changed. Of course, most of the recent stress about the ranch was financial in nature. An operation the size of the Tipped Z required a lot of cash. Even if we turned a profit most years, it only took a string of perfectly normal but expensive events happening with unusual frequency for us to start to feel the pinch. Two grand a month would be enough to make a difference.

Clint turned halfway around to look back at me. "What about when you're not here?"

I opened my mouth to say I'd only be gone when the horse was gone too. But then I realized this wasn't true. There could be trips like the one I'd taken to Dallas, where perhaps the TruGlide Girl would need to be present without her horse.

I stopped and gaped helplessly at my brother.

It was Erin who spoke, her voice sounding in a cool, unruffled tone from the other side of the hay bales. I hadn't heard her come in but now she walked around to stand next to me. Because I was paying attention, I could see a little stiffness in her stride. But I didn't think Clint noticed. "I'll do it," Erin said. "It's only fair since Nora has been putting in so much time helping me with my filly."

I felt a flood of relief. I'd told Erin about Jay's purchase, of course, but my plan to board it here had formed during my subsequent exchange of details with Jay. She didn't know what she was signing up for but she'd come to my aid.

Clint stood frozen for a moment, stymied by being faced down by both his wife and his sister. Then he strode over and kissed Erin softly on the mouth, the anger fading out of him like shadows swallowed by the sunrise.

I heard a jaunty whistle. I looked to see Wyatt returning from turning the horses out. He strode through the open bay doors, seeming to be the only one of us who wasn't totally stressed out. His hat was pushed back on his forehead. I recognized the whistle as the melody from a Garth Brooks song about a man who's convinced he's fallen in love with a girl he met the night before.

Wyatt stopped when his eyes fell on Erin and Clint, and his whistling fell silent. Then, he raised his eyes to meet mine.

Slowly, deliberately, Wyatt winked.

Chapter 6

I leaned on my shovel, feeling the sweat trickle down my back under my shirt as the sun hammered down from above. The tip of my spade bit into the dry earth, making a sharp crunch. I levered the handle, picked up the dirt, and flung it to the side.

Next to me, Erin threw a scoop of dirt after mine. She paused, squinting at the bottom rim of the door we'd unearthed. The wood was stained from having been buried for so long but otherwise it looked like it was perfectly intact and undamaged.

It was Monday morning, and it felt like I'd spent the entire weekend at the ranch. My new horse was scheduled to arrive in about an hour. Mostly, we had the place ready. The puppies had graduated from their stall and were now at large in the hay room, frolicking under the watchful eye of their mother. The double stall was prepared to receive its new occupant.

The door Erin and I were trying to unearth opened into a holding pen that hadn't been used in years. It was a space isolated from other horses. The overhang of the barn roof provided shade and it was large enough a horse with pent up energy from time in a stall could stretch his legs. It was the best place we had for a horse that needed to stay pristine, unblemished, and ready to perform at all times.

The pen was accessible via an exterior gate, but the door we were trying to open also led into the pen. Erin and I had surveyed the situation after working with her filly on Friday, agreed it would be easy to get the door functioning again, and put off doing anything about it until today. Now, although we'd dug out all the blockages, the door remained as fixed as if it was actually a wall disguised to look like a door.

Erin, face bright with exertion, wiped her forehead and approached the door to wiggle it hopefully. It was a sliding door, hung from above and set on a horizontal track. We had inspected the door, inspected the track, and inspected everything in the general vicinity. We couldn't figure out what was keeping the door shut.

In the three days since my father's stroke, some equilibrium had returned to the ranch. My father, though he still seemed to avoid using his left hand, remained stoic in his determination to carry out his normal duties. Clint seemed to have regained his temper. Whatever had made him angry the day I'd asked about the TruGlide horse appeared to be in the past. He'd even thanked me for helping when he'd seen me and Erin leaving the round pen with her filly in tow the day before.

Today, Erin had started in high spirits. In the cool of the morning, she'd climbed back on her horse for the first time since her wreck. This time, everything had gone smoothly. In no time at all, she'd had the filly walking around the round pen, showing no signs of trouble.

Now, however, the satisfaction of that ride was wearing thin in the face of the door that would not budge. Erin wiggled a little harder, then gave the base of the door a frustrated kick. A hollow boom sounded through the barn but otherwise the door did not respond.

"What the hell?" Erin set her shovel down to walk back and forth, bending over to stare at the base of the door in search of the obstruction. Erin was one of the most even-tempered people I knew but this puzzle was taxing even her considerable patience.

I leaned on my shovel again. My hair was heavy with sweat. I wondered for a moment what Jay would think if he could see me right now. I was wearing an old t-shirt that had belonged to my brother at some point before he'd been entirely full grown. It had a logo on the front so faded and cracked as to be no longer recognizable. My jeans were baggy, stained and dirty, and the boots I was wearing were blunt-toed clodhoppers.

For my part, I was ready to give up. There was probably a reason use of this door had been abandoned in the first place. I realized in the despondent clarity of hindsight it might have been intelligent to ask my father why it had been closed for so long before starting our excavation. "It doesn't matter," I said to Erin. "I'll go around."

Erin, however, was not to be diverted. She stood glaring at the door as if its very existence was a personal insult. "But that's ridiculous. If you go around you have to go through the hay room, all the way around the outside of the barn, and through two gates. If this door worked you could open his stall and the horse could walk out on his own."

It was true. Still, at the moment the thought of leading a horse through two extra gates on a twice-daily basis sounded more appealing than continuing to invest time and energy in this fruitless, sweaty endeavor.

I opened my mouth to speak again. Before I could say anything we heard the sound of an approaching whistle. Wyatt, it was turning out, was a habitual whistler—a fact I had come to find very distracting. When he was around the barn, it kept me acutely aware of where he was at all times. When he was not near the barn, I found myself straining for the whistled melody that would announce his return.

Today, Erin and I both turned as the sound drew closer. A moment later, Wyatt appeared, stepping around the side of the barn and stopping to look at us. His eyes flicked over the closed door, the freshly oiled gate, the repainted pipe of the pen, and the mound of soft earth we'd dug out from around the doorway. He stopped whistling to start singing. "Sha la la la la laaaa. Goodbye, Earl." Wyatt released the notes in a surprisingly high, sing-song voice, then stopped and said in his normal tone, "And hello, ladies. Pen looks good."

Wyatt, it had seemed to me, had been in an exceptionally good mood over the past few days. He seemed to be always at the edge of things, whistling and smiling. I'd noticed a large number of small, neglected tasks getting seen to. The broken handle on the bay doors leading into the hay barn was gone, a shiny new one in its place. The cracked tile on my parents' porch had been removed and replaced. The rusted pipe that carried water to one of the near pastures and sprung leaks at least twice a year had been dug out and hauled away. A new, insulated tube now carried the water, coated in some kind of rubbery substance that looked impervious to the elements.

As Erin returned Wyatt's greeting, I realized I was staring. I was staring because Wyatt's appearance was markedly different than usual.

Namely, he was bare-chested. His bronze torso was sweat-slicked and gleaming, the low relief of his abdominal muscles distinct in the early light. His t-shirt was partly crammed into the back pocket of his jeans, hanging out behind him like an off-center, floppy tail.

I found myself drawing certain comparisons between Ted and Wyatt. Ted was not bad to look at with his shirt off. He was relatively fit. He spent enough time in the gym that he was firm and contoured in the right places.

Wyatt, though. Wyatt was another story. Where Ted was adequate, Wyatt was impressive. In his snug jeans and bright spurs, he looked like a Wrangler model.

As Wyatt walked to the pipe of the pen and gave it an experimental touch with his finger to see if the paint was dry, I blinked and forced myself to look away.

The pen, I reflected, did look nice. This morning it had been a weed-choked holding area for old dog kennels, abandoned tires, and all manner of other junk that had somehow accumulated here instead of getting hauled off to the dump. Now its pipe railing gleamed in the sun, rust splotches concealed under the new paint. Considering the pen was visible from the drive and the approach to the barn, it was an improvement to the overall aesthetic of the place to have it cleaned up.

"Except this freaking door won't budge," Erin said. She appeared to be unaffected by the sight of Wyatt's gorgeous torso. She released an exaggerated sigh. "Nora thinks we should give up."

Wyatt, who'd pulled his shirt out of his pocket to wipe the sweat off his face, stowed the shirt again and dipped through the fence, the muscles in his back flexing beneath his skin as he moved. I was staring again. I couldn't seem to help myself.

Wyatt approached the door, reaching out to set his hands on the metal edges. He shook. The door held firm He shoved. It didn't so much as wobble. He heaved to the side. Although the chords in his neck popped into sudden evidence as his whole back flexed and strained impressively with his effort, the door did not yield.

At last, Wyatt's hands fell away. He stared at the door with the same stymied confusion Erin and I had been feeling for hours. "Weird."

My new colleague stepped off the trailer with a quiet snort. He stood with his head high and eyes wide as his ears rotated to take in his new environment. "If you'll sign here," the driver was saying, tapping a line with a capped pen, "and here."

I turned away from the horse as it took a dancing step to the side. I winced as the handler cracked it across the nose with the halter. I signed my name as quickly as I could and handed the clipboard back. "Thank you."

The horse's arrival had been delayed. After giving up on the sliding door, Erin and I had spent the previous afternoon sitting on my parents' porch drinking coffee and waiting for the trailer to arrive. When it hadn't shown up two hours past the appointed time, I'd texted Jay. He'd eventually texted back with the information the delivery service had experienced a delay in Colorado. The horse wouldn't arrive until the following day.

Now it was Tuesday morning and the horse was here at last. He was here, but so wrapped up in a sheet, a hood, and hauling boots I could hardly get any sense of what he looked like beyond being generally horse-shaped.

The handler gave me the lead rope and backed out of the way, his body-language expressing the idea that he considered the horse to be untrustworthy. I considered the hauling boots with a mild feeling of consternation. The horse had been on a trailer for days. I would have preferred to turn him out right away. But the boots were massive, padded, ungainly things. I didn't want him tripping himself up in his enthusiasm at being able to move freely again.

I was alone on the ranch. Erin had ridden out with my brother, my father, and Wyatt that morning. My mother's car was not in the driveway. Only the puppies and their beleaguered mother remained. I'd confined them all to a stall in anticipation of this horse's arrival.

"And here you go." The driver handed me a green plastic folder, ostensibly containing important documents like the horse's papers and vet records. I accepted the folder with my left hand, keeping hold of the lead rope with the other. The horse had temporarily gone still and was staring off at a distant pasture with a rigid neck and upright ears.

"Thanks," I said again.

The driver and the handler were both youngish men. Something in their manner suggested they were somewhat hesitant to leave me alone with this blanketed and padded animal. This would have been sweet if it hadn't been so insulting. "If you follow the drive, there's a turnaround loop back there." I pointed with the folder to indicate the best way to get the gigantic semi and stall trailer off the property.

The guys seemed to take the hint. They turned away to see to the task of getting the trailer closed up and back on the road. The horse, startled out of his frozen pose by the clang of the ramp retracting into the trailer, whipped his head around and took a few more dancing steps to the side. I let him find the end of the rope, holding my arm firm. I was disappointed but not surprised to see him brace and lean on the halter, trying to push through my boundary rather than yielding to it.

With a small sigh, I crammed the folder between my thighs, put both hands on the lifeless nylon rope, waited until one of the back feet was leaving the ground, and gave the rope a firm pull with all the strength in my frame. I didn't jerk. I was smooth, using my body as a counter-weight to propel the horse's hind end out from under him, cause his back to bend and his front to step around. He ended up facing me, somewhat confused, with a look in his dark eyes suggesting he'd just noticed me for the first time.

Behind him, the truck roared to life. The horse's momentary attentiveness vanished. He wheeled around to stare, bug-eyed, towards the departing vehicle. I took the slack out of the rope and hauled, once again maintaining steady pressure until the horse swiveled and looked at me.

For a moment, I wished one of the guys would get back out of the truck. Not so he could help me with the horse but so he could take the bloody folder and put it in the tack room. I was convinced I was going to need two hands to handle this monster and I didn't think Jay would appreciate it if the first thing I did with his fancy $10k dunalino was lose its paperwork.

The semi's engine revved and the trailer rattled as it bounced away. The horse tensed. I cursed, stooped, and set the folder on the ground. I picked up a gritty rock and set this on top to anchor it down. As the horse began to dance again, this time towards me, I straightened, got both hands on the rope and looked at the frantic horse. He was large, he was distracted, and he had no respect whatsoever for my personal space.

For a moment, I felt annoyed. I was annoyed at Jay, for purchasing an animal without consulting me. I was annoyed at the drivers, for being late and delivering this creature when no one else was around. And I was annoyed with the horse, for being so irrational.

It was that last thought that checked me. I seemed to hear my father's voice, speaking to me after my first horse had dumped me into the arena sand by turning more sharply than I was prepared for. I could still remember the moment perfectly, even though it must have happened when I was six years old or even younger.

I'd hauled myself out of the sand, stood up, and stormed towards my waiting horse, seething with frustration. "Stupid horse," I'd said, reaching up to grab the dangling reins.

But my father had caught my wrist, stopping me in mid-swipe. "Nora." He spoke quietly but in a tone that meant business. "You never, ever touch a horse when you're angry. Understand? What happens with a horse is never the horse's fault. The horse does either what nature tells him will keep him safe, or what he's been trained to do. If you want him to do something different, it's your job to show him how."

The truck began to pull away. The horse skittered into my space. I stepped out of his way and he kept going, hauling on the rope when he ran out of slack. The sun was hot and bright. The folder on the ground fluttered behind me on the breeze.

I moved with the horse, let go of all that anger and annoyance. I waited, watching the horse's feet until I could once again bring his head towards me with a well-timed pull as his hind foot left the ground.

This time, when the horse faced up, I made sure my body was soft, my mind free of anger.

The horse looked at me, blinked, and licked his lips.

"Well." I wiped sweat off my forehead as the sound of the delivery truck's engine faded. "It's a start."

"Wow," Ted said, making his way across the arena and stopping to stand next to me. "He's ..." Ted trailed off. "He's called Snoopy?"

I gave a little laugh. Chrome Zippo Whiz, aka Snoopy, and I were finishing up with our fifth groundwork session. It was Friday afternoon and we were both covered in sweat.

On one level, I had to agree with Ted. The name, at a glance, didn't seem to suit.

After the trailer had driven off on Tuesday, I'd gotten the horse calmed down, unwrapped, and turned out in his pen. At that point, I'd been forced to admit he was remarkable, at least in the looks department.

Snoopy was a sooty dunalino—which meant his coat was pale gold overlaid with rich brown dappling. His mane and tail were silver. His legs were barred with delicate horizontal stripes and he had a sooty dorsal that ran from his withers to his rump.

In short, he looked like a horse out of a fairytale.

Which was appropriate, I supposed, because, training-wise, the horse belonged squarely in kindergarten.

To be fair, I had yet to ride Snoopy. I imagined he did know how to run around and slide to a stop. Call me old fashioned, but I like my horse to exhibit signs of sanity *before* I climb onto his back. So every day since Snoopy had arrived, we'd been doing groundwork to instill such

basics as, "Follow when led," and "Don't trample your handler."
Sometimes we did multiple sessions a day. I'd decided the name was
fitting.

Now it was Friday, which meant Snoopy and I had known each
other for several days. The horse stood in the afternoon light, dripping
luminous silver sweat. But he also stood with his hind leg cocked at a
goofy angle, eyes drooped halfway closed.

"He seems to have two modes," I told Ted. "He flips from
'convinced of imminent death' to 'completely not interested in
anything' at the drop of a hat."

Ted chuckled and stepped forward, walking up to pat the horse on
the shoulder. I had to resist the urge to grab his arm and yank him back.
Snoopy wasn't dangerous, particularly not now that he was all tired out
and docile. Still, Ted was one of those people who seemed to view horses
as big, hoofed dogs. It never seemed to occur to him that he should
approach a new one with caution.

Snoopy swiveled an ear toward Ted as my boyfriend gave him a slap
on the neck that was apparently meant to be affectionate. To certain
things, such as rough or abrupt handling, the horse was utterly
desensitized.

Still, I found Ted's proximity to the horse grating. "Come on," I
said. "It's time to get him cleaned up and turned back out."

Ted turned willingly enough. He'd gotten back into town and had
driven straight out to the ranch to see the new horse. He was excited
and a little triumphant Jay had taken my advice after all. He seemed to
view Snoopy's very existence as incontrovertible evidence my new career
was well launched and guaranteed to succeed.

I wasn't so sure. But, I had to admit, Snoopy's arrival had confirmed
Jay wasn't as unwilling to adapt as he'd seemed. Sure, left to my own
devices, I would have chosen a different horse. But hadn't I told Jay I
was a horse trainer? If I was so good at making horses do what I wanted,
the raw material I started with shouldn't make any difference at all.

It was a relief to get out of the sun. Snoopy sighed as I led him into
the hay room and tied him up in the aisle next to his stall. I began to
untack. Ted fell in next to me. He "helped" by getting a kink in my
halter as he handed it to me, failing to tie my latigo up correctly, and

getting in my way at every turn, all the while chatting gaily about his trip and the new marketing initiative his client was launching.

Finally, Ted heaved my saddle and pad off Snoopy and carried them into the tack room. I picked up a curry and began to work the saddle stain on Snoopy's back.

In the tack room, I heard Ted's phone ring. He picked up. A moment later, I glanced to the side to see him standing inside the tack room. He rolled his eyes, pointed at the phone, and closed the door, retreating within to have whatever conversation trumped spending time with me.

I had just finished laughing at myself for being annoyed with Ted for being there one moment and annoyed with him for withdrawing the next when I heard a distant whistle. I froze in my rubbing, straining around to stare at the hay room door. My heart rate increased approximately tenfold. Even the dull Snoopy twitched an ear in my direction, as if wondering why I'd gone stiff.

A moment later, I heard the jingle of spurs. A moment after that, I heard a sigh and a thump as Wyatt dismounted. Then he strode into the hay room, leading Sally.

Sally was my horse. Clint had once given her to me in much the same fashion he'd given Erin her new filly. I'd been recently out of college and it was one of Clint's early efforts to lure me back to the ranch. It had even worked. I'd started Sally in the snaffle and graduated her to the hackamore. She was a solid mount these days.

But she was five now and I had to admit I hadn't been putting in the time lately to see to her continued growth and improvement. By my brother's standards, she should have been well into the two-rein— progressing on her path to being the one-handed bridle horse my dad and brother revered so much.

For my part, it seemed if I could get it done in the hackamore, why bother monkeying around with two sets of reins?

Now, though, my heart gave a weird little tumble and lurch when I saw a set of romal reins carefully looped around the horn. Wyatt was leading Sally by a finger's width little get-down rope, attached to the delicate bosalita under her bridle.

Wyatt saw me standing with Snoopy. His whistle died on his lips. He looked momentarily sheepish. Then he cleared his throat and started forward again. He led Sally into the aisle, parking her so she stood parallel to Snoopy but was not close enough for the two horses to get any ideas about saying hello.

I gave Sally a quick once over. She was a nice looking horse, well made in the using ranch style. She wasn't all silver and gold but she was correct and athletic—elegant in her own way. As I watched, Wyatt gently lowered the spade out of her mouth, stroking her face with gentle fingers as he eased the large bit past her teeth. I had to admit, she'd looked good in the sophisticated gear.

"Clint says you started this one?" Wyatt's tone was casual, as if we'd been hanging out together all day.

I bristled. I turned my back and continued my work on Snoopy, who appeared unaffected by Sally's arrival. "She's supposedly my horse." I couldn't keep a bit of sharpness out of my tone.

Wyatt didn't seem to notice. He'd already gone on. "She's amazing, Nora."

Something about his tone made me turn around. Wyatt was standing with one hand on Sally's withers. He was looking at me over her back with one of the most earnest expressions I'd ever seen. "Clint's been trying to get me to care about finishing horses for years," he said. "He convinced me to try to get this one going in the two-rein, said she's been ready for ages. So I gave in, mostly to get him to leave off bugging me." He stopped and gave a little laugh.

Behind me, Snoopy sighed and shifted his weight. I could hear the muffled undertones of Ted's conversation in the tack room but I couldn't tear my eyes off Wyatt's face.

"Clint gave me a crash course in the two-rein this morning. I have to say, this horse is incredible." He looked down at the old silver bit in his hand, then back at me, as if some secret truth had been revealed to him. "I never realized ...."

Wyatt broke off as the tack room door opened. Ted stepped out, shoving his phone into his pocket and saying, "I swear, the people who call themselves professionals in this industry ...."

I turned in time to see Ted see Wyatt. He broke off mid-sentence and went still. Simultaneously, all the wonder and openness drained out of Wyatt's face. "Ted," Wyatt said, hanging the bridle on the saddle horn and removing the bosalita.

"Oh. Hi, Wyatt," Ted looked at me, looked at Wyatt, then looked at me again. "Anyway," he continued in a less maligned tone, "are you about done here, honey? I could use some lunch."

I reached down to give Sally's neck an absent pet. "Good," I said to Erin. "Now I'm going to move into a trot. You hold onto that night latch and see if you can get your filly to move out after me."

I glanced back, containing a smile at the bug-eyed look on Erin's face. I eased Sally into a slow jog. Behind me, Erin's filly continued to walk as if nothing had changed. "Give her a little more leg," I instructed.

It was Tuesday morning. Erin and I were in the round pen. Erin had been getting on her horse regularly for many days now and walking around in circles before getting off again. It was high time for her to explore some different gears. Seeing Wyatt on Sally a few days before had made me realize I could do more to support Erin from the back of my own horse than from the center of the round pen.

Now, I put a little more life in my seat, encouraging Sally into a larger trot. My mare moved out beneath me. After the highly unrefined rides I'd had on Snoopy this weekend, I was more appreciative than ever of the agile way she responded to my subtle cues.

I glanced back again at Erin. Her filly's ears were tipped back and the horse was walking faster, but she clearly wasn't sure if she could trot with a rider on her back. "More leg," I said to Erin, "or I'm going to come around behind you and pop that horse on the butt with my rope. Keep up with those rhythmic bumps."

Erin's face firmed up. She tightened her grip on her night latch and bumped a bit harder. The filly, at last, broke into an awkward shuffle-trot, then lapsed back into the walk almost at once.

"Good," I said, turning Sally. "That was a try. Give her a break. Pet her."

Erin petted her horse. She looked at me with those wide eyes of hers. "We trotted." Her voice came out in a disbelieving whisper.

I smiled. Without warning, the image of Wyatt rose up behind my eyes—the look on his face after he'd taken Sally's bridle off. *This horse is amazing.*

I felt a shiver run through my body though the sun was bright and hot on my shoulders and hands. Erin's eyes narrowed under her hat as she looked at me. "What on earth are you thinking about? I've never seen that look on your face before."

I blinked, turning Sally to walk off. "All right, let's try for the trot again."

Erin made a sound of protest but followed my lead. Soon we had her filly moving out again, maintaining the trot for more than a few awkward strides this time.

We worked on trotting for the next twenty minutes. As the sun beat down, all four of us in the round pen worked up a solid sweat. But Erin can have an inconveniently long memory. There was something speculative about her expression after we finished our ride. She watched me as we untacked our horses and turned them out. When we were done, she suggested I come down to the house to cool off and eat something before I started my tasks involving Snoopy. I was too hot to decline.

So it was I was sitting at Erin's kitchen table sipping a tall glass of ice water when she said, "Clint told me Wyatt rode Sally in the two-rein the other day. He said they both did really well."

Erin was situated across from me with her own tall water. Between us sat a large wooden bowl of tortilla chips and a smaller glass dish of salsa. When I had chips at my house, I didn't bother with the bowls. But then, Erin had always been a little classier than I was.

Her comment caused me to pause in my chewing of a chip. "Have you thought of a name for your horse yet?"

Erin took a sip of water. She still had that look on her face, as if she was harboring some secret conviction. I considered the idea of leaving before she could voice that conviction. But the AC was deliciously cool on the back of my neck and the salsa was fresh and tangy.

Erin ignored my attempt at changing the subject. She gazed at me, drumming her fingers on the tabletop. "Nora, I'm just wondering, did anything ever happen between you and Wyatt?" She spoke with deceptive innocence, her tone indicating nothing more than mild curiosity.

I thought of the gentle way Wyatt had stroked Sally's face as he'd lowered the bit out of her mouth. I thought then, simultaneously and unflatteringly, of the way Ted had blundered up to Snoopy and whacked the large horse on the shoulder.

"Damn it, Erin." The words burst out of me of their own volition, erupting with unnecessary force. "I don't *want* a cowboy. All my life it's been ranch first, everything else second. I don't want that to be it forever."

Even as I spoke the words, though, I wasn't so sure. What was the alternative, after all? TruGlide first? Ted's job first?

Erin blinked, taken aback by my outburst. She delicately selected a chip from the bowl. "It's just the way he looks at you when you can't see him, the way he talks about you when you're not there."

The wound that had been in my heart for as long as I could remember split open in a sudden rush of pain and longing. It filled me with its sharp bite, clawing in my chest like a caged, angry creature. I rose, unable to sit still, the cold air abruptly unsettling instead of comfortable.

"Erin," I pushed in my chair, hoping she couldn't tell I was fighting to hold back tears, "if Wyatt wanted me, he'd maybe once in all these years have hung around long enough to ask me out on a date or something."

I stood there for a moment, trembling with contained emotion. Then, aware I was behaving like my brother—someone who typically dealt with intense feelings by fleeing from them—I said, "Thanks for the snack." I turned and walked towards the door.

I was halfway across the kitchen when Erin spoke. Her voice was low now, and a little sad. "I think you're wrong," she said. "I think you've got it exactly backwards."

I said nothing. I did, after all, have a lot to do today. I hadn't cleaned Snoopy's stall, or brushed out his ridiculous silver tail, or done any groundwork, or ridden him.

I kept walking.

I had my hand on the handle and was in the act of pushing open the front door when Erin said, at last, "I think I'm going to name my filly Esperanza."

I punched in the key code that opened the gate, then sat as the motor whirred and the entrance to the Tipped Z was unbarred. I waited until there was room for my Dodge to ease through, then moved forward with an unnecessary revving of the engine. I tore up the dirt road, kicking up dust, only slowing when I was close enough to the barn I'd have blown grit all over Snoopy, who was standing splendidly in his pen in the luminous morning light.

I was revving my engine and generally behaving like a teenager because I was annoyed. I was annoyed because of Ted. When I'd gotten up at 4:30 AM this morning and begun to pull on my jeans, he'd eased himself up onto his elbow and gazed blearily at me. We'd spent the night as his place, which meant I'd started my day further away from the Tipped Z than usual. Which meant I'd needed to get moving early if I wanted to muck out Snoopy's stall in anything less than soul-crushing heat.

He'd blinked at me a few times, mumbling in a sleepy voice, "Where are you going?"

"To the ranch." I pulled on my tank top.

He woke up a bit then and spoke in an annoyed tone. "Really? We have a morning we could spend together and you're going to the ranch before the sun is up?"

I stooped to pull my socks on. "I have a horse there I have to take care of. It belongs to the TruGlide Corporation. In case you'd forgotten, me becoming the TruGlide Girl was your idea, not mine."

Perhaps my tone carried a bit more of the inexplicable frustration I'd been feeling the last few days than the situation demanded. Ted sat up all the way. His dark eyes were sleepy but concerned. "Nora?" His tone went gentle. "Is there something we need to talk about?"

Somehow, his solicitous words made it worse. "No." I tied my hair back in a ponytail. "What I need to do is go take care of the damn horse."

I'd stalked out, driven through the sunrise, and now I was here, the horse in question watching me through the pipe fence.

Which was odd, now that I thought about it. According to the contract Jay had drawn up, Snoopy was to be kept indoors at night. When he was outside, he was required to be wearing a fly sheet at all times so as to preserve his perfect coat against disasters like sun bleaching and fly bites. I'd left Snoopy in his stall the night before, munching on sweet-smelling hay.

Now, there he was, fly-sheeted and spry-looking, standing at the bottom of his pen.

Which was when I noticed something else—something more perplexing.

The door Erin I had spent an entire afternoon trying to unstick was open. It was open and a lean, Wrangler-clad figure was propped against the doorjamb.

It was Wyatt, broadcasting smug satisfaction in approximately a one mile radius in every direction.

I killed my engine, the frustration and annoyance draining away more quickly than they'd come on. I stepped out of my truck, walked to the pen, and ducked through the pipe fence. I straightened to see Wyatt still leaning there. I wondered if he'd been hovering around for a while just so he could situate himself this way when I drove up.

I gazed into the dim reaches of the aisle, disbelieving. "The door. How did you fix it?"

Wyatt's eyes were creased at the corners, his mouth turned up at the edges. He turned to set one square hand on the doorjamb, tilting his head to look up towards the track at the top. "You know, sometimes it takes a man to do a job right."

He was already laughing before I smacked him on the shoulder. His t-shirt was thin. I could feel the warm heat of his body through the fabric. My mind scrambled. Had I ever touched Wyatt before? I must have, but I couldn't recall. Now my fingers seemed to thrum, as if they'd absorbed some sort of elemental energy straight out of him.

Wyatt's chuckle faded. "Actually, it was three nails—driven straight through the bracket there at the end that keeps it from blowing outwards when it's closed. I guess someone nailed it shut once before a storm or something and then everyone forgot. You could hardly see the heads because the entire bracket had been buried and was all over rust." He held up three gritty nails as he spoke, as if I might not believe him without evidence.

I shook my head in wonder. Behind me, Snoopy ambled over to his water trough, which was full, and began to take a noisy drink. "And you put Snoopy's sheet on, filled his water, and put hay out for him?"

Wyatt shrugged, dropping the nails into his pocket like souvenirs. "Don't get your hopes up. I didn't muck his stall." He met my eyes, grinning. Then the grin faded. When he spoke again, his voice had shifted—lowered and turned more serious. "You seem a little stressed. I thought I'd ease your morning a bit."

My heart gave a strange, swelling throb. Inexplicably, I felt the prickle of tears behind my eyes. I thought of Ted's resentful comment in his dark bedroom. *You're going to the ranch before the sun is up?* Then his quieter, kinder one. *Is there something we need to talk about?*

I looked at Wyatt. He was looking at me. His eyes were steady and serious. For a moment, it felt as if all the years between us were a bond and a connection. Not a rift, as I'd always thought. For a moment, I thought not of all the times he'd left but of all the times he'd been here. Times like now.

My phone in my pocket chimed to let me know I had a text. I blinked and fished it out, staring down at my lock screen.

It was a message from Ted. "I love you."

I saw Wyatt look down, saw him see the screen. I saw him read the words.

Something went out of him. He turned away, patting the door frame like an old loyal dog. "Anyway." There was something defeated about his tone and a strange droop in his shoulders. "Seemed like the least I could do, for letting me ride your horse."

He walked off, leaving me standing there, phone in hand, heart full of so many conflicting emotions I couldn't even find the voice to thank him.

Chapter 7

I stood beneath the shade of a large umbrella, staring at the parking lot and trying not to chew my lip, rub my eyes, touch my hair, or do anything else that might cause Maggie to sigh, storm over, and fix whatever I'd mussed. I had also been instructed not to sweat, which was impossible to begin with and growing harder by the minute. The sun was rising. The camera crew was assembled behind me. Jay was pacing around the edge of the parking area. I was glancing down at my phone every five seconds.

I'd woken extra early this morning to head to the ranch, make sure Snoopy was still as clean and polished as I'd left him the night before, hook up the trailer to my truck, and borrow Erin's car to head back into town to meet my stylists at the hotel where Jay and the rest of the TruGlide team was staying. Maggie and her assistants had transformed me into the TruGlide Girl and we'd headed out to meet the photographers.

Now we were on site for the shoot. The only thing missing was my horse.

The shoot had been Jay's idea. He was now super on board with the idea of pushing Snoopy into the limelight. I had tried to explain Snoopy's groundwork had made a lot of progress in a week, but the horse wasn't exactly bombproof at this point. Jay had brushed me off. Since I needed to be the TruGlide Girl—un-mussed and immaculate—I hadn't been able to load and haul Snoopy myself. I'd asked Erin to help out.

But she was late. And I was now busy imagining every horrible scenario which might have led to my crazy dunalino murdering my sweet sister-in-law.

I turned to glance at Jay. Erin was only eight minutes late at this point, but eight minutes was an eternity in Jay's world. He expected everyone to be not only punctual but early. He'd arrived excited, keen to see the horse. Now excitement had given way to annoyance.

I looked back down at my phone. Today I was dressed in an outfit of pure black, with a pair of red chaps and tons of bling. In the sun, my shirt glittered and reflected light with my every nervous breath.

The lack of text or phone call was a good thing, I told myself. It meant Erin was running a little late. I'd warned her about Jay's crazy timeline expectations, but life on the ranch was unpredictable. Snoopy and I had practiced loading the night before. He'd walked into the trailer like an old pro. But Erin wasn't me and today wasn't yesterday. Things can change in a heartbeat when it comes to horses.

I shoved my phone back into my pocket and again resisted the urge to touch my own face in a way that would disrupt my immaculate appearance. The black shirt was hot on my back. I knew I'd be dripping sweat underneath the fabric in only a matter of time. I was tired, too. I'd been up since before dawn. I hadn't slept well because I'd been so worried I'd sleep through my alarm.

Jay had just turned from his conversation with one of the photographers and taken a step in my direction with an expression that promised I would not enjoy the conversation we would soon be having when I heard the familiar rumble of my old Power Wagon's ancient engine. I turned, relief flooding through my veins like a drug.

The location of the shoot had been chosen for its proximity to the ranch. Erin still wasn't exactly a pro at operating machinery and the old Dodge was a bit temperamental, but it had been such a short distance she'd been confident she could make it. She'd said it would be good practice.

I hurried across the parking lot as Erin navigated the truck off the road. Jay had rented a section of a local golf course for the shoot, so there was an entire bay of parking spots set aside for the truck and trailer. I directed Erin into place. She killed the engine as I hurried over to her door.

Erin's face had a harried look as she stepped down from the truck. "I'm so sorry I'm late." Her face was flushed and her voice had that trembling quality it took on when she was upset.

I fell in step beside her as she headed towards the back of the trailer. I could see Snoopy's big brown eye gazing out the window. "Was he a monster for loading?"

There was one hitch in Erin's step as she looked at me in some confusion. "Snoopy? Oh, no. He was a doll. It was Clint. He asked me to help him pony in a few horses this morning. He wanted it done before your dad was up. I guess your dad almost got in a wreck yesterday. He fumbled the reins when a colt he was working from horseback got upset, then couldn't pop his dallies. The young horse went nuts and almost hauled your dad's saddle horse off his feet."

We'd arrived at the back of the trailer. I reached up to unlatch the door but Erin batted my hands away. "Don't you touch anything." She paused, seeming to take in my appearance for the first time. A series of expressions flickered across her face, all too transient and too strange for me to understand. "Wow," she said as she propped the door open. From inside, Snoopy nickered. "Wyatt said they transformed you. He was right."

As Erin stepped into the trailer, I turned to see Jay approaching. I didn't have time to try to decipher Erin's strange tone before he was there, all smiles now, eager to see the soon-to-be-famous TruGlide Horse.

"And then," Jay swirled his glass of wine and looked at Ted with an expression of relaxed outrage, "they said the project scope hadn't included anything about an interactive print ordering system. I said how else were people supposed to order autographed photos?" He then turned as the server approached, holding up his glass to indicate he wanted it to be topped up from the open bottle which sat on the table. "Anyway, so now it's going to be a few more days. They can't tell us how many, exactly, because they don't have the photography yet."

Ted made a noise of commiseration and thanked the server, who'd also refilled his glass.

My glass did not need refilling because I'd not been keeping pace with my two dinner companions. My long day had more than caught up with me. The shoot, once it had started, had gone well. Snoopy mostly took the strange environment, the flashes, the snapping shutters, and the people, with equanimity, though Erin had to remove him from the general vicinity of all the fragile people to do a little groundwork to get him resettled a few times. Jay, fortunately, appeared to be so happy with how the horse and I looked together, his good mood had established itself and stayed in place all day.

After the first part of the shoot, which featured me and Snoopy pretending to have some deep emotional bond, I'd tacked up and ridden around on the pristine golf course grass. It was not an environment that made sliding stops possible, however, so from there we'd loaded back up, hauled to a reining arena, and proceeded to collect photos of Snoopy doing the thing our product supposedly enhanced.

Finally, the photographers called a wrap. Erin and I loaded Snoopy again. I'd sent her off with my truck and profuse thanks. I'd been stripped of my clothing and make-up, had time to go home, shower, hurry to the ranch to swap Erin's car for my truck, and get back to my apartment in time for Ted to pick me up for dinner.

I'd spent the last two hours watching Ted and Jay eat and drink. At first, Ted made regular attempts to include me in the conversation. He'd given up, however, at my repeated failure to rally. Now I felt like little more than an accessory.

The server emptied the last of the wine into Ted's glass. He hovered until Jay looked at him. "Would you like another bottle?"

"Yes, the same," Jay answered without consulting either Ted or myself. He took a sip from his glass and turned to Ted as if to continue their conversation about how annoying web developers were.

I stood up. Ted looked at me with surprise, as if he'd forgotten I was with them at all. I ran a hand through my hair, which was dry and stiff, though I'd done my best to wash the product out. I looked down at the little table bearing the remnants of dinner. "I'm sorry, guys, but I need to head home."

Jay looked at me as well. He wore one of his blank expressions.

Ted began to scoot back his chair. I held up a hand. "No, no. You guys stay. It's not all that often you have a chance to hang out like this. I'll Uber home."

Ted looked like he might protest but Jay shifted to reach into the inner pocket of the jacket that hung on his chair. He pulled out an envelope and offered it to me.

The envelope was made of thick, creamy paper and was sealed shut. Uncertain, I accepted the envelope. The rhinestones still affixed to my fingernails flashed in the subdued light. "There's a company credit card in there for you," Jay said, "for work-related expenses. Please save all receipts. Also, there's a bonus for your recent significant contribution to the development of the TruGlide brand identity." He winked.

I held the envelope awkwardly now, feeling the off-center weight of a hard piece of plastic in one end. *Significant contribution?* I wasn't quite sure what Jay was talking about. My eyes flicked to Ted. He mouthed an exaggerated, silent, "Snoopy."

I understood. Now that it appeared to have worked out quite well for the business, Jay was making amends for stealing my idea of getting a TruGlide horse on board.

I felt myself blush. "Thank you."

Jay sat back, looking pleased with himself. "We've booked your first performance with Zippo at a local event. It's a rodeo thing downtown. That's on Sunday. Then you'll have two weeks to prepare for your first major appearance, which will be the *Start the Horse, Connect the Heart* colt-starting competition in Oklahoma City. A trailer will arrive to pick Snoopy up two weeks from today."

I froze in the act of stooping to gather my purse, dismay rippling through me. *Start the Horse, Connect the Heart?* In two weeks? Sure, Snoopy was settling in. But that was one of the most well-known, well-attended colt-starting events in the country.

I recovered from the shock, slipped the envelope into my purse, and straightened. I plastered a smile on my face. "Wow. That's a big one."

Jay gave a slow nod, taking another sip of wine. "We were lucky. One of the opening acts canceled at the last minute and our marketing team got wind of the opportunity. We think it will be worth the expense."

A mild headache bloomed behind my eyes. "Cool," I said, my voice sounding syrupy and fake even to me. "We'll be ready."

I turned, waving Ted back into his seat again when he tried to rise to accompany me to the curb, and escaped into the bustling solitude of a downtown Tucson night.

I pulled my phone out of my pocket as I stepped outside, realizing with surprise it was only 8:00. I rubbed my gritty eyes. It felt more like midnight. I let out a long, tired breath as I glanced up and down the street, then pulled up Uber.

I was waiting for the app to load when my phone chimed, letting me know a text had arrived. My heart went into violent spasms when I saw the name "Wyatt" appear in my notification bar.

The message was short and opaque. "Where are you?"

The restaurant Jay had chosen for our meal was on 4th Avenue. As I stood on the narrow street, a group of laughing girls passed by on the opposite sidewalk and a car passing in the street honked its horn. The girls hooted and laughed. The car revved its engine and sped on.

It took me a moment to recover from my stunned surprise. I texted back. "4th Ave. Why?"

I stood then, waiting, for what seemed approximately an age. Finally, my phone chimed again. "I'm at the District Tavern."

I blinked. Behind me, the door to the restaurant opened. A couple stepped out into the street. He held the door for her, then set an arm around her shoulders as they walked off together.

I knew where the District Tavern was. It was on Congress Street, a trolley ride away from where I was now. But what on earth was Wyatt doing downtown? He wasn't one to go out drinking, as far as I knew.

And why was he telling me where he was? I read his message again and again. Was it an invitation? A cry for help?

Another text came in. "I had a date."

My heart, which had been hammering this whole time, stopped beating for several seconds. Then it spasmed into a staccato double-time that nearly dropped me to the street. I texted back a single word. "Had?"

Wyatt's reply was quick this time. "Ended Bali."

As I tried to decipher this cryptic response, a breeze stirred my hair into my eyes. I shoved my phone into my pocket, tied my scorched hair into a ponytail, and dug my phone out again. Wyatt had texted again. "*badly."

The door behind me opened again. I glanced back, convinced it was Ted coming to ask why I was still standing here on the sidewalk. It wasn't Ted. It was a group of four young professionals. I started to walk anyway, drifting with uncertain momentum in the general direction of downtown. I stopped underneath a streetlight to compose my eloquent response. "Oh. Sorry."

I waited. The trolley clattered by, full of laughing people. The wind kicked up again, blowing a discarded Starbucks cup off the curb and into the street. I could smell heat and dust and stale beer. I stared at my phone. Its screen turned itself off.

I stood there for what seemed like an eternity. My heart began to recover, slowing from a hammer to a steadier rhythm. I stood in the pool of light, waiting, until I realized Wyatt wasn't going to text back. This was what he did. He would pop up in my life without warning, we would have some inexplicable interaction, and then he would disappear.

A chill seemed to flood over me. I closed my messaging app and opened Uber again. I had just punched the "set pickup location" bubble when another text arrived.

It was Wyatt. "Where on 4th?"

Adrenaline surged through my veins. Some movement caused me to look up. The trolley had stopped at the top of the street and people were streaming off. As the crowd dispersed, one man did not move. He stood alone under a neon sign, his hat brim bathed pink, his chin lit by his glowing phone.

I texted back. "Look up."

I waited. I felt, somehow, as if this was all taking place in a suspended bubble of unreality. It occurred to me this would look very bad if Ted happened to come outside in time to see Wyatt. It would look like it had been planned.

Across the street, Wyatt looked up. I seemed to feel an electrical current as his eyes raked down the street and settled, at last, on me. He put his phone away, looked both ways, and jogged across the street, the tiny hitch in his step giving his gait a particular off-beat rhythm.

As he approached, my whole body seemed to go warm. He hopped up onto the curb next to me, saying in his typical, relaxed tone, "I heard about your shoot today."

I thought of the envelope in my purse—the credit card and the bonus check. "Yeah." A warm breeze blew over us, bringing with it the clang of the trolley as it started up again. "Erin hauled Snoopy all by herself."

Wyatt began to walk. With one guilty glance back at the restaurant where I'd left Ted and Jay, I went with him.

The boots Wyatt wore had good heels. His stride was confident and sure as we moved together down the sidewalk. "Erin's the one who said you might want a ride home."

I felt my face flush. I'd sent Erin a pathetic text from the bathroom about half an hour before.

With Wyatt's words came sudden understanding. Understanding that caused all the heat and excitement to drain out of me.

It was Erin who had thought of me, stuck out with Ted and Jay, exhausted, wanting to go home. She must have known Wyatt was downtown, must have heard his date had been a disappointment and suggested he pick me up. It all fell into place. Wyatt hadn't been sitting somewhere nearby on a date with some strange woman, wishing he could be with me.

No. He'd been ready to head back to the ranch and my sister-in-law had suggested I might want a ride home.

That was all.

My fatigue, which had been banished by the sudden rush of emotion that had accompanied Wyatt's first text, came back in a sudden rush. A headache swirled in my temples again. My steps faltered.

Wyatt stopped too, looking at me with an inquiring expression. He looked very good, standing there in his jeans and button-down. My tone, when I spoke, was cold. "I was going to take an Uber home."

Wyatt's brow furrowed under his hat. He said nothing, only looked at me in the still way of someone waiting for developments.

I felt a sudden twinge of remorse at the sight of his confusion. I made a gesture back towards the restaurant. "Ted's just ... I mean he might not ..." I stopped talking, unsure what I was trying to say.

Wyatt's expression darkened. He took his hat off, ran a hand through his short hair, and settled his hat back on his head. "Nora." His tone was low. "Are you telling me your man is so insecure he won't let you catch a ride home with an old friend?"

It was the way he put it that made me angry. I lifted my chin, starting forward again. "Ted's not in a position to let or not let me do anything."

Wyatt moved to stay with me. "I'm glad to hear that."

Snoopy jerked, raising his head as a group of noisy children passed by outside the warm-up arena. I reached down and patted his neck, doing what I could to soothe him while feeling in need of soothing, myself.

It was Sunday: three days since Wyatt had picked me up downtown and driven me back to my apartment. Since then, I'd spent a good deal of time with Snoopy, doing my best to get him ready for our first real performance. The bonus check had turned out to be generous. Accepting it had filled me with a sense of urgent anxiety. I was still certain the company's investment in a TruGlide horse would pay off. I just wished Snoopy and I didn't have quite so much ground to make up.

In the desert in the summer, an animal can only take so much exercise. Snoopy and I did what we could. He improved, slowly but steadily. And now it was time to show off what we knew.

I sat waiting, listening to the distorted voice of the man on the loudspeaker and the waves of applause and cheers as competitors passed through the big performance arena. Snoopy was warmed up. I was in full TruGlide regalia. We were as ready as we were going to get.

I took deep breaths and put conscious effort into keeping my legs loose and relaxed. When Snoopy quivered, I reassured him. Until, at last, the arena doors swung open.

Snoopy tensed but didn't move. The announcer's voice boomed in. "And now for this special message from our sponsor."

I took a deep breath. That was our cue. I gave Snoopy one last pat and asked for a gallop.

The big horse was up to full speed by the time we rocketed through the gate and into the expansive arena. The first thing I did was run down the middle of the space and ask Snoopy to slide to a stop.

He did as I asked. It was the one thing he was actually pretty good at. Still, I had to make an effort not to wince as he buckled up beneath me, skidding so hard he blew a wave of sand up around us. Sliding stops were hard on horses. As one reining trainer I knew had once put it, "Every horse has a finite number of these in his body. I try to use mine wisely."

The crowd, however, wasn't interested in that kind of pesky detail. They went wild. Snoopy came to the end of his slide. I rocked him a few steps backwards, then hopped him out into the canter.

Doing much other than sliding on a horse wearing TruGlide's patented reining shoes is a bit tricky. The shoes are optimal for sliding and sub-par for everything else. Fortunately, the footing was good and we had space. As the announcer boomed through the prepared script about all the ways in which TruGlide shoes are better than any other reining shoe, I put Snoopy through the routine we'd been practicing the last three days.

The stands, I had time to notice as we moved around, were less than packed. Jay had gotten wind of this little reining event and decided we should perform—an act I was now profoundly grateful for considering I would be called upon to produce a more impressive display in front of a vastly larger and more critical crowd in two weeks' time.

I still hadn't fully processed Jay's announcement that I would be riding in *Start the Horse, Connect the Heart*. It seemed there was a strange quality of suspended reality to my life since that dinner with Ted and Jay. On the surface, everything seemed to be continuing as it had been before. I went to the ranch. I helped Erin with Esperanza. I worked with Snoopy. I cleaned Snoopy's stall. I made sure every silvery gold hair on Snoopy's body remained unblemished, immaculate, and properly aligned.

But something was different.

We finished with some trotting patterns. I pushed Snoopy into another gallop. We whipped around the perimeter of the arena. As we careened past the stands, I tried without any hope of success to pick out familiar faces. Erin and Wyatt had said they'd try to come today if they could get their morning work done in time. The knowledge the two of them might be watching made me more nervous than the attention of all the other fans combined.

The night Wyatt had driven me home from downtown, nothing had happened. Nothing had happened at all. We'd chatted on the way home. I'd explained about my long day and leaving Ted and Jay to do their thing without me. Wyatt had absorbed this without comment. But there had been something in his eyes that made me feel agitated, as if I'd divulged a tremendous secret and now had to trust him to keep it.

We'd talked about unimportant things for the rest of the drive. He'd pulled into my apartment complex. We'd said goodnight. I'd gotten out of his truck, gone inside, and gone to bed.

Nothing had happened.

And yet, something was different. Since that night, there had been a change in Wyatt's demeanor when he saw me or spoke to me. There was a kind of patience about him now—a quality of waiting, of watching, of biding his time. He was no more or less present at the ranch than he'd been for the last few weeks. Nevertheless it seemed he was always there, just around a corner, just riding out, always looking back to flash me one quick grin before disappearing.

I lapped the arena, turned Snoopy towards the center, and executed another sliding stop. The change in Wyatt was imaginary, I told myself. My big fat imagination was getting itself all wound up over nothing.

And even if it wasn't nothing, it couldn't become anything more than what it was. Ted had been ultra-sweet the last few days, apologizing the morning after his dinner with Jay, saying he shouldn't have let me go home alone. Since then, he'd been showing me every little thoughtful courtesy he could come up with, as if we'd fought and I expected him to make amends.

It was actually a little annoying.

The announcer approached the end of his speech. I spun Snoopy, took one more lap around the arena, and we surged into one final gallop. As the last words of the TruGlide catchphrase faded, the crowd burst into applause. Snoopy and I barreled through the open gate, out of the limelight, and into the suspended quiet of the warm-up arena.

No one was watching anymore. I eased Snoopy down to a trot, then a walk, and let him walk a few laps to cool down. He was amped and sweating. I could feel his jittery energy.

For my part, I was feeling more relaxed. It had been a small crowd, yes, and a modest performance. But we'd made it through without embarrassment or disaster.

It was a start. As time went on, perhaps I could refine things, find more horsemanship-centric riding to work in and demonstrate during my routine.

I reached down, patting Snoopy's neck. "Maybe this is all going to work out after all."

I gave Snoopy's shoulder one final rub and stepped back, letting the halter fall away from his face. Free, the silvery horse turned with a look of mild anticipation. He moved across the double stall to the generous pile of hay in the corner. I watched for a moment, feeling almost fond of the silly animal.

It was early evening. I was back from my long day being the TruGlide Girl at the reining event. Although I'd done my best to remove all traces of my other identity from my body, my hair still reeked of product.

Still, it didn't bother me as much as usual as I stepped out of Snoopy's stall and hung up his halter. The long sliding door at the far end of the aisle was open. We mostly left it open now we had the option. Stained clouds holding the last colors of sunset lay on the horizon like jeweled marshmallows.

I stood watching the sky for a moment. In the hay room, one of the puppies gave a quick, playful bark and scampered in my direction. It bumped into the back of my legs with a soft, clumsy thump. I smiled and squatted to rub the little fellow's ears. As I did so, my stomach growled. I was beyond hungry.

The puppy was one of the males. He was a mottled combination of gray and black and white markings with a big blotch across one side of his face that gave him an off-balance look. We'd dubbed him Lop. He was, in my opinion, the pick of the litter.

As I rubbed my hands in his warm, soft, puppy-smelling coat, I said to him, "I wonder if there's anything to snack on in the fridge?"

Lop, who'd been leaning against my legs, collapsed onto the ground the better to give me access to his highly rubbable belly. I laughed and rubbed a minute longer. Then I straightened, groaning in a geriatric fashion, and made my way into the tack room.

The tack room at the Tipped Z doubled as a sort of lounge. It was a spacious place, well-sealed and insulated, unlike the rest of the barn. The room was full of tack. There were two full walls of hackamores and bridles, sorted by bit type. There was a row of saddles set on racks, pads hanging above them. There was also a good deal of miscellaneous tack, spare parts, and materials, all organized in drawers and on shelves tucked back in the far corner.

More importantly for me right now, there was a refrigerator. Next to the refrigerator was a long counter overhung by cabinets.

For the most part, my father's training philosophy didn't include giving horses treats. The fridge mostly contained things hungry and thirsty humans might like to consume at the end of a long day in the saddle. Humming to myself, I opened the door and peered in. I found the interior surprisingly well-stocked with beer. There were also a couple of ancient cans of Coke and a jar of pickles.

This last drew my attention. I investigated the plastic drawer under the top shelf and found two baggies, one containing roast beef, one deli cheese. I also found a jar of mustard. I opened the cupboard above the counter to discover a loaf of bread.

My mood brightened further. Still humming, I began to set the sandwich makings out on the counter.

The counter ran the length of the wall. Down at the far end, in the corner, stood a computer. This was a recent addition to the place, and a little-used one. As my activity sent small tremors through the counter, the screen lit. I turned in surprise at the sudden light, realizing it must have been left on.

Then I froze in the act of opening the mustard.

The screen was fully occupied by me. Or, then again, maybe not. I both recognized myself and did not recognize myself. I was a smoothed out, enhanced, burnished, perfect version of myself.

It was not Nora on that screen. It was the TruGlide Girl.

Appetite vanishing, I took a few steps down the counter, staring at the computer in confused disbelief. I was not alone on the screen. Snoopy was with me, resplendent in his silver and gold hues. To the left, above our heads, the TruGlide logo sat next to a list of menu options. "Home, The TruGlide® Story, Our Patented SureSlide™ Technology, Find a Dealer, Contact TrueGlide®."

It was, I understood at last, the TruGlide website. And Snoopy and I were front and center.

I stood motionless for long enough the screen turned itself off again. I blinked. My mind seemed to unfreeze. I felt a strange sense of shock. Of course, I knew photos had been taken of myself and Snoopy. I had known these were going to be used on the website. But I hadn't, somehow, envisioned us being, essentially, *the whole* website.

In the distance, I heard the thud of a horse's hoof on dirt. Wyatt's whistle drifted in from the hay room. I startled as if I'd been caught in the act of doing something unsavory. It occurred to me the TruGlide webpage had not magically opened itself on the computer in the Tipped Z's tack room. Someone had opened it. Since Clint and Erin had a computer in their own house and my parents thought of computers much the same way they thought of time travel and cryogenic freezing as a route to immortality, that meant there was only one person who would have had reason to turn this particular computer on.

My heart seemed to compress, a strange sensation of weakness spreading out from my chest and coursing through my muscles. If Wyatt had pulled up the TruGlide website, it certainly hadn't been because he was interested in shoes.

I heard the sharper clops of a horse walking on concrete as Wyatt led his mount into the aisle to untack. I turned, suddenly frantic. I focused on my sandwich creation, trying to summon up a look of blasé concentration while I waited for Wyatt to appear.

Wyatt's whistle broke off as he pushed through the tack room door. I looked up to see him standing at the end of the narrow hallway that opened into the wider room. He was hatless, hair damp with sweat. He carried his saddle under his arm. The narrow hackamore and full bridle of a two-rein set-up hung over his opposite shoulder.

Wyatt's eyes flicked over my array of sandwich-making materials. It occurred to me this bounty was undoubtedly his. Clint and Erin had their own kitchen, as did my parents. They'd never before shown any inclination to keep such food items in the tack room fridge.

I felt my face heat with awkward realization. Beyond that, I was acutely aware of the computer at the end of the counter. My activities had jostled it to life once before. If that happened again, Wyatt would know I knew he'd been looking at the TruGlide website.

"I'm sorry," I blurted as soon as Wyatt looked at me. "I wasn't thinking straight." I stared down at the piece of bread I'd already slathered in mustard.

Wyatt's face lit with his easy smile. "No worries, señorita." He moved past me towards the wall of saddles. "I'm always grateful for the opportunity to feed the hungry. Help yourself."

I turned to watch Wyatt as he passed behind me. He set the saddle on its rack with practiced ease, then moved to hang up the bridle. He wore a pair of light chinks. The fringe swayed around his legs as he walked. I'd always thought there was something indescribably sexy about a man in chinks.

Wyatt turned around, saw me looking, and ran his two blunt hands through his damp hair. "You can leave all that out," he added. "I'll make one in a minute."

With that, he was gone again, heading out the door and picking up his whistling. I glanced at the computer as if it was an ornery, unpredictable cow who might choose at any moment to act out and make my life more difficult. I considered my situation, weighed the pros and cons, then set two more pieces of bread onto the counter.

By the time Wyatt returned with his pad, having groomed his horse and turned it back out, I had two fully assembled sandwiches set on old plastic plates, one orange, one red.

Wyatt strode through the door, carried his saddle pad to its place, then turned to look at the sandwiches with an appreciative air. "You know your way to a man's heart." He walked across the room, which felt a good deal smaller now that he was in it. He stopped quite close to me and asked in a low, intimate tone, "Which one's mine?"

I felt paralyzed. I could smell the faint scent of horse sweat and worn leather rising off him like a dusky cologne. I was acutely aware that if either of us shifted our weight a little, our bodies would collide.

"Either one." My voice felt dry and papery. "They're the same."

Wyatt picked up the red plate and stepped around me to the fridge. He opened it, stooped, and grabbed a can of beer. He thumped the beer down on the counter. "Making sandwiches is thirsty work. You'll need one of these."

Down on the end of the counter, the computer screen turned on.

I snatched up the cool can, as if doing so would cause the screen to turn off again. Heart hammering, I tried to position my body between Wyatt and the ridiculous photo of Snoopy and me. Why, I wondered with frantic recrimination, hadn't I closed the web browser when I'd been alone in here? I wasn't sure why I didn't want Wyatt to know I knew he'd been looking at the TruGlide website, only that I really, really didn't want him to know.

Wyatt straightened, a second beer in his free hand, and bumped the fridge closed with one hip. Before he could say anything, I forced a false smile onto my face. "We should eat on the patio." Wyatt, I imagined, was the sort of person who ate standing up a lot. I didn't think my heart could survive the strain of the two of us being near the computer for more than another minute.

Wyatt grinned. "Nora," his tone was playful, "is this a sandwich eating date?"

I felt my face go scarlet. The combination of my gnawing hunger, the knowledge of the glowing screen behind me, and Wyatt's sheer proximity all seemed too much. I wanted to shove him out the tack room door. Instead, I stood there, my face and ears radiating embarrassed heat. I couldn't think of a single thing to say.

Wyatt's grin faded a little. He shifted his weight, as if to turn towards the door.

Then he saw the screen. I saw him see it—saw the sudden change in the tension of his body. Involuntarily, I followed his gaze.

There I was, bejeweled, airbrushed, and painted to perfection. My hair was arranged in a loose tumble of artful curls. My eyes seemed oversized in my pale face. For the first time, I wondered if Wyatt had been looking at the photo because he found it attractive. Jay, after all, was in the business of providing what men found beautiful. What if Wyatt preferred the TruGlide me to the real one?

Wyatt drew in a breath, letting it out in a slow sigh. He set his sandwich and beer down on the counter, moved to the computer, and closed the browser. All the playfulness had left his face when he turned around to look at me. I became aware of my plain jeans, my fried hair, my make-up free face.

Wyatt took one step forward. He picked up his beer. He rotated the can between his two palms. He looked away from me, eyes going a bit distant as he looked at the wall upon which the fine silver bridles hung, collected and kept by multiple generations of my family.

I watched. My mind was oddly blank. It occurred to me I should say something to make the moment less awkward. I didn't. It is the curse of my family, to stay silent when we should speak.

Wyatt let out a short, frustrated breath. He spoke in a low tone that carried a strange undernote of anger. "These guys in marketing." He paused, rubbing the back of his head with his hand. "They've got it wrong. Most men don't care for glitter and shine." He paused. Something firmed up in his face. He raised his eyes. I felt that familiar shock as his gaze found mine. "They do you an injustice with all that make-up and Photoshopping."

I felt as if all the air had gone out of the room. His words seem to fall into my stomach like warm stones. I blinked, remembering Jay's words. *Boobs and butts. That's what sells.*

Wyatt picked up his plate and seemed to stir himself, pushing aside whatever deeper emotion had spurred him to speak. His grin returned as he headed towards the door. "I think there's a picnic table out back that could use some company."

Chapter 8

○

I parked my truck and dropped my keys into my purse, drawing in a fortifying breath as I looked towards the lit windows of Ted's house. Behind me, the sky was stained with a lurid sunset as the heat of the summer day faded from the air.

It was Monday evening. I was tired. Ted had called me the night before, not long after my time sitting at a picnic table with Wyatt, eating sandwiches and talking about nothing particularly important.

Ted had told me all about some big plan he'd cooked up for today. He wanted to do a morning hike, a midday swim, and finally a romantic evening out. He'd sounded revved up and excited about the plan. To me, it sounded exhausting.

It was Snoopy who saved me. I explained to Ted the performance we had coming up was a major one. A couple sliding stops and some galloping around wasn't going to cut it this time. The other shows at the *Start the Horse, Connect the Heart* event would be nationally and internationally known, displaying multiple kinds of horsemanship and showmanship. "One year, a woman did an entire reining pattern without a saddle or bridle," I told Ted, unable to keep a frantic edge out of my voice. "And there's this guy with one arm who trains bison to run up onto his trailer and do tricks. I need to get Snoopy to the point that we can at least reliably accomplish a flying lead change or two."

Ted sounded none too pleased. He said, "I thought this horse cost a small fortune. Isn't he trained already?"

I sighed. "He can do a sliding stop. And he can gallop. Anything more refined leaves a lot to be desired. I don't think Jay would appreciate it if I went to this event and didn't at least make an effort to perform somewhere near the same level as everyone else."

The reminder this was all Jay's doing seemed to mollify Ted a bit. He agreed to ditch the plans for the day so I could work with Snoopy and do my other ranch chores. But he'd insisted on the romantic dinner. He would cook, he said. He'd make something special. I should dress up a little.

So now I headed up the short sidewalk to Ted's front door, feeling uncomfortable in the clinging dress I'd selected for the evening. I wondered at myself a little as I walked. I'd bought the dress less than a year ago. At the time, I'd been excited. I'd imagined wearing it on just this sort of occasion. It was a flattering cut and comfortable besides. Back then, I'd enjoyed putting on nice clothes and makeup. I'd looked forward to evenings out with Ted and nights on the town with girlfriends.

What had changed? Now what I wanted to do was drive home, wash my face, toss the dress into my hamper, and put on sweat pants. Instead I steeled myself, walked to Ted's front door, and let myself in.

Ted's house was in one of the older neighborhoods on the east end of what could possibly be called downtown Tucson. It was not new, but it had been well cared for. It was on the small side, with a traditional layout. Ted had made up for this by outfitting it with spare, modern furniture of minimalist design. There was no clutter and a fair bit of open space. The art on the walls was abstract, each piece occupying a single wall that was otherwise blank.

"Hello?" I hung my purse on one of the brushed metal hooks behind the door. Off in the kitchen, I could hear the mellow tones of some jazzy music. I could smell dinner, something sweet and spicy. Ted had a bit of a knack for Asian cuisine.

"Nora." Ted came striding out of the kitchen with a huge smile on his face. He was wearing a pair of tailored slacks and a shirt that probably cost more than my dress, sleeves rolled up to reveal his tanned forearms. His shoes were buttery brown leather. They gleamed in the low light. "You look great, honey." He delivered this compliment with easy nonchalance, crossed the entryway, kissed me lightly on the mouth, and handed me the glass of wine he'd been carrying. "It feels like it's been so long since we had a nice evening to ourselves."

I accepted the wine and the compliment, trailing after Ted as he returned to the kitchen. I considered his words, wondering if this was all some sort of elaborate apology for the night he'd stayed out with Jay.

In the kitchen, Ted stirred a pot of simmering soup. "Everything's pretty much ready." He gestured at an array of covered dishes arranged on a side table. He picked up a spoon, tasted the soup, then nodded and turned off the burner. He set the spoon in the sink and retrieved his own glass of wine. "We can unwind for a few minutes before we start eating. How was your day?"

As he spoke, Ted moved from the kitchen into the sitting room, which was populated by a low, sleek couch, two slim armchairs, a glass coffee table with nothing on it, and a single narrow lamp. I settled onto one of the chairs as Ted sat on the couch. I took a sip of my wine. It had a complex, rich flavor that made me think it was expensive.

"Fine." I ran my mind back over my day, trying to think of something noteworthy enough to tell Ted. Mostly, though, it had been routine. He wouldn't want to hear about the manure I'd hauled out of Snoopy's stall and wouldn't understand a dissection of the slow but steady progress Erin was making with Esperanza. Nor would an in-depth discussion of the way I was working to correct Snoopy's balance and make him less defensive about his mouth be of much interest. "Snoopy and I are making progress. How was yours?"

Ted leaned forward, setting his glass onto the coffee table with a sharp click. He didn't answer immediately. He looked good, sitting there with his soft hair and his tailored shirt. Looking at him, I wondered why I couldn't seem to see him in a flattering light anymore. Every time I looked at him I seemed to find fault in stupid little things he had no control over.

There was something unreadable in his eyes—something deep and serious that made my heart start to beat a little faster. He stood, left the room, and came back a moment later, concealing something in his hand.

He walked toward me. Without warning, he knelt on the gleaming floor beside the coffee table. I stared at him, too startled to think, too startled to act, too startled to realize what was about to happen.

Ted gazed up at me from his low vantage point. I could see the sincere emotion in his eyes. "I was going to save this for later, but I can't wait." He lifted his hand. There was the small creak of a tiny hinge opening. Suddenly, Ted was presenting me with a ring.

The song that had been playing ended. In the brief silence between tracks, I missed my moment. That was when I should have stood up, or at least started talking. That was my chance to explain to Ted why I couldn't say yes.

I missed my moment, though. I sat like a stump, silent and rooted in place. Ted began to talk instead.

"I know this can't be much of a surprise." His face wore a small smile. His tone was relaxed and conversational, as if we'd long ago agreed he would present me with a ring tonight. "I've been meaning to formalize things between us for a while. Something about seeing you perform, though—watching that whole stadium cheer for you." He gave a self-conscious little laugh. "I guess I'll feel better about you going to these things with a ring on your finger."

I still hadn't found my voice. While it was true Ted and I had discussed marriage as something we both wanted to do, I certainly had not considered the question all but settled.

"Anyway." Ted turned the box around and pulled the ring free of the slit in the velvet cushion. "I'm serious about you, Nora. I'm serious about the life we're building together. I love you. I want to be with you, always."

As he spoke, he set the box aside. Ring in one hand, he reached forward with the other. He still had that relaxed quality about him, as if it had never occurred to him I might say no.

Ted's fingers hooked under mine. He guided my left hand forward. I watched my hand move as if I was watching a movie—as if I had no control over that appendage. Ted held up the ring. He was going to slip it onto my finger.

I should have done something, should have protested, tried to explain, anything but what I did—which was straighten my finger so he could slip the cold band of metal into place.

The ring was beautiful. Simple yet classic, it featured a generous diamond on a platinum setting with several smaller diamonds arrayed around the centerpiece. Unable to help myself, I moved my hand, holding it up to watch the way the stones caught the light.

And why not marry Ted? Isn't this what I had wanted, a scant few months ago? Hadn't I thought as I'd watched Erin prepare for her wedding that I would be organizing my own in the not so distant future? What reason on earth did I have to refuse Ted? He was attractive, kind, talented, and well-employed in a job that didn't involve spending most of every day out in the heat or interacting regularly with large and potentially dangerous four-legged animals.

Ted was a catch. And he was looking at me. His expression was expectant, growing the slightest bit strained. I realized I hadn't spoken since he'd gone down on his knees. His position on the hard floor was probably uncomfortable.

I opened my mouth. I tried to say, "Yes." I tried, but the word didn't quite come out. It got stuck in my throat like a burr in a mane. I made a colossal effort and managed to say, "I love you too."

It seemed to be enough. Ted leaned forward, kissing me. Then he pulled back with a grimace. Using the arm of my chair, he levered himself to his feet. "Good thing I didn't prepare a longer speech." He rubbed his knees, straightened his slacks, and stood upright. He looked down at me for a moment. I felt awkward in the dress again. I became aware of my exposed shoulders, the way I had to sit with my legs tucked primly to the side so the slit in my dress didn't do embarrassing things.

Ted stood there and gazed at me. I was reminded with a sudden, unpleasant twinge of the way Jay had regarded me that first time I'd ever been dressed up in my TruGlide costume. He'd looked me over with the critical eye of a man looking at something he has created and still might find a way to improve.

Now, Ted's expression seemed much the same. I had to resist the urge to do something bizarre, like stick my tongue out at him. Instead, I sat and waited, feeling like a vase or a framed photograph.

Ted let out a little sigh. "You're so beautiful, Nora."

I blinked. My eyelashes were heavy with the mascara I'd put on before coming over. I thought, jarringly, of the words Wyatt had spoken in the tack room. I'd been a mess then, wearing my worn jeans and thin t-shirt. *I think they do you an injustice.*

I managed to turn my head and force my face into a smile. It was unfair, I told myself, to fault Ted for finding me attractive. After all, hadn't I just been looking at him the same way a moment before, noting his nicely toned forearms and his soft hair?

I looked down at the ring on my finger. It was big—bigger now that it was on my hand instead of in a box. The stone had slid slightly so it was pointing off to one side. I straightened it. *Engaged.* The word seemed to echo in my head.

I'd somehow gotten myself engaged.

Erin swung down from Esperanza's back and turned to smile at me. "Well." Her voice was somewhat breathless. "That went well."

It was a hazy late morning with a blank, white sky. The heat was duller than usual. I arranged my reins and stepped off my horse as well. "It did."

Erin and I were in the Tipped Z's outdoor arena. This morning, I'd issued Erin an ultimatum. No more riding in the round pen. The round pen was a tool to get a horse started. In most cases, a few rides in that space was enough to get one ready enough to move on. The longer a horse stayed in a confined space, the more a change of venue would startle her later.

Though things with Esperanza had been going smoothly since the bucking incident, Erin still lacked confidence. She'd been clinging to the round pen, using it as a crutch. Today, I'd put an end to that.

I was riding a rangy four-year-old gelding named Dom who had a fair bit of ranching on him but not any arena work. He was on the list of horses Clint had asked me to work with if I had the time, whom I had never previously touched.

Dom was a chestnut. His coat was a deep, burnished copper. He had four socks, two short, two tall, arranged on opposite diagonals. Over the course of the day, I'd discovered he had a sweet temperament and an energetic, eager-to-please personality.

Like all the horses at the Tipped Z, he'd been started well. He was soft to the bit, responsive to the seat and leg, and didn't have any anxiety about his job. Throughout the ride, while Erin and Esperanza gradually gained the confidence to explore the expanse of new space, Dom and I felt each other out.

Now we were both a little sweaty. I pulled my get-down out of my belt with a feeling of satisfaction. There was something about getting in sync with a new horse that always filled me with a relaxed sense of accomplishment.

I reached up to pat the glossy dark neck and a sparkle on my finger caught my eye.

The relaxation drained out of me in a heartbeat. Erin was still speaking but her words were dim in my ears. "I guess I shouldn't be surprised. She probably would have been fine out here weeks ago."

I stared at the ring on my finger for a helpless moment, then dropped my hand and turned towards the barn. "She wouldn't have been fine if you hadn't been fine. There's nothing wrong with taking it slow. Just so long as you keep moving forward."

I began to walk towards the barn, Dom ambling behind in easy contentment. Erin came up next to me, leading Esperanza. The bay filly had filled out a good deal in the last few weeks. She'd put on muscle in the shoulder and haunch. Her brilliant coat gleamed in the sunlight.

"I don't know how I'd have done this without you." Erin spoke in a sincere tone as we made our way through the arena gate, across the yard, and into the barn. "I don't think things would have gone nearly so well."

I walked into the hay room. For a moment, the interior was impossibly dim as my eyes adjusted from the brightness outside. "Don't sell yourself short." I navigated into the large space. "You know more than you think you do."

Behind me, I could hear the clop of Dom's hooves. The puppies ran out from their favorite corner to dance around my feet, their mother looking on with a harried expression from her perch on top of the hay bales—a vantage point her young were still too small to reach.

"Knowing how to do all this in theory is one thing." Erin's tone was genially argumentative. "Remembering to do it when you're on the back of a young horse is something else."

We'd reached the aisle. I eased the hackamore off Dom's face and hung it on his saddle horn. I removed a halter from its hook and slipped it into place. I was about to respond to Erin's comment when I heard a gasp.

I turned to see Erin staring, wide-eyed, at my hand. "Nora." Her voice was breathless, carrying a tone of mild accusation. "Why didn't you say something?"

For a moment, I didn't know what she was talking about. Then the cold glitter of the diamonds on my finger caught my eye and I understood. She'd noticed my ring.

On the one hand, it was a bit surprising it had taken her this long. For my part, all morning I had felt like I was walking around with a brand on my forehead or wearing sandwich boards that announced, "This person has been claimed by another."

In reality, though, it would have been easy to overlook. In the dim light of early morning, Erin and I had both been yawning and focused on the task of getting our horses saddled and out to the arena. Working with a green horse left very little room in one's mind for anything else.

Now, I loosened Dom's girth and turned to Erin. Her face had a suspended look to it, as if it could not decide what expression to assume. It was, in large part, the way I'd been feeling all morning. Today, I'd woken up in Ted's bed with Ted's ring on my finger. I'd made my way out of his house despite his sleepy protests that it would be nice to sleep in, for once. The night before, over dinner and wine, I'd almost convinced myself I was happy about the engagement.

This morning, I wasn't so sure. Seeing Wyatt's truck parked in front of the barn had sent a sharp stab of pain through my heart. Now I stared at the ring in a sort of blank confusion. "I guess I sort of forgot."

Erin let out a strange, strangled sound. "This family," she said in an exasperated undertone as she ducked under Esperanza's head. "You did not forget." As she spoke, she walked up to me. Without hesitation, she wrapped me in a warm hug. "Congratulations. You must be so excited. Tell me everything. How did he propose? Have you set on a date?"

Inexplicably, Erin's warmth made my eyes go hot and prickly. I gave her an awkward pat on the back.

She returned to her horse but kept rattling off questions. "Have you told your parents? Your brother?"

I shook my head, struck dumb by the interrogation. "You're the first to know."

It must have been the movement that caught my eye. There was a shift in the shadows in the hay room and the light thud of a boot heel on dirt. I looked up. My heart seemed to shrink and shrivel when I saw Wyatt standing there in the shadow of the hay, his body as rigid as if he'd been jabbed with a cattle prod.

Before I could do anything, before I could think of something to say, Wyatt turned and walked out the door. A moment later, I heard the deep rumble of his truck engine growling to life.

The next day when I arrived at the ranch, Wyatt's truck wasn't there. I noticed this with a strange feeling of alarm. As I parked my own truck and killed the engine, I told myself there were plenty of reasons the truck might not be there at that particular moment. But deep down, I knew better.

The truck was gone all day. By the time I finished my chores and rode Snoopy, Wyatt had not put in an appearance.

When I returned the following morning, it was still gone. And when I arrived again the morning after that, there was a different truck in its place.

I found Erin tacking Esperanza in the aisle. She'd brought Dom in for me. The two horses stood in the dim aisle as Erin rubbed a soft curry over Esperanza's coat. I moved towards them, stopping to give Esperanza a rub as I greeted Erin.

I made my way over to Dom and gave the gelding a pat on the neck. I couldn't help it. I'd resisted asking about Wyatt for three whole days. I'd assumed if something significant had changed about his position at the ranch, someone would have told me. But communication has never been one of my family's strengths.

I let the question slide out casually as I selected a brush from the grooming caddy. "Did Wyatt get a new truck?"

Erin paused in the act of rubbing some dried sand from Esperanza's knees. She looked at me, an expression of pure surprise on her face. She blinked, straightened, and regarded me from over her filly's back. "That's Kyle's truck."

I felt a spasm of mixed frustration and fear. The emotions bloomed through me in an unpleasant wave right as my phone gave off its text message chime. Muttering a curse under my breath, I tried to fish my phone out of my pocket. My ring snagged on the lip and my hand got stuck. I had to set my brush on Dom's back to assist with my other hand. As I unlocked my phone, I said, "Who the hell is Kyle?"

The text was from Jay. It was a photo of a glittering black outfit displayed on a dummy. It was even more extravagant than my usual TruGlide attire and included a new innovation—a short cape that would swirl out from my shoulders as Snoopy galloped around.

My stomach clenched further. I put the phone away. Looking up, I saw Erin staring at me with a look of mystification. "He's Wyatt's replacement." She spoke slowly, as if she was attempting to communicate with someone who was not fluent in her language. "Wyatt left first thing Wednesday morning. I'm sorry I didn't mention it. I thought you knew."

I turned away from Erin and retrieved my brush. Dom's coat was warm and smooth beneath my hands. The delicate light of the sunrise spilled in through the large door Wyatt had figured out how to open. Around me, the barn smelled of hay and dust and horses.

The sting of learning Wyatt had left without bothering to say goodbye was a real pain. It was sharp and harsh.

It was also utterly familiar.

How many times had Wyatt made me feel this way? How many times had Wyatt shown, unequivocally, that he did not care about me? Not only did he not care about me the way I'd always cared about him, he also didn't even care enough to follow the most basic rules of social convention.

"Nora?" Erin's voice was tentative. I felt self-conscious. Not only was it rude, it was also embarrassing. Wyatt had left without telling me he was going and how his disregard for me was publicly revealed.

I opened my eyes and busied myself with Dom's already clean coat. "Wyatt is Clint's friend." I made my tone brisk and devoid of emotion. "There's no reason he should keep me informed of his movements."

As I worked the brush over Dom's coat, the diamond on my ring glittered in the weak light. I stared at it, thinking with a bitter twist of my gut that at least I hadn't been fool enough to refuse Ted only to have Wyatt leave me in the lurch a few days later.

In fact, I told myself as I moved through the comforting process of getting a horse ready to ride, this was good. It was better. Wyatt was a distraction and a source of pain. That was all he'd ever been, all he was ever destined to be. Sure, he was good for the ranch. But he was not good for me. This new Kyle guy, I was certain, would be just as helpful. He could do the work Wyatt had done without loading me down with emotional baggage every time I heard him walk by, whistling.

Still, Erin's silence made me think she wanted to say something she knew I didn't want to hear. I did not look at her as I finished with Dom's coat, picked his feet, and brushed out his mane and tail. At last, I was ready for his pad. Which I couldn't retrieve without going into the tack room.

Erin was looking at me when I turned around. I couldn't avoid making eye contact. "It was a prior engagement," she said. "Some colt-starting job he committed to over a year ago. He might come back when it's over, although Clint couldn't get him to commit."

I stood for a moment, blinking, trying to decide if this made it better or worse. So Wyatt hadn't just up and abandoned his duties here at the Tipped Z. He'd known he was going. But still, he hadn't felt the need to say goodbye.

"Good for him." My voice was falsely cheery. "I'm sure he'll do exactly what he wants. He's good at that."

I accepted Snoopy's lead rope from the handler, thanked him, and led the big silvery gold gelding towards the stall area. Snoopy was fully swathed in his traveling get-up. He wore a sheet, a hood, and big padded hauling boots strapped on over his legs. His distinctive coloring was hidden underneath the swathes of white fabric, a fact for which I was grateful.

I was also attempting to go unrecognized. I wore a baseball cap Jay had given me. Though it did have the TruGlide logo stitched on the front, that in itself was not a big enough clue to give me away. I had my hair back in a ponytail and I wore a pair of old jeans and a ragged shirt with a faded Arizona Wildcats logo blown to such huge proportions it didn't fully fit on the fabric. I was going out of my way to look as unlike the TruGlide Girl as possible.

I was doing this because we were now on site in Oklahoma, in the gigantic arena facility that was to house the *Start the Horse, Connect the Heart* event where Snoopy and I would give our first major performance. It was only Thursday morning, so the place was relatively quiet. But as I walked through the unloading arena with Snoopy, there was plenty of activity around. Crews of men were erecting temporary structures that would be used for not-yet-revealed purposes. There were horses as well. Many of the other performers were already on site. As we passed the opening to the large arena, I glanced out to see a prominent natural horsemanship trainer cantering around on a big black gelding.

I reached up to pat Snoopy's clothed neck in a reassuring manner. "This is the big leagues now, buddy."

Snoopy, for his part, was taking the shift in venue well. Sure, he was moving in a stiff approximation of his usual easy amble. His ears were up and his eyes were wide. But he wasn't coming undone. He was curious and attentive, but that was all. I wished I could say the same thing for myself.

"Come on," I said to the horse. "Let's get those ridiculous boots off you."

I fought down a wave of fatigue as I proceeded to our assigned stall. It had been a harrowing week. Perhaps unsurprisingly, Kyle was not working out well. My dad had already fired him twice for being too rough with the horses—incidents Clint then had to go in and smooth over. Now Clint was trying his best to keep Kyle and my father from crossing paths at all, which was difficult on an operation as small as the Tipped Z. Clint was hoping Kyle would adjust and shift his way of thinking about horses before he did something truly irredeemable. From what I'd seen of the guy, I wasn't holding my breath. He seemed like the sort of cowboy that already knew everything there was to know. Therefore, although he might spend his next 20 or 30 years in the saddle, he would gain no new experience and would not improve.

So there was that, plus getting Snoopy's routine polished, and keeping Snoopy himself in impeccable condition. And also, there was the engagement.

I'd been under the false impression getting engaged was a simple thing. There was a ring and a question. And then it all sort of went away for a while.

This is not how Ted viewed engagement. The ring and the question were only the beginning. Since the night I had not prevented him from putting the ring on my finger, Ted had been collecting information. Midweek he'd invited me over for dinner. After we'd eaten, he'd cleared the dishes and returned to the table with a selection of glossy brochures. "A lot of these places are booked out over six months in advance," he'd told me. "We'll want to pick a venue soon so we don't end up stuck with the dates no one else wants."

I'd stared at the brochures in a sort of uncomprehending haze. I'd been up since 4:00 AM and had been feeling somewhat proud of myself for managing to stay upright throughout the dinner. As Ted had opened the first brochure, I'd felt a sensation of exhausted hopelessness settle over me. "Please, Ted," I'd said. "Not tonight. I'm too tired."

He'd gone stiff and disapproving. I could almost see him gearing up for some lecture on how I wasn't seeming to take the engagement seriously. I hurried on, saying, "It's this event. I'm so nervous. Snoopy and I still have so much we could improve. It's taking up all my time and focus."

He took my hand, face softening. He said kind things about how he understood, and he was being selfish, and he was so excited he couldn't help himself. Then he kissed my cheek and took the brochures away.

Now I thought about Ted with a sensation of confusion as I made my way out of the unloading area through the maze of wide hallways that led to the massive stall barn attached to this place. We passed wash racks and tack rooms, grooming stalls and a livestock scale. A horse called in the distance. Snoopy didn't call back. Impressed with his stoic reserve, I patted his neck again.

We reached our stall and I clipped a single cross-tie underneath his chin. Then I stooped to remove his hauling boots. They were a maze of Velcro and padding and I hadn't got the trick of them yet. It seemed whenever I got one part of them loose, some stray bit of Velcro managed to reattach itself to the other side.

I persevered. At last, I set his front boots to the side of the stall and moved to the back.

It was when I unwrapped Snoopy's hind legs that the feeling of dread settled in my stomach. I realized with sudden sick clarity Snoopy hadn't been walking with a short, choppy stride because he was nervous. He'd been walking that way because his hocks and ankles were a swollen, hot mess.

Chapter 9

I trudged through the shallow sand in the warm-up arena, Snoopy's rope in one hand, my cell phone in the other. For the first time in my life, I wished I had one of those Bluetooth earpieces that let you talk with your phone in your pocket.

I had removed Snoopy's leg wraps, hosed his swollen hocks with cold water, and was now leading him in aimless circles, hoping without much conviction the swelling would go down as quickly as it had come up—that this would turn out to be a strange, isolated event that would have no bearing on Snoopy's long-term health or soundness.

I'd spoken to our vet on the phone. In a brief discussion in which he'd sounded distracted and not totally interested in the details of my situation, he'd suggested giving Snoopy 2 grams of bute and turning him out in a small pen where the horse could move freely but not cover a lot of ground. I should leave him for the night and see how things looked in the morning.

The trouble was, I had neither bute nor such a turnout area. The idea of leaving Snoopy in this strange place and waiting for morning to see how big a disaster this was had no appeal whatsoever.

Perhaps it revealed my sheer rookieness, but I'd brought no first aid equipment of any kind. I'd somehow assumed there would be support available on site for these kinds of extremities.

And perhaps there was, but I didn't know how to find it. Other than the cheery girl who'd given me my stall number and made me sign a waiver attached to a clipboard, I'd been left to my own devices since I'd arrived in the vast, echoing facility that would be overflowing with fans in a few days' time. Jay had asked if I wanted any staff to assist me upon my arrival. I, stupidly, had said I'd be fine on my own.

Now I was loathe to leave the swollen Snoopy in a strange stall while I tromped around looking for someone who might have some bute. I'd been leading him around this pen for half an hour, trying to build up the courage to call Jay. I'd finally done it. Now his phone was ringing. With each ring, I grew both more hopeful and more fearful it would go straight to voicemail.

But, at last, Jay answered. "This is Jay." He spoke in that distracted way that suggested he was dealing with something vastly more important than whatever you were calling about.

"Hi Jay. It's Nora." I said this knowing he already knew it was me. This was the age of smartphones, after all. For all I knew, one of those airbrushed TruGlide photos popped up on his screen whenever I called him. I'd already texted him to let him know Snoopy had arrived safely—before I'd unwrapped the legs.

There was a confusing jangle of background noise and some beeping. "Crissy emailed your hotel details a few minutes ago. She was supposed to do that yesterday. They should be in your inbox now."

"Oh." I rounded the corner of the warm-up pen and continuing along the top wall. "Okay, thanks. Jay I ..."

I was cut off by more background noise—a chatter of voices, the sound of car doors slamming, Jay's irritated voice. "Keep it down people, I'm on a call here."

Things quieted. "Nora, you there?"

I stopped walking. Snoopy drifted to a halt beside me. I'd removed his hood. Now he wore only his sheet. I stroked his glossy neck as the words tumbled out in a rush. "Snoopy may not be able to perform."

The ill-advised sentence fell out of my mouth without authorization. As soon as I said it, I knew it was the worst possible way I could have brought this up. Jay did not like to be told what could and could not happen. Jay was the one who weighed variables, took stock of situations, made final decisions.

There was a long, prickly silence. Jay's voice was hard when he answered. "Nora. What are you telling me?"

I started babbling then, explaining about the swelling and my lack of bute and how bute would possibly only mask the symptoms anyway, not necessarily solve the problem. And how I couldn't leave Snoopy in a stall because he needed to walk because most likely it was standing in the trailer for so long that had gotten him so stocked up in the first place. Confining him again would make the problem worse.

Jay cut me off mid-stream. Whatever activity had been taking place on the other end of the line had quieted. I could almost see his rigid shoulders, his frosty expression. "Nora." His tone was clipped, sharp, all business. "Nora, calm down. Talk to me in smaller pieces. You are telling me you need a drug? Is that it? Advil for horses or something?"

I paused, drawing in a deep breath and looking around the empty space. There was still the work crew off in the performance arena. Now and then I'd hear the distant slam of a door or call of a horse. But I felt as if Snoopy and I were the only living creatures in this strange, concrete maze.

"That's what my vet recommended." My voice wobbled a little. I realized with horror I was on the verge of tears. This was unlike me. I normally kept my cool in a crisis. But all week I'd been feeling as if my life was building towards some kind of catastrophe. Now I looked listlessly towards my left hand. My engagement diamond twinkled like a frosty beacon in dim space.

"Okay." I could hear Jay gathering his wits, preparing to deploy his fix. He excelled at crisis management. "This is okay. I will find someone to get you this stuff. Tell me exactly what it is and how much. We'll make it happen. Look, Nora? Talk to Spencer, okay? He's going to write down what you need and someone is going to bring it to you within an hour. Got it?"

I knew we already had staff on the ground here in Oklahoma City. I wasn't sure where Jay was. He wasn't officially scheduled to arrive until tomorrow.

I felt absurdly grateful to have at least part of this problem taken out of my hands. "Okay." Before I could say anything more, Jay handed the phone to Spencer.

It was more like two hours later, but the bute did come. It was delivered by the girl with the clipboard. Snoopy and I were back at the stall by then. I was sitting on a TruGlide folding chair and pretending to read my Kindle while I listened to the sound of Snoopy in his stall, munching hay and sighing now and then.

The girl strode up to me, boot heels thumping on the concrete. She stood looking down for a moment. "Nora, right? Someone left this for you." She handed me a round plastic canister, white with a lavender label. On the front, in large black letters, it said, "Phenylbute Powder."

I stood, relief flooding through me as I accepted the canister. The white tub was cool and heavy in my hand, and reassuringly familiar. We kept a stock of the exact same tubs in the medicine cabinet at the Tipped Z.

The girl looked behind me at Snoopy, who had raised his head to look through the bars of his stall. "There will be a vet on call here starting tomorrow morning. I can give him your name when he arrives if you want him to look at whatever you've got going on?"

I hesitated, uncertain. In the last two hours, the facility had become less empty. I was not the only performer who'd come in early. In the distance, I heard the slide and bang of stall doors and the mixed mutter of many voices talking. Snoopy and I were still alone in our branch of the hallway, though. I suspected Jay had asked we be kept out of the way of things, which was fine by me.

The girl was looking at me, face curious. "Yeah, that'd be great." Then I remembered something. I reached for my purse, fished around inside for a moment, and found the slim case I'd stashed in an inner pocket. I snapped it open, removed a card, and handed it to her. It was *my* card. It had the TruGlide logo in the corner, plus my name and relevant contact information.

Giving someone my card was something I'd never done before. I hadn't had a card until my last day in Tucson. They'd been delivered to me then, along with some other items Jay felt I needed to take with me to Oklahoma. The number printed on the card was to a cell phone that had also been in the package, which I was to keep with me at all times I was not performing or mixing with the crowd. It was for business use only and would prevent me from having to give my personal number out to vendors or facilities operators or anyone else who might need to reach me for professional reasons.

The girl took the card, glanced at it, then did a double-take. She looked between me and Snoopy for a minute, blinked, and recovered. When she spoke, her voice was higher and a little chirpy. "Okay, great. I'll ask Dr. Warren to come by as soon as he arrives."

She walked off, leaving me to wonder if I'd made a mistake. Jay, I knew, was cagey with information—particularly if it was information of the "not unequivocally good" variety. The clipboard girl now knew the TruGlide horse needed bute for something. Was that bad?

Determined not to worry about it, I turned my attention to the tub of medicine in my hand. Suddenly, I was riddled with doubt. Bute, I knew, was very effective. It was so effective it could mask a good deal of pain. If I gave Snoopy bute now, it might help with the swelling. It also might make it harder for the vet to figure out what was going on with him.

I glanced around the empty hallway. In the distance, there was a heavy clang, a shout, and a round of laughter. I felt unbearably alone.

I fished my phone out of my pocket and stared down at the screen. Calling Jay again was not an option. He would not be interested in a nuanced discussion of the pros and cons of giving a horse pain-masking drugs. Our vet, realistically, could not help without being able to see the problem. I didn't want to call Ted, either. Somehow I couldn't imagine trying to explain the situation with Snoopy and having him respond in any way that would help.

I scrolled through my contacts list. The photo next to my brother's number was one I'd snapped of him quite a few years before. He'd been working with a fresh colt—a young stud who'd been quite a handful. In the photo, they were sharing a quiet moment. The stud was standing with his head lowered, Clint's hand resting on his forehead.

There had been an undeniable distance growing between my brother and me for the last few months. Life had been busy enough I'd been able to ignore it, perhaps even succeed in convincing myself it wasn't there. Now, looking at Clint's face, I tried to remember the last time I'd talked to him about anything other than the logistics of the ranch. I couldn't. Not that Clint and I had ever been prone to having long, in-depth, heart-to-hearts. Always before, though, there had somehow been time for small conversations about life, the horses we were riding, the weather, and all the other irrelevant things you talk about with the people you see every day.

I took a deep breath and tapped my phone, telling it to call my brother.

I let myself into my hotel room with a long sigh. As I dragged the wheeled suitcase Ted had given me over the plush carpet and propped it up against the wall, I felt exhaustion settle over me like a shroud. I bent to pry my boots off my feet.

It was nearly 8:00 PM. I had finally left Snoopy alone in his stall.

When I'd called my brother, he hadn't answered. This shouldn't have surprised me, but it had been a crushing blow anyway. I'd sent him a short text, saying something was up with Snoopy and I could use his advice. He'd called back less than a minute later. He'd been out on horseback but he'd talked to me for fifteen minutes, listening when I explained the situation in unnecessary detail, then calmly telling me what he considered to be the pros and cons of giving bute. Hearing Clint's steady voice had soothed me tremendously.

In the end, with Clint's help, I'd decided to wait on the bute. I'd spent another hour leading Snoopy around the warm-up arena, cold hosed his hocks again, walked some more, and left him in his stall for the night. Clint's reasoning was that the horse was accustomed to spending time in a stall and this had never caused his hocks to swell before. Giving him bute would make it unclear in the morning whether he'd recovered on his own or if the drug was masking symptoms.

Finally, I had felt easy enough to leave my co-star for the night and retire to my own accommodations, which turned out to be a spacious suite in one of the nearby hotels. Barefoot now, I wandered through the rooms, gazing around in mystification as I tried to figure out what Jay thought I would need so much space for. Then I remembered this was going to be my staging area. My entire staff would be descending on these rooms first thing Saturday to transform me into the glittering TruGlide Girl, who would then sally forth to dazzle the massive audience of *Start the Horse, Connect the Heart* into buying truckloads of reining shoes.

I found my way into the bedroom and collapsed onto the massive beast of a bed. A strange blend of exhaustion and trepidation warred for control of my internal landscape. If Snoopy wasn't much better in the morning, we were going to have a real problem. And that problem would be entirely my fault. This, I realized with sudden clarity, was why TruGlide had worked with regional vendors in the past. Sure, if disaster struck you might end up with a horse that wasn't the ideal color. But at least you'd have a horse that could put on a show.

My phone began to ring. I rolled over, fishing it out of my pocket to see Ted's face smiling at me out of my screen. I felt a minor stir of irritation which I instantly felt guilty about. The guilt, more than anything, was what made me answer the call.

Ted's tone was comfortable and warm when I answered. He started by telling me some dorky marketing joke he'd read on the internet, which I didn't get though probably could have if I'd tried harder. When I managed to produce a wan chuckle in response to the punchline, Ted shifted gears. "You all settled in there? How's the suite?"

The question startled me on multiple levels. It revealed two things. 1) Ted had known I was in a suite but 2) Ted did not know about Snoopy's condition. Increasingly, I was finding it difficult to measure Ted's friendship with Jay. On the one hand, it seemed like they were in touch a little more than they needed to be from a strictly professional perspective. On the other, they clearly never shared the sort of personal details one would assume might pass between people in any kind of friendship. For instance, Jay had not yet congratulated me on the engagement. This seemed to suggest he did not know about it. I hadn't seen him since Ted had given me the ring, but I'd talked to him quite a lot.

I told Ted about Snoopy. As I explained about the swelling and the bute, his brief respondes took on the distracted quality that meant he was dinking around on the internet, half-listening. It always annoyed me when he did this but tonight I found it more than usually insulting. I segued from a description of the swollen hocks into hyperbole. "So then I had to shoot him." I kept my tone mild, cadence steady. "And that's a real problem because now I don't have a horse to ride."

Ted's answer came back as expected, mild and sympathetic. "That's no good."

I said nothing. Something had gone a little cold and hard inside me. There was a long pause, then Ted began to scramble. "Wait, what? You shot a horse? Jay's horse?"

Still, I said nothing. I rolled of the bed and walked to the large windows that opened along one side of the room. Beyond them lay the lights of Oklahoma City, brilliant and expansive in every direction. "You're not even listening." I spoke in a dull tone. "I've had this horrible, traumatic day. I didn't call you because I knew you wouldn't give a shit. And now you've proven I was right."

There was some background noise through the phone—the creaking of a desk chair. Ted's voice was a little less smooth when he answered. "Nora, wait. That's not fair. I'm sorry. You're right. I was distracted. I didn't realize we were talking about something that was so important to you."

His words irritated me further. I hadn't turned on any lights and the room was dim. I looked down at the ring on my finger, the ring I didn't want there. "It might be nice if you would assume any time I'm talking to you, I'm doing so because I want you to listen."

There was a long silence, a slow sigh. "Okay," Ted said. "I'm sorry." But his tone sounded more irritated than apologetic. "You didn't shoot Jay's horse, right? You just said that to get my attention?"

The comment made me furious. Why did he keep calling Snoopy Jay's horse? Why couldn't I shake the feeling he was only concerned about this from a marketing perspective?

I turned my eyes away from the twinkling expanse of Oklahoma City's skyline. I lifted my right shoulder to awkwardly clamp my slim phone in place below my ear. I removed Ted's ring from my finger.

"Snoopy is fine." This wasn't really true, but I had exactly no energy for explaining that to Ted at this point. "And Ted, I'm sorry to do this over the phone, but we need to take a break." I set the ring down on the bedside table with a soft clink.

Ted's voice was definitely not relaxed anymore when it came back over the line. "Break? Wait, Nora? Honey? What are you talking about?"

I realized with sudden clarity I had wanted to break things off with Ted for weeks. I had been confused into thinking it had something to do with Wyatt. But it hadn't been Wyatt at all. It was Ted. It was Ted who had shoved me into this job, Ted who seemed to think it was great rather than embarrassing that my position required no skill other than the ability to play an elaborate game of dress-up and pose for photos. Everything about my life I didn't like right now traced back to Ted.

But when I was actually with Ted, it didn't seem so bad. He was so sweet. So kind. So good looking. So reasonable.

"I'll give the ring back as soon as I return to Tucson." My voice was firm and steady now. All the fear and anxiety I'd been feeling over the course of the day were utterly gone. I felt certain about this—more certain than I'd felt about anything in a long while. "This isn't working for me," I added, just to make sure he understood what was happening.

There was a long, long silence. It was so long, I started to wonder if the call had dropped. When Ted spoke again, his voice had a vaguely frantic edge. "I should have gone with you." He sounded as if he'd lit on the solution to a complex puzzle. "You're feeling abandoned and alone. I can come right now. I might be able to get on a flight tonight."

"No, Ted." My voice gained a little volume. "That is not what I want. That is exactly the opposite of what I want. This isn't a work situation you can smooth over or talk your way through." I looked down at the ring. It seemed small and insignificant against the dark wood of the table. "What I need is some space."

There was another pause. I could practically hear Ted's internal dialogue, scrambling to parse this, trying to tidy it up. "Okay," he said. "You're right. It wasn't the right time for the engagement. I see that now. I was pushing too hard. We can put the wedding on hold. And we'll talk about the rest of this when you get back. Sound good?"

I closed my eyes. I didn't want to talk about the rest of it. But I also knew Ted was right. We had a good thing, mostly. Maybe I was being hasty to discard that because I'd had a bad day. "Yeah," I said. "That sounds good."

○

Dr. Warren turned out to be an affable man in a cowboy hat who introduced himself with a handshake, smiling through his gray beard. His palm was rough and calloused. After listening to a summary of the problem, he asked me to lead Snoopy out of his stall and walk him around while he watched, frowning under his hat brim.

Snoopy's condition had improved somewhat during the night. The swelling had gone down and he seemed to be walking with a little more ease. Still, after leading him around for a minute and coming back to look at the vet, I felt my heart sink as I took in his expression.

"How long have you had this horse?" The question wasn't a red flag, in and of itself. But I thought it was not an auspicious starting point.

I nervously arranged Snoopy's lead rope into small coils in my hand. I thought back. "About a month." I found my own answer surprising. Could it be so little time had passed since my first TruGlide event? It seemed more like a year, for all that had happened.

The vet, still frowning, stepped forward to massage one of Snoopy's hocks. The horse swished his tail. "Who did the pre-purchase exam?"

I felt my stomach sink further. "This isn't actually my horse." I felt the need to explain. "I had nothing to do with buying him. So ... well ... my boss didn't ask for a pre-purchase exam."

The vet straightened, pausing to lift his cowboy hat, run a hand over the short-cropped hair beneath, and set the hat back in place. He looked at me, holding my gaze for a moment. Then he said exactly what I'd been hoping he would not. "My guess is distal tarsitis, more commonly known as bone spavin. A fairly advanced case. We'll need x-rays to be sure."

The news landed on my psyche like a falling piano. Of course, I'd considered the possibility of hock degeneration. Snoopy had obviously been started young and hard. All those sliding stops tended to leave a mark. Still, the news was so resoundingly bad it left me speechless.

When I received his diagnosis with nothing more than a glassy-eyed stare, the vet went on. "I'd guess he's had injections for a while." His voice was kind but mild, as if he hadn't noticed the news he was delivering was very, very bad.

I gave Snoopy's neck a dull pat, trying to parse this in practical terms. "He's a reining horse," I said. "He needs to perform tomorrow."

The vet's eyes were gray and they were kind, but there was a firmness behind them. "You said you haven't given him anything? No bute?"

I nodded. The vet sighed, turning from me to gaze off towards the performance arena. I didn't envy the man his position. There is a blurry place where ethics and commercial interest collide. Most of us only encounter that zone now and then. This man spent practically his whole life there.

The vet walked over to the medical kit he'd brought in, returning with a thermometer and a stethoscope. We didn't talk for a while as he did a slow, thorough general exam, making note of Snoopy's vital signs as he went along. Finally, he put his tools away and looked at me again. "You say he's four?"

I nodded, biting my lip. "Just." Around us, the facility was significantly more lively than it had been the night before. As I spoke, I had to scooch Snoopy to one side of the aisle as a young man led another horse by, this one prancing and snorting on its lead.

The vet took another moment to adjust his hat. "I'll be honest with you," he said at last. "There isn't a good answer. We could bute him for the next three days and get him through the weekend. After that, you could inject his hocks to keep the discomfort at bay. There's a chance, with the right treatment, his hocks could fuse. But that can take a long time, if it works at all. There is the option of surgery if he doesn't respond to more conventional methods. That isn't always successful, either. Joint degeneration is not reversible, in any circumstances. If this horse retires now and his symptoms are managed properly, he might make an okay trail horse or pasture buddy for quite a few years. But he's nearing the end of his useful life. The harder he's used, the less time he'll have."

I closed my eyes. The words didn't surprise me. I knew the vet was right. Nevertheless, they were difficult to accept.

The vet continued. "I could be wrong," he said, backpedaling a little. "Like I said, we need x-rays to be sure. And some vets would tell you hock fusion is a miracle cure. With the right steps, we could keep the horse performing. But I see a lot of these young performance horses. They blow up like this all the time. It's what happens when you put so much strain on the joints before they're finishing growing." He set a grizzled hand on Snoopy's rump in a gesture of consolation.

A dull sense of resignation settled over me. After I'd gotten off the phone with Ted the night before, I'd spent over an hour scouring the internet, reading about hock problems in horses. What the vet was telling me wasn't any different from what I'd found online.

I looked at Snoopy, who was gazing towards the warm-up arena with an air of mild curiosity as several horses and riders moved in lazy circles around the ring. In retrospect, it seemed I should have done more. There had been days, of course, where Snoopy had seemed tight in the hind. But I'd attributed that to the time he spent in his stall. Why hadn't I had our vet come out and give him a thorough examination the day he arrived?

I turned to Dr. Warren. "Thank you. I'll need to talk to the horse's owner before I can make any decisions."

The vet nodded, pulling a card out of his shirt pocket and passing it over to me. "If you'd like to write his number on here, I can call him directly to give my opinion."

I stared at the man's kind face, feeling absurdly grateful for this offer. I scribbled Jay's number on the vet's card and gave it back. Then we shook hands and he walked away.

"Oh Snoopy," I said as the vet disappeared into the main aisle, "this is not good."

The tall horse turned his head to sniff at me when I spoke. It was remarkable, now that I thought about it, how much he'd changed in so short a time. I remembered the day he'd been delivered. The memory made me smile. The men who'd unloaded him had been treating him like he was some sort of hooved demon.

But then my smile faded. If Snoopy had come from the sort of place that started horses so hard they caused advanced joint degeneration in animals that hadn't yet turned four, he'd been treated with very little generosity in his life before now. I gave the horse's withers a rub, feeling the weight of this bad news resting heavily on my heart. "You're a good guy." I spoke quietly, thinking about something my father always said. I'd heard it so many times when I'd been a kid, I'd come to hate the phrase. Every time I'd looked at my dad and said my horse did this or didn't do that, he'd have the same answer. "The horse is always available. It's the human that has trouble changing."

With a sigh, I led Snoopy back into his stall. I removed his halter and closed the door, then collapsed back into my TruGlide folding chair. I would have to call Jay, and soon. But for the moment, I didn't have the energy.

All morning I'd been noticing the absence of Ted's ring. Though I'd worn it for less than two weeks, somehow I'd gotten used to its feel. My hand felt bare without it.

I rubbed my eyes. I hadn't slept well and now I had precious little to do other than sit around and worry about all the things going wrong in my life. I pulled my phone out of my pocket and looked at the screen. It was just past 9:00 AM. I didn't have any official TruGlide duties until tomorrow morning and now the question of whether or not I'd be able to complete them was totally up in the air.

I looked up as a man with a flatbed cart full of hay bales trundled by. I pulled my toes in to keep clear of the wheels. Around me, the performance arena was coming to life. There would be vendors setting up in the concessions area. All the competitors would be putting on shows tonight. Then, in the morning, the real event would start.

Restless, I reached down to pick up the folder I'd left on top of my ice chest the day before. The clipboard girl had given it to me when Snoopy and I had arrived. I'd set it aside without so much as a glance. Now, picking it up, I realized I'd paid no attention to the details of this event I was to have some small part in. I knew the flavor of big-name trainers that usually competed, but I hadn't heard who was slated to appear this year.

The folder had been sitting on my ice chest, face down. I picked it up and flipped it over. It was fat and heavy in my hands, replete with promotional materials. I glanced down and nearly dropped the thing.

Because there was Wyatt's face, staring back at me from the lower right-hand corner of the folder.

For a moment, I was so confused it felt as if my entire mind had ground to a sudden and complete halt. I blinked and stared, trying to convince myself this was not Wyatt. It was only someone who looked a good deal like him. But no, his head and shoulders were set inside a sort of crest-shaped badge. The name "Wyatt Lewis" was stamped in clear block letters below his photo.

My eyes flicked over the rest of the faces. All the others were familiar to me as well, though not in a personal context. There was Tim Moriarty, the darling of the natural horsemanship world, Keith Walker, a famous name from Australia, and Lea Norther, a woman known for riding bareback and bridleless.

And then there was, somehow, Wyatt.

I continued to stare, utterly confused. Wyatt was certainly good at what he did. But he hadn't exactly achieved national or international recognition.

I gaped at the folder for almost a full minute, becoming slowly convinced I was dreaming. The thought had appeal. Maybe none of this was happening at all. Maybe I'd never let Ted talk me into taking this ridiculous job. Maybe I'd not accepted his marriage proposal only to change my mind about it two weeks later. Looking back, none of the events that had taken place in my life lately seemed any more plausible than Wyatt appearing in an event like *Start the Horse, Connect the Heart.*

Then, however, my eyes settled on a little piece of text floating to the upper left side of Wyatt's head. It said, "Wildcard Competitor."

Finally, I understood. I'd even read about this in some horsemanship magazine earlier in the year. The competition had opened up one slot and let anyone apply, then they'd selected a regular old person to compete alongside the industry's biggest names.

And apparently, that person was Wyatt.

Feeling strangely breathless, I set the folder aside. "This is insane," I mumbled under my breath.

At the same time, however, I couldn't help but look towards the warm-up arena and search among the distant figures to see if I could spot Wyatt's familiar form.

He wasn't there, of course. This venue was massive. I could likely go the whole weekend without running into him.

Since my arrival at *Start the Horse, Connect the Heart,* I'd been so consumed by my worries about Snoopy I'd hardly even looked around. Before I discovered Wyatt's face on the folder, I hadn't been all that curious about the event. My family considered colt-starting competitions to be gimmicky affairs, built around the fact that bringing ignorant people and shows-offs together usually produces revenue.

It blew my mind Wyatt would participate in such a thing. After seeing his face on the outside, I'd opened the folder and read through the rules and terms of the competition. I learned each competitor was assigned an unstarted colt. The colts were practically wild, having been raised on a large ranch and handled little or not at all. Each competitor had a few hours with their colt on Saturday and a couple more on Sunday morning. Then on Sunday afternoon, they had to guide their horse through an obstacle course and complete certain riding milestones. The trainer whose colt was deemed most proficient by the judges would win the day. And also, perhaps not insignificantly, $100,000.

After I turned up the information that Wyatt could perhaps be nearby right now, I found myself unable to sit by Snoopy's stall any longer. I wandered out into the concessions area, drifting past the vendors getting ready to open. Wyatt was not there.

Telling myself I was only trying to get familiar with my surroundings, I took to ambling up and down the rows of stalls, glancing at the horses I passed. Wyatt must have brought a horse. All competitors would be putting on one performance tonight and another in the morning. But I had no idea what horse he'd have brought with him. He hadn't had his own mount at the Tipped Z.

I didn't see Wyatt in the stalls, nor did I see any horse I recognized. I continued to walk with aimless energy, constantly glancing at my phone. Presumably, Jay's discussion with the vet would yield a plan of action for the weekend. This meant decisions about Snoopy and his future were out of my hands. I felt wretchedly grateful for this fact even as I worried about what Jay would decide to do.

After an hour of walking hadn't yielded any discovery of Wyatt's whereabouts, I gave up and returned to Snoopy's stall. I put the horse's halter on and led him to a second arena I'd discovered. It was deeper in the bowels of the facility but quieter than the warm-up arena, which was becoming crowded. Once there, I walked Snoopy in circles, glancing up any time I saw a man in a cowboy hat. There were a lot of men in cowboy hats around. None of them were Wyatt.

Finally, I stopped walking. I felt trapped in some strange, suspended reality. I checked my phone. The screen was blank. I sighed, put my phone in my pocket, then took it out again. I unlocked the screen, feeling a sort of nervy anticipation begin to grow in my chest as a thought occurred to me. I opened my text messaging app and scrolled down to Wyatt's name. I tapped his photo. The conversation from the night he'd found me downtown popped up—the night Erin suggested he find me and give me a ride home.

I scrolled through our message history. Above the messages from the night downtown was a text he'd sent me after he'd arrived in Phoenix with the horse he'd found for Jay to borrow. Before that, there was nothing. I hadn't even had his number.

There was a clang as another horse and rider entered the quiet arena. Snoopy raised his head in curiosity. I glanced up to see a girl in jeans and a t-shirt leading an agitated bay mare and looking overwhelmed. "Hi." She sounded breathless. "Is it okay if I ride in here a little?"

"Be my guest." I returned my attention to my phone. Seeing the text message history made me realize something. I always faulted Wyatt for being elusive, distant, hard to pin down. But the fact was, I'd never called him, never sent him a single text. I tended not to acknowledge him when he entered a room because I was busy waiting for him to acknowledge me. When he didn't, I got my feelings hurt.

I stood there, leaning against Snoopy, chewing on my lip. Across the arena, the girl tried to mount her wound up mare. The horse danced to the side and the girl had to pull her foot out of the stirrup to make the horse stop moving. I frowned as I watched. Then, in a sudden fit of courage and determination, I tapped out a brief text. "Hey, are you in OK City right now?"

Before I could think about what I was doing, before I could convince myself not to follow through, I sent the text. Then, heart hammering, I shoved my phone into my pocket and looked up in time to see the girl make it onto her horse's back only to get unseated immediately as the horse spooked, leaping hugely to the side. The girl tumbled out of the saddle to fall hard on her back in the shallow sand of the arena. The horse thundered towards me and Snoopy at a dead run, loose reins and stirrups flapping, a look of panic in her eye.

Chapter 10

For the next quarter-hour or so, I was occupied enough I didn't have time to obsessively check my phone. I caught the girl's horse, tied Snoopy to the fence, and returned the wayward mount to where the unfortunate youth sat in the sand, looking more embarrassed than injured. As the girl wobbled to her feet, I did what I could to calm the horse.

The girl thanked me as she dusted off her jeans, explaining she was here to ride in one of the performances tonight—a showcase for local youth riders. "I don't know what I'm going to do if I can't get Chelsea calmed down by then." She had sand crusted to the backs of her arms and a quaver in her voice.

She did not, however, ask for my advice. So I helped her straighten her saddle. When she displayed determination to get back on, I held her horse as she mounted. Personally, I would have done a few things from the ground to get the horse in a better state of mind, but I kept my mouth shut. I thought of something else my father had told me a million times. *Offer a man advice and he will scorn you. Wait until he asks and he will listen.*

So I said nothing as the girl got on, tightened her reins, and kicked the nervous horse into a punitive canter. I walked over to Snoopy and led him back towards his stall.

My phone rang as I walked through a deserted aisle, causing my poor heart to leap into painful spasms. I pulled out my phone to see it was Jay. I answered with a feeling of dull trepidation, but the conversation was crisp and businesslike. Jay said the vet had recommended two grams of bute, twice a day, and as little riding as possible until we could get Snoopy back home and collect some x-rays for a more certain diagnosis. He pronounced this treatment plan as if reading it from a notepad. When he was done, there was a pause. "Got it?"

I turned the final corner and saw my folding chair and the folder on the ice chest. "Got it."

"I'll be there in the morning." Jay's tone was neutral, bland, and rushed. Clearly, he did not want to discuss the bigger picture of Snoopy's long-term prognosis. A fact for which I was just as happy.

We said good-bye and hung up. I put Snoopy back in his stall and looked around. It was 11:00 AM. I'd planned to use this day working with Snoopy, practicing our routine and putting in a lot of mellow saddle time to get him accustomed to the new environment. Except now I couldn't ride him any more than strictly necessary.

I gave Snoopy his first dose of bute. After that, I had exactly nothing to do. I'd never been to Oklahoma City before. It occurred to me a younger, more energetic version of myself would leave the arena and head out to explore. A more intelligent version of myself would go back to the hotel to spend the day lounging by the pool or making good use of the suite in some way.

Somehow, the me of the moment couldn't find the motivation to do anything but collapse back into the folding chair and stare at my phone.

Ted had been notably silent since I'd broken off our engagement. I'd stowed his ring in the safe in the hotel suite but the thin depression in the skin of my finger was still there. I wasn't sure what to think of the fact he hadn't been back in touch. I suspected it meant he was busy preparing some grand reconciliation event. As I sat by Snoopy's stall, I tried to figure out if that was what I wanted. Somehow, my feelings for Ted and our relationship had gotten so mixed up with my feelings about my job, I could hardly remember the way I'd felt about him before there was Jay. Jay and Snoopy and my stylist and photos of a perfect version of myself all over the internet.

My phone chimed. I jerked in my seat in surprise even though I'd been staring right at the screen. Then my heart did the thing where it leapt into frantic spasms.

The text was from Wyatt. "Just arrived. Getting settled. What's your stall number?"

I stared at the phone as if it possessed some sort of wondrous magic. I had texted Wyatt. He had texted back. Could it be this simple?

Fingers clumsy, I tapped out my stall number and asked for his. I sent the message on its way. Then I waited.

And waited.

The minutes dragged by. My hopeful excitement faded by degrees, degrading down to frustrated annoyance. I set my phone on the ice chest and pointedly looked away. I reached into my purse and fished out my Kindle. I opened the book I'd selected for this trip and stared at the first page, too distracted to read.

Then, at last, my phone chimed again. The message was from Wyatt, containing nothing but, "C43." I took in the number, using my recently gained understanding of the stall complex to envision where he was. It was an aisle I'd walked down earlier. It had been empty then.

Once more, I set the phone aside. I picked up my Kindle but was even more distracted than before. I felt ridiculously uncertain about what to do next. Wyatt had asked for my stall number and he'd given me his. Did that mean he was coming here? That I should go there?

For a moment, all the stress and uncertainty nearly overwhelmed me. I felt an overpowering urge to leave. Sure, I was on contract with the TruGlide Corporation. But what was a contract, really? It was only words. I could stand up right now, walk out of this place, and take the shuttle back to the hotel. I could pack my things into my little rolling suitcase and go to the airport. I could fly back to Tucson. I could leave

Snoopy and Jay to their fate. I could flee from all the stress and uncertainty.

I heard the thump of boot heels. I turned in my chair, looking down the aisle. A man was there, walking towards me. He was a well-made man, with just the right amount of lean muscle on his frame and a little hitch in his step. He wore jeans, boots, and a hat. The fringe of his chinks swayed around his legs as he walked.

My heart seemed to pause, then shudder into greater life. I stood up as Wyatt approached. As he drew near, the shadows under his hat brim grew lighter until I could see his face. He was smiling that little smile of his. "Why hello, Nora." His tone was playful. "Fancy meeting you here."

A rush of endorphins flooded me at the sound of his voice, as if he'd declared his undying love and devotion instead of making some lame quip.

I found myself smiling back. "Wildcard entrant, huh?"

His smile lifted on one side. "Ridiculous, right? It happened last summer. Five of us were up at the Catskills Ranch. We had 50 head of colts to start and a week to do it. One night we got to talking about these kinds of competitions. Someone said he thought any one of us could win one of these things, hands down. He was talking a bunch of crap about professional clinicians. Anyway, one thing led to another. A different guy piped up about this wildcard slot. Suddenly we were on someone's phone, putting in our applications right then and there. By the next morning I'd all but forgotten the whole thing."

He was close by then. He'd stopped walking a few paces away from my chair. He smelled of leather and horses and dust. "But they picked you."

Wyatt gave a modest shrug. "Can't think why." He said the words in a light tone. But the smile had faded and there was something serious about the way his eyes held mine. I rubbed my denuded ring finger. I saw his eyes follow the movement.

The fact of my bare hand registered in his eyes. I saw him blink and go still, like a horse trying to decide whether it needs to brace for pain or yield to pressure.

He seemed to look at me more closely, then. He took in my lonely chair, the single folder, the canister of bute sitting on the ice chest. His eyes came back to my face. "You all right, here?"

And just like that, I was talking. At first I made an effort to frame it all in a way that made sense. But the story dissolved into a disorganized torrent of words. I told him about Snoopy and the vet and Jay. I told him about Ted proposing and not saying yes but somehow accepting anyway, then breaking it off over the phone.

Wyatt listened. He never interrupted, never gazed off into the distance as if he'd rather be somewhere other than here. I heard his phone chime but he didn't look at it. When I had finished my disjointed summary, he spoke. "You know what helps almost every problem on earth?"

I shook my head. As soon as I stopped talking, I started to feel embarrassed. What had I done? Poor Wyatt had probably come by to be polite and here I was dumping the entire saga of my recent life onto his shoulders.

Wyatt's small smile reappeared. "Sandwiches." His face was so handsome, his eyes so friendly, I felt my brain sort of short-circuit.

Was it just me, or was he making no sense?

He continued. "Let's go get sandwiches. We can eat them. While we do, we can pick apart this grand tangle into its smaller pieces and figure out how to make each piece right."

"Sandwiches." I repeated the word, realizing I was ravenously hungry. I glanced at Snoopy but the horse was fine. I turned to Wyatt and matched his smile. "I knew there was a reason I turned to you for help."

The thunder of the crowd broke over me like the waves preceding a tsunami. Light glared down from above. Snoopy, his pain masked by drugs, was in fine fettle. I'd done quite a bit of light groundwork with him but had put in minimal time on his back. As we started through the final lap of our routine, he still had plenty of energy.

The announcer's voice boomed over the sound of the music, so loud it was hard to hear. I pushed Snoopy into our final gallop. The ridiculous black cape Jay had added to my outfit flared out behind me as we gained speed. Then I asked for one final, sliding stop in the center of the arena. Sand sprayed up from around Snoopy's haunches as he doubled over with the effort.

The crowd cheered. The announcer's voice boomed. "Let's hear it for Chrome Zippo Whiz and the TruGlide Girl!"

I was done. Or, I was done with part one of my job for the day. I gave Snoopy a moment to recover, then pushed him into a smooth canter. I took my hat off and waved at the crowd as the announcer moved smoothly into one final spiel about TruGlide shoes. He explained more information about the product and the flashy Chrome Zippo Whiz and his gorgeous rider could be found on the TruGlide website.

I passed out of the main arena. The sound of the crowd shifted and faded as I eased Snoopy down to a trot and steered him through the warm-up area. Where this place had been empty the day before, it was now overflowing. There were people and horses everywhere. There were the competitors, of course, but there were also support riders and other performers and all manner of people and horses whose role I couldn't quite pin down.

Start the Horse, Connect the Heart was in full swing.

I eased Snoopy down to a walk. We paced a few circles at the bottom of the warm-up arena, working near the cage of chickens placed there for some inexplicable reason. A moment later I dismounted and finished cooling Snoopy out from the ground. I looked at his hocks and his stride with a critical eye. He seemed fine.

Still, I felt a sort of dull pressure in my chest as I led him. He seemed fine, but I knew he wasn't. He wasn't fine, but I'd asked him to do something I knew was bad for him for the sake of putting on a show.

I'd modified my routine to make it less taxing on Snoopy. But when I'd suggested to Jay we remove sliding stops entirely, he'd nearly gone apoplectic. My boss had arrived that morning, sweeping into my hotel suite with a host of support staff. As my stylist had gone to work on my hair, I'd talked to Jay about Snoopy.

Unsurprisingly, we had mismatched opinions about what to do. My thought was to get Snoopy through the weekend with as little exertion as we could manage, then figure out how to find him a retirement home while he was still sound enough to be comfortable. Jay's thought was to figure out a drug and injection regimen that would keep him going as long as possible.

I recognized this weekend was not the time for the broader discussion on the ethics of masking pain in horses so they could keep doing their job until they were too broken down to go on. The stakes were too high. I kept my focus on the short term. I haggled with Jay over sliding stops like a used car salesman, bringing the number in the routine lower and lower until he genuinely looked like he might die from an aneurism. He kept saying, "Sliding stops are the *whole point*, Nora. If we don't do them, we might as well be saying, 'Don't buy our product. It doesn't work.'"

We agreed on a total of six, three in each routine. I thought it was way too many. Jay thought it was way too few. But that, I supposed, was the definition of compromise.

I attributed the fact I'd been able to stand up to Jay at all to my sandwich date with Wyatt. That easy afternoon had cleared my head and prepared me to hold my ground.

The day hadn't been anything remarkable. Wyatt and I had walked out of the arena together into the bright expanse of one of the parking bays. Wyatt's truck had been there, already unhitched from a trailer I didn't recognize. We'd headed off in search of sandwiches, finding a little shop in a strip mall. We'd sat together and ate. And we'd done what he'd promised. We'd talked about each of my problems. Somehow in talking about them, they became smaller.

We hadn't stayed out long. He'd been due back at the arena for a photoshoot. As we drove back in his truck, he explained in apologetic tones he was expected to be involved with the event until pretty late and then back to the arena first thing in the morning. I told him that was fine, of course. We returned to the arena and went our separate ways.

Although I'd returned to my lonely vigil by Snoopy's stall, my situation had seemed less bleak.

Now, I was through one performance. Today I had to work the crowd, which shouldn't be as difficult this time. Jay had secured a booth that had space for Snoopy. The horse would function as an oversized silver and gold billboard, encouraging people to stop and ask questions about our shoes.

Snoopy and I made it back to the stall, where several nervous-looking girls Jay had brought to assist me with horse matters did more to get in my way than help. I removed Snoopy's saddle and brushed him down, oiling his nose and hooves back to a perfect shine. Jay wasn't there. He was probably putting the final touches on the booth.

I was feeling around my crispy head trying to determine if my hair was still in place when my phone chimed. My phone was not in my pocket. It was in my purse, which was tucked near the stall with my other personal belongings and ostensibly being guarded by the two girls. I went over and fished it out.

The text almost made my heart stop.

It was from Wyatt. "Love the cape." I could almost hear the sardonic tilt of his voice. Then, as I stared down, starting to feel stung and hurt, another message followed the first. "We're off the hook tonight. You free for dinner?"

I stood in front of my hotel room mirror, critically aware of the traces of my TruGlide getup which had proven to be impossible to remove. My hair smelled like product. My eyes bore the vague shadow of the heavy makeup I'd worn earlier. My fingernails had little glittering rhinestones stuck to them. I seemed to hear Wyatt's voice. *They do you an injustice.*

I'd spent nearly an hour trying to decide what to wear to dinner only to finally settled on blue jeans and a slim black t-shirt. I'd called Erin midway through the process. I'd told her about Snoopy and Ted. And I'd wanted to ask her opinion on Wyatt. Was this a date? Or was it a thing we were doing because we were old friends and we were in the same place that wasn't home?

Somehow, though, I'd been unable to tell her Wyatt was here at all. Did she know? I couldn't tell. She didn't bring him up and neither did I.

Erin was sympathetic about my predicament with Snoopy, but I told her it was going to be okay. The afternoon following my performance had been a resounding success, with more people coming to the TruGlide booth to see Snoopy than even I had expected. We reached our target saturation without effort. Jay had to send attendants back to the van several times for more promotional materials. Finally he let me go early, as happy as I'd ever seen him.

The knowledge Snoopy was on borrowed time had weighed heavily on my heart as I'd led him back to his stall and tucked him in for the night. I returned to the performance arena and watched a little bit of the competition, seeing the last half hour of Wyatt's work with his colt before the timers stopped for the night.

Now it was almost 7:30. Wyatt was due to arrive any minute. When he'd asked where I wanted to go to dinner, I'd said we should start here. What was the point of having a hotel suite, after all, if you didn't have any fun with it?

I'd called room service. A bottle of red wine sat breathing on a table on the balcony. I had the doors open. An evening breeze was weaving its lazy way through the room, the distant bustle of the city drifting in. I didn't know if Wyatt liked wine. But there was also a stash of beer in the mini-fridge.

Jay had invited me out to dinner with the rest of the TruGlide staff—an invitation I'd declined, pleading fatigue. He'd been too happy about how the day had gone to push the issue. So here I was, alone.

I walked out of the bathroom, flipping off the light and pausing to take in the scene. The room wasn't the Ritz, but it was a nice enough space. The door opened into a hall with a coat rack, then expanded into a sitting area with a sofa and a coffee table. To the left stood the mini kitchen. Straight ahead, the balcony doors opened onto a view of the cityscape.

The place was done up with modern décor—nice without being overdone. I had stowed all the gear my TruGlide team had left behind in the oversized closet. Ted's ring was still in the safe.

I was ready.

Behind me, there was a tap on the door. I waited a moment, feeling the need to pretend I hadn't been standing in the middle of the room waiting. Then I strode across the soft carpet and worked the heavy handle.

Wyatt stood in the hall looking not at all like a cowboy except for his boots. He was wearing the old baseball cap from his truck. I felt instantly relieved I hadn't dressed up. Wyatt had changed into clean jeans. But other than that he didn't appear to have gone out of his way to make himself attractive.

Feeling a strange dip of disappointment, I moved back so he could enter. Wyatt stepped into the room and closed the door quickly, then turned to me and took the hat off. "People have been recognizing me." He said this in a horrified tone as he set the hat on the table near the entryway, dropping his truck keys on top of it and pausing to smooth his hair, which was damp and a little rumpled. "Like, they stop me and ask for my autograph."

It was the look on Wyatt's face that made me laugh. This was a man who wasn't in the least bit afraid of the prospect of getting a half-wild colt ready to complete an obstacle course in a few hours' time, yet he found the prospect of interacting with strangers terrifying.

"Well, you're safe here. There will be no fawning adoration from me. I've seen you get bucked off more times than I can count." I led the way into my suite as I spoke. I wondered, belatedly, where Wyatt was staying. The event staffers might have hooked him up with somewhere even more lavish.

Wyatt stepped off the carpet of the entry onto where the floor transitioned to wood. His boots made soft, solid thumps. I thought his tiny limp was more pronounced than usual. He looked around but made no comment.

I found myself suddenly jittery. The day before, when we'd gone for sandwiches, things had felt natural and easy. Now I was acutely aware I'd never been alone with Wyatt this way before.

"Would you like a glass of wine?" I made the offer, then backpedaled. "There's beer too, if you'd prefer."

Wyatt seemed to be relaxing by degrees as he trailed after me through the sitting area and onto the balcony. He was tired, I could see now. I tried to imagine the level of stress he'd dealt with over the course of the day. Handling young horses was difficult enough before you factored in high stakes, a ticking clock, and an entire arena of spectators. "Wine is fine." He paused by the balcony railing, gazing out over the city. "Good. Wine is good."

I reached the small table and poured two glasses, turning to hand him one. I raised my glass to clink my rim against his. I could see the fatigue around his eyes and a slight droop in his shoulders. Wyatt was exhausted.

I raised my glass a little higher. "To connecting the heart." I meant it as a sarcastic quip about the ridiculously awful name of the event, but it sounded strangely sincere as I spoke.

Wyatt didn't laugh. He raised his glass as well, then took a sip. Embarrassed, I did the same. Then we stood there, listening to the hum of the city. Yesterday, I'd had so much to say to Wyatt I'd been unable to stop talking. Today, the very air between us seemed to sing with emptiness.

My mind scrambled around, trying out different conversation topics only to discard them. Finally, I managed, "How did it go today? I barely got to watch."

Wyatt shrugged, taking another sip of wine. He ran a hand through his damp hair again. The smell of light soap drifted to me on the evening breeze. "The colt is good minded. But then, they all are. I don't think Moriarty is any kind of threat. For the other two, we're going to have to wait and see."

I'd heard enough chatter about the day to learn Tim Moriarty's colt had bucked him off twice, prompting the trainer to fall back on the primitive method of tying up one foot and forcing the horse to lie down. He'd run out of time and hadn't gotten back in the saddle. Wyatt, I knew, had gotten into the saddle and worked his colt at all three gaits. The other two trainers had experienced similar success.

"It's a lot to throw at a colt so fast." Wyatt was still gazing out over the city, voice subdued. "It's not good for them, to be honest. By the end of the day tomorrow the main thing they'll all be is exhausted."

I couldn't think of an answer to this. The conversation lulled again. Wyatt sagged into one of the balcony chairs. He set his wine on the table with a click, glancing up at me. "Would you be terribly disappointed if we didn't go out tonight?"

I felt a dip in my chest as he spoke. Had I screwed things up that badly? Two sips of wine and he didn't want to hang out with me anymore? Maybe I should have tried harder to learn about how to pick a good bottle from Ted.

I was too disappointed to answer. Wyatt gestured out at the city. "I'm afraid I'll get mobbed out there. We could order in instead? Chinese food? Or pizza? Whatever you want, it's on me."

Wyatt picked up a crab wonton and maneuvered it onto his plate, setting it down, then repositioning his chopsticks to twirl them in his fried noodle dish. I watched with vague fascination as he collected a tidy mouthful and raised it to his lips.

I had abandoned my chopsticks approximately ten seconds after unwrapping them and was now using the silverware I'd found in the kitchen to attack my steaming plate of cashew chicken. I watched Wyatt for a moment. "You're good with those."

He winked at me as he chewed. "I dated a girl from China. Lived with her for a couple of years. She always ate with chopsticks when we were home. It seemed like a good thing to learn."

I stared at Wyatt as if he'd confessed he was an alien form of life that had perfected the guise of seeming human. I blinked, trying to cover my surprise by snagging my own wonton. Wyatt had had a serious girlfriend? He'd lived with her? For a couple of *years*?

"How did I not know this?" I meant this as a joke but it came out sounding somewhat accusatory.

Wyatt's eyes flicked up to meet mine. They held mine for a fraction of a second, then returned to the table. "You never seemed interested."

After we'd decided to stay in, the atmosphere between me and Wyatt had relaxed. I realized he hadn't been stiff and nervous about me. He'd been dreading braving the streets of Oklahoma City and facing the hordes of people who'd been staring at his face on the jumbo screens in the performance arena all day. He'd perked up as we sat on the balcony in the light of the falling sun, sipping wine and chatting.

After one glass of wine, however, we both switched to beer. The bottle I'd ordered wasn't very good.

The beer, however, was just fine. We sipped our hoppy brews and pulled up the menu of a local Chinese place on my phone, sitting shoulder to shoulder as we decided what to order.

Now the food had arrived. I was one glass of wine and half a beer into feeling very relaxed. Or, at least, I had been relaxed until Wyatt's most recent comment.

Had he really said *I* hadn't been interested? This, coming from the guy who couldn't even be bothered to say hello when he called to speak to my brother?

"When was this?" I poked at my food, trying hard to keep my tone neutral.

Wyatt set his chopsticks down and studied me from across the table. He was perkier than before but I could still read the fatigue in his face. We'd moved indoors but I'd left the balcony open. The soft breeze toyed with the gauzy curtains as he spoke. "A few years ago. You were dating the guy in the band."

A felt my face flush. I picked up my beer to cover my embarrassment. I'd had an unfortunate fling with a musician. It wasn't that musicians were inherently deficient, just this particular one had been a good deal older than me and not exactly a catch. Though not particularly talented, he'd had an ego the size of South America—the region he claimed to have studied extensively and thus influenced his musical aesthetic.

"Ah. Right." I set my beer down, wondering how Wyatt knew about the musician. I knew for certain the two of them had never met. Clint had disapproved of that relationship so tremendously I'd never even brought the guy to the ranch.

The fact Wyatt knew at all, then, meant I'd been at least somewhat wrong about his level of interest in me. He must have either asked about me at some point when he talked to Clint or Clint must have told Wyatt about the relationship, unprompted. I couldn't decide which seemed the less likely scenario.

We were quiet for a time. The buzz of the city was a distant thrum of background noise. I ate my cashew chicken with a fork. Wyatt cleaned his plate with the chopsticks. Finally, I stood and stretched, collecting our empty plates and carrying them into the kitchen. "Would you like another beer?" I asked over my shoulder as I walked across the wooden floor to the chrome sink.

Wyatt also rose. In answer, he went to the mini-fridge and took out two more bottles. He set them on the counter as I washed the dishes. They hissed as he popped the tops. "This will have to be the last one." He tossed the jingling caps into the trash. "I need to rest well tonight."

He pushed one bottle towards me along the counter, raising the other to take a sip. The kitchen was small. I was suddenly aware of how close he was. All he'd have to do to touch my shoulder was reach out a hand.

I set the final plate in the drying rack. I turned off the water, drying my hands with a paper towel. As I tossed the towel into the trash, Wyatt spoke. It was as if he'd heard my earlier thoughts. "I always asked about you, you know. Every time I talked to your brother."

I turned in the narrow space. Wyatt's body blocked the way out of the kitchen. His eyes were on me.

Feeling flustered, I reached for my beer. As I stretched my hand towards the cool glass, Wyatt's fingers got in the way. I felt a strange sensation of shock as his hand found mine and his rough, firm fingers wrapped around my palm.

He shifted. Suddenly he was very, very close. He wasn't more than a few inches taller than me. But he was broad and firm in a way that was different from the taller men I was usually around.

"Nora." Wyatt's voice was little more than a whisper, his mouth mere inches from my ear. I felt my heart in my chest, hammering for all it was worth. My eyes kept trying to find something safe to look at, something that wasn't Wyatt. Because I knew what would happen if I looked at him now.

I heard the clink of a bottle being set down. Wyatt's other hand lifted. He set one gentle finger beneath my chin and tilted my head up and to the side.

It was too much. I gave in.

I looked into Wyatt's face. His eyes were earnest. I felt that shock. It shot through me with more force than I'd ever experienced before. It raced down my spine like a current of electricity, turning my whole body into a livewire. I looked at Wyatt and Wyatt looked at me.

A thought snaked through my mind. *He's going to leave now. Somehow, he'll get a text or a phone call and he's going to have to go, just like always.*

But this time, Wyatt didn't leave. He bent forward. I felt the brush of his lips on mine.

At first, the kiss was soft. I melted into it, my thoughts dissolving into formless things. Wyatt's hand left my chin and trailed down my back, coming to rest on my hip. His mouth was cool and tasted of hops. I felt the light scratch of stubble against my chin.

Time seemed to slow. I felt overwhelmed with a sense of giddy disbelief. *This is happening,* I thought. *Wyatt is kissing me.*

Then I thought about Ted, how crushed he'd sounded on the phone. The electric feeling snapped off as if a switch had been flipped.

"Wait." I pulled back. The magic of the moment shattered, falling into fragments around us. "I'm sorry. I can't. I mean, Ted."

Wyatt's chest was moving up and down with more force than usual. There were high spots of color on his cheeks. His eyes had a dark, hungry look I'd never seen in them before. He stared down at me, his whole body full of restrained desire. As if words were beyond him, he lifted his hand from my back and used it to trace the shallow indentation my ring finger still bore.

"I called off the engagement," I hurried to explain, "but we didn't break things off entirely. He wants to talk about it."

Wyatt swallowed. His eyes cleared a little, but his voice was rougher than usual. "What's to talk about?"

I felt overwhelmed. I thought of sweet, patient Ted and all the times he'd been there for me. I thought of wild, sexy Wyatt, who was always where you least expected him.

Earlier, he'd said he always asked about me when he talked to my brother. But why, then, didn't he ever talk to me?

The aftershocks of the kiss were still shuddering through my body. On the one hand, I wanted nothing more than to fling myself back into Wyatt's arms. On the other, I felt like the very least I owed Ted was a clean break.

Wyatt watched me for another moment. Then all the energy and excitement seemed to drain out of him. I saw him shut down, saw him pull back, saw him close to me once again.

He glanced around as if he'd forgotten where he was. Then he looked at his watch.

"Look," his voice sounded a little angry. "I have to go."

He began to move, collecting the few items he'd left around the room. I watched him, frozen with horror at what I was doing.

This was Wyatt. He'd kissed me and I was letting him go.

Wyatt stopped one last time before heading towards the door, looking towards me with a final question in his eyes.

Say something. The thought hammered in my head. No words came to my lips.

I saw another shift in his eyes—a cooling. "Good luck tomorrow."

And then he was gone.

Chapter 11

I listened to the slow snick of the latch on the door closing behind Wyatt. Then, as if the sound stirred me out of a stupor, my brain seemed to wake up.

My thought process of a moment before seemed suddenly ridiculous. Wyatt was right. If I didn't want to marry Ted, what else was there to say? I knew what would happen when I got back to Tucson. Ted would put on a big show of being sorry. He'd arrange some grand event to make it all up to me. And then we'd be right back where we were before. He'd hold off for another six months, maybe, planning an even grander proposal next time. But sooner or later he was going to ask me to marry him again. And, chances were, I wouldn't feel any differently about that idea then than I did right now.

I closed my eyes, raising a hand to touch my lips where Wyatt's mouth had so recently touched mine. For a moment, I let all the defenses I'd built up, all the half-truths and barriers I'd constructed around my heart fall away.

I admitted something, if only to myself.

I *loved* Wyatt.

I'd always loved him. At the core of all the confusion and frustration and longing was that one simple fact.

Was I really standing here, leaning against a kitchen counter, letting the man I loved walk away from me, disappointed?

Suddenly, I was moving. I raced around the edge of the counter, all but flinging myself through the narrow hall to fall upon the door. I cranked on the cumbersome handle and dragged it open, darting out into the hall. I was wearing only socks—I'd taken my shoes off some time after we'd ordered the Chinese food. The carpet in the hallway was a thin dark red strip bordered in dull brown tile.

I looked one way, towards the elevator.

The hallway was empty.

I looked the other, towards the stairwell.

Wyatt was pulling open the door. "Wyatt." I called his name and my voice echoed in the empty hall.

Wyatt paused. He stood looking towards me. I could see the tension and fatigue in his broad shoulders. There was a sort of dull pain in his eyes. I saw his hand touch his back pocket, as if he was wondering if he'd forgotten his wallet and I was bringing it to him.

Other than the two of us, the hallway was deserted. But the walls were lined with doors. I wondered who was behind them right now, what small dramas were playing out just out of sight.

But I didn't wonder about that for long. I'd been overthinking Wyatt for far too long. Now, it was time to act.

I darted forward, running down the hall on light feet. It felt good to move, as if I was doing something useful for the first time in my life. I ran to Wyatt, intending to fling myself into his arms. As I neared him, however, my courage failed. I stopped close to him. But not quite close enough to touch.

He stood utterly still, watching me. His face still wore that guarded expression. He had made the first move. I had rebuffed him. If there was going to be another start, it had to come from me.

I took another step forward, feeling hesitant as I entered his space. I caught the light scent of soap again. Through the stairwell, I heard the distant murmur of voices and a heavy door closing far below.

I stepped right up to Wyatt, slipped my hand around the nape of his neck, and kissed him.

For one sliver of an instant, Wyatt stayed still. I had time to fear it was too late. I'd made my mistake, missed my one chance. I was going to have to give him up after all.

Just when I was about to draw back, something changed. Wyatt seemed to explode with life. He kissed me then with far more energy and passion than in the kitchen. His body pressed against mine. He let go of the door. As it swung closed, I took a step back until I was pressed against the hallway wall.

Wyatt's lips left mine and traveled down my neck. I felt hot all over, full of brilliant energy. I seemed to lose myself in the sensation of his rough chin on my neck, his hands on my waist.

Then the sensation ceased. I opened my eyes to see Wyatt looking at me. He'd pulled back a little, but the fire was back in his eyes.

He took another step away, giving my hand a gentle tug. "Maybe we should go back inside." His mouth lifted in a small smile.

I'd all but forgotten we were in the hallway. Embarrassed, I started forward as the elevator doors at the end of the hall opened with a quiet ding, disgorging a harried mother and two kids. I blushed more deeply, mortified at how closely they'd come to seeing us.

I let Wyatt lead me back across the hall to the door of my room. He moved with quick steps, stopping when he was within reach of the handle. He looked at me with an expression of expectation.

The door was closed, of course. Hotel doors do not stay open on their own. I felt my heart seize in deeper mortification. "Oh no."

I patted my pockets. It was useless. I knew where I'd left the hotel key cards. They were on the side table, just inside the bedroom door.

Wyatt and I were locked out.

I woke to the sound of banging. I gasped, sitting up in a spasm of confusion. For a moment I sat in the broad, white expanse of the massive hotel room bed, utterly disoriented.

I blinked. The room was bright with the sunlight falling in through the large windows. They were open, with morning air moving lazily through the screen.

The banging came again—a rhythmic series of thuds. Faintly, in muffled tones, I heard the distant sound of a voice that seemed familiar yet too quiet to make out.

For one more moment, I sat there suspended in a timeless instant of forgetfulness.

Then it all clicked together.

The hotel room. The colt starting event.

Wyatt.

I gasped, reaching for my phone. It wasn't on my bedside table, where it should have been.

Also, I was completely naked.

"Shit." I glanced feverishly around the room. There was a clock on the other side of the bed, red numbers giving off a baleful glow. 7:05.

It took a moment for this to register. Then, I cursed again. "Shit shit shit." I scurried out of bed. I should have been up ages ago. My team of stylists was supposed to have arrived at 7:00.

The banging came again. "Oh, god. They're outside." I mumbled this to myself as I scampered around the room, hurrying to collect my clothing from the night before. My jeans lay in a ball at the foot of the bed. My bra was draped over the armchair by the window. The door to the outer room was open. Lying in the center of the living room floor was my black t-shirt.

As I scrambled to dress, memories of the night before came back to me in a hot flood. My face flushed as I buttoned my jeans. I crept out into the living area to snatch my shirt and dash back to the bedroom.

When we'd discovered the locked door, I'd been certain Wyatt would leave. He had a big day coming up, after all, and the spell that had been cast over us when we kissed had now been twice broken.

But Wyatt hadn't left. He'd grinned and led me down to the lobby.

It had taken an inordinately long time to convince the hotel receptionist to let me and Wyatt back into the room. The problem was the room had been booked by the TruGlide Corporation. I could confirm neither the contact phone number nor the last four digits of the credit card which had been used to reserve to room. I also couldn't produce any ID to prove my identity as the person the room had been reserved for.

The receptionist was a twenty-something girl with a bored aspect and a band-aide over her eyebrow that likely hid a piercing. Apparently unmoved by the sight of me standing on the hard tile in my stocking feet, she'd offered to call the number on the booking. I had hastily asked her to refrain, explaining my boss was at dinner and I didn't want to disturb him.

I offered a compromise. I would tell her exactly where the keys were in the room, and where my purse was. She could go in and get the keys and my purse. I would take my ID out of the purse and show it to her. She would then have proof we'd been in the room mere moments before, and I was who I was claiming to be.

I'm pretty sure the girl would have refused me. But Wyatt had spoken up after I made my request. He'd been silent throughout my exchange with the receptionist, though I'd been acutely aware of his body only a few feet away from mine.

"We'd really appreciate your help." He said the simple words, in his smoothest, friendliest tone.

The girl blinked, shrugged, and gave in. "Okay, fine. It's not like it's busy down here anyway."

When the keys had been on the side table, as I'd said, and my purse had been on the chair in the living room, as I'd said, and my Arizona driver's license proved to have my name on it, as I'd said, the girl shrugged our thanks away and sauntered out. Wyatt and I waited until the door swung shut, and clicked.

Then we fell upon each other like wolves.

My discarded clothing told the story of our journey to the bed. The part missing was the trail of discarded clothing he had also left. There was no evidence of Wyatt in the hotel room at all—not so much as a stray sock. The side of the bed he'd slept in was turned up and tidied.

It was as if he'd never been here.

Out in the kitchen, my phone began to ring. At last wiggling into my black shirt, I scrambled out and retrieved my phone from where it had been sitting all night on the counter. It gave off its low battery chime as I picked it up.

The photo of Jay sprawled in the TrueGlide chair was glowing on the screen. I hurried to answer. "Jay," I said. "Sorry, I ..." I almost said I'd been in the shower but stopped myself just in time. Jay was outside my door right this instant and my hair was demonstrably not wet.

"Nora?" Jay's voice was irritated. "Are you in there? Your stylists are wandering the halls like stray sheep. They say you're not answering the door."

I glanced around the kitchen, doing a critical sweep for any telltale items. I didn't know where Wyatt was but it seemed he was no longer here.

After we tumbled into bed the night before, we stayed there a long time, exploring each other in a way I'd never explored anyone before. Wyatt's body, freed of shirt and jeans, had been even more beautiful, even more touchable, than I'd expected.

Eventually, we wore ourselves out and fell asleep. I'd woken up a few hours later to hear him out in the kitchen, tidying up the neglected Chinese food. I sat up in bed and watched the shadowy outline of his form through the open door. He'd returned to bed, his mouth finding mine again in the darkness.

"I'm sorry, Jay." I tried to push the feverish memories aside. "I overslept. I'm coming."

Jay's response was testy. "Aren't you supposed to be a rancher? Ted says you're always out of bed before the sun."

The mention of Ted's name was like a punch in the guts. A flood of remorse pooled through me.

What had I done? I'd slept with Wyatt. Whether I'd called off the engagement or not, I had definitely not left things with Ted in such a way that this turn of events was in any way defensible.

Whatever happened, I had to make sure Ted didn't find out about Wyatt from Jay. I needed to tell Ted about this myself. I owed him at least that much.

As I headed for the door, I noticed a small pad of hotel stationery on the kitchen counter, a ballpoint pen sitting next to it. The note was in Wyatt's slanted hand. "Had to run. Call me later?"

Jay stalked into my room the moment I managed to get the door open, my gaggle of stylists in tow. He stopped near the kitchen counter, resting his hand mere inches from the notepad off of which I had just ripped the top sheet. Wyatt's note was in my pocket. The suite, as far as I could tell, bore no traces of his stay.

Still, I was jittery as Jay's icy gaze swept the room. My style team filed past and began to set make-up bins and garment bags all around. For a moment, Jay's eyes flicked away from me. "Let's go, people." He spoke in a loud tone that was apparently supposed to be motivating. "We're running late, so we need to be efficient. Maggie, where's Spencer?"

Maggie looked up from hanging a garment bag over the back of the door that led into the bedroom. Beyond the door, I could see one of my socks poking out from beneath the bed. "Getting coffee and bagels. He'll be here in a minute."

Jay let out a short sigh and returned his attention to me. His eyes raked over me, narrowed slightly. "Nora." He dropped his voice so it wouldn't travel over the clatter and chatter of my style crew. "Is everything all right with you? I got a call this morning from the hotel manager. He said you got locked out of your room last night?"

I felt my face flush with embarrassment. "I was hoping they wouldn't bother you with that." I tried to look only marginally embarrassed but the knowledge of the note in my pocket was bright and uncomfortable in my mind, as if I expected a pat-down. "It was a stupid mistake. I went out into the hall without a key and I let the door close behind me."

Jay's expression did not change. His gaze made me want to squirm like a child who is blatantly lying to a parent who is not fooled in the least. He seemed to be trying to decide whether or not to push further. The question, "Why did you go out into the hall?" would have been an imminently logical place to start.

There was a tap on the door. One of the crew moved to answer. Spencer appeared, balancing a coffee caddy and clutching a bag of bagels to his chest.

Jay looked away for a moment, then back at me. He took in a slow breath. "You do realize the entire reason I'm on the ground here is to help you?" His expression as he spoke was as unreadable as ever. "The success of this event is important to the brand, and you are important to the success of this event."

I couldn't help but notice Jay's choice of words stopped short of saying I, personally, was important to the brand. But I didn't point this out. I did my best to look contrite.

"What I'm saying, Nora, is the reason I'm here is to fix it when you get locked out of your hotel room. Next time, call me. Got it?"

I looked up, unable to decide whether he was being supportive or invasive. "Got it."

Maggie stepped up behind us, clearing her throat and tapping her wrist, though she wasn't wearing a watch.

"Right." Jay turned from me and glanced towards the balcony doors. "Team," he raised his voice, "work your magic. I'm going out on the balcony to make some calls."

Jay strode across the room. Maggie stood with one hand on her slim hip, taking in my rumpled appearance.

I could imagine how I must look. My shirt was wrinkled from the night it had spent on the floor. My feet were bare. Wyatt's hands had spent a good deal of time in my hair last night. My lips felt a little raw from all the kissing.

I swallowed, wondering if it was obvious to all the people who were crammed into the suite but studiously not looking at me that I'd had sex last night. I looked at Maggie. Was it my imagination or was that the hint of a sly smile at the corner of her mouth?

I resisted the urge to attempt to smooth my hair. "I'm sorry about the late start."

Maggie pursed her lips, cocking her head to one side to look me over. "Don't apologize." Her tone was all business. "Sit your ass down so I can get started."

I moved, chastened, towards a chair. But as I brushed my hair back behind my shoulders, I got a telltale whiff of Wyatt—his fresh soap smell, and also something a little more masculine.

I changed my trajectory at the last minute. "I need to go take a quick shower first." I spoke hurriedly, scurrying towards the bedroom at speed, hoping no one here would believe they had the authority to stop me. I could see Jay on the balcony, gesturing and pacing as he spoke on the phone. "I'll be right back."

I darted into the bathroom and closed the door. I leaned against it for a moment, heart pounding, eyes shut. For a second, I let myself remember Wyatt's lips on mine. I felt a shudder of recalled pleasure

Then, with a sigh, I slipped out of my clothes and stepped into the shower.

I sat on the cold bleacher seat, wearing a baseball cap and a t-shirt. Although I could still feel remnants of my overdone make-up on my face and my fingernails still glittered with rhinestones, my duties as the TruGlide Girl were done for the weekend.

My ride on Snoopy had come early in the day, before the competitors had started work with their horses. I managed not to visibly wince each time I asked the horse to slide to a stop. The cheers had been a tad less thunderous than last time—a fact I blamed on the early hour. Nevertheless, Snoopy was once again well-received in our booth. During the break between the last hours of training time and the first competitor's obstacle course ride, droves of people came by to pose for photos and accept baggies of promotional materials.

Now, it was over. After that first break, Jay decided we'd done enough. Jay, who wasn't going to stay in Oklahoma another night, wanted to oversee Snoopy's departure for some unknown reason. The hauling service arrived less than twenty minutes after Jay released me and Snoopy from our booth in the vendor's area. It was a bit of a scramble to get his boots and blankets on and load him up.

Jay left shortly after Snoopy, as did my style team. The only other TruGlide representatives left were two bouncy girls who'd stayed to sit behind a table in the vendor area in case someone wanted more information about our product.

The day had been so busy I'd hardly had a chance to think about Wyatt, much less try to watch him work with his colt. I knew the day had been exciting. There had been cheers and moans from the crowd. Once or twice, I'd heard Wyatt's voice booming over the speakers or seen his face on one of the oversized screens that hung in the vendor area. But I hadn't been able to gather any kind of assessment on who was ahead, or who was behind.

The final rides had started by the time I was loading Snoopy. The competitors had drawn numbers. Wyatt was to compete last. Some riders would have considered this a disadvantage as it meant his horse would have the most rest before the obstacle course. Wyatt, however, had told me over our Chinese food the hardest part of this kind of competition was not wearing the horse down through over-exertion and stress. He liked them to still have something in the tank at the end. I thought he would be pleased with the order.

I'd had to return to my hotel with my style team during the second rider's final ride and had chafed at the delay as they'd denuded me of my costume. They'd left, I'd taken a second hasty shower, changed into the most nondescript outfit I'd brought with me, and dashed back to the performance arena.

As it was, I almost missed the beginning of Wyatt's ride. But I didn't. He stepped into the round pen where his horse waited as I settled myself into the empty row of seats Jay had reserved for our staff. Nobody, as far as I knew, had actually used them the entire event. They were good seats. I felt briefly guilty they'd been wasted.

Soon, however, I was too occupied in watching Wyatt to think about anything other than what was coming to pass in the arena below. Wyatt's colt was a tall, squarely made sorrel gelding. He had a small white star on his forehead but otherwise his burnished coat was a solid expanse of deep red. Wyatt, I knew, had chosen the colt for his athleticism.

Around me, the stands were full. I caught little snatches of the conversations taking place nearby. "... does this for a living ... " and "... think he'll win?" and "... he's so hot."

This last made me turn my head. The speaker was a teenaged girl. She sat amidst a cluster of her friends, all of them staring down with a kind of wistful hunger as Wyatt caught and saddled his horse.

I turned away from them, feeling a small, secret smile on my lips— the lips Wyatt had kissed last night.

A little rush of remembered emotion surged through me as I sat and watched Wyatt work his magic. I'd seen him start colts before, of course. I'd watched him do this dozens of times. A dozen more times, I'd been doing the same thing with another colt, me and him and Clint and my father all in the round pen together, working the youngsters as a group so they wouldn't feel so alone.

Wyatt had always loved putting those first rides on a group of young horses. It had been a contrast between him and my brother. Clint didn't mind the beginning of the training process, but it was the end he was really interested in. Clint started a lot of colts. Only a handful made the cut and progressed all the way into the bridle. It was the culmination of the journey that gave my brother satisfaction.

Wyatt always seemed to prefer the beginning. And I suppose it was an illustration of the irony of life that Clint always had more horses to start than he could quite keep up with while Wyatt had to rove around the country looking for people who would pay him to do what he loved.

I watched Wyatt as he saddled his colt, mounted, and began his ride. From where I sat, it looked effortless. Sure, the horse was obviously green. Watching him, I saw the shortcuts, the places he'd pushed more than he would usually have done in order to make things happen the way they needed to. But the horse wasn't stressed or troubled. At the end, after completing the obstacle course with plenty of time, Wyatt took off his hat and let the horse gallop around the arena, waving his hat at the cheering crowd.

Then he dismounted and his horse was led away. He went to stand with the other competitors.

Only the question of who would win remained.

Wyatt, I knew, didn't believe he would be given the victory. The event, after all, could hardly be judged without a degree of partiality. Unless only one competitor managed to complete the ride, he believed the judges would skew towards the big names.

I thought about this belief as I sat and waited for the judges to tally scores. The arena was cleared of the obstacle course. A trophy saddle, an easel with a giant painting of a herd of horses running, and various other gaudy prizes were carried out and set up on display. I couldn't help but think Wyatt's ride had seemed as flawless to me as you could expect from a horse that green.

I hadn't seen the other rides but I knew Tim Moriarty's horse refused two obstacles and he'd taken the longest time. It seemed Wyatt's previous assessment about that trainer had been correct.

As far as I knew, the other two competitors, Keith Walker and Lea Norther, hadn't made any serious errors. Which meant Wyatt was right. It was more likely to come down to factors more subtle than the question of who had the best final ride.

Around me, the arena was hushed. The announcer, filling time, went through a brief recap of previous winners, the evolution of the competition's rules, and thanked a short list of sponsors and important people. I waited, feeling my stomach kink with anxious concern. From the way he'd spoken the night before, I knew Wyatt didn't expect to win. But that didn't mean he didn't want to.

I tried to think about what a win like this would mean for Wyatt's life in practical terms. It seemed unlikely he'd have trouble finding work for a while. With the level of recognition this kind of event would give him, he'd probably have more than he could keep up with. He might be able to have people ship their horses to him, which meant he would travel less.

The thought popped into my head just like that—a thought I'd been trying to avoid all day. I tried to push it out again. But it was as stuck as a colt feeling a halter for the first time. It dug in and wouldn't budge.

Wyatt was going to leave.

This was a fact. It wasn't a question of if, but one of when. I knew this because Wyatt always left. He'd been doing it my entire life. One day, he'd be there—his smiles and easy conversation a stark contrast to my brother's quiet, solemn ways. It would seem, for a while, he was always there. I'd turn around to see him watching me. There would be moments he seemed to turn up in places just so we could exchange a little flurry of bantering remarks. This would seem to happen more and more. I'd accumulate a list of things to grow excited about. I'd track them, add them up, and try to measure their worth.

Then, when I was convinced, finally, there *was* something between Wyatt and me, he would leave. It would be months before I saw him again. When he came back, the cycle would start all over.

Wyatt was standing between Tim Moriarty and Lea Norther. I was too far away to see his face but his stance looked relaxed. The other three competitors had tension in them. Not Wyatt. Wyatt looked like he couldn't care less who walked away with this victory.

In a few minutes, that tension would be broken. The announcer would open an envelope and read a name.

Then what? Would Wyatt go back to his truck and drive out of my life again? Or would he go back to the Tipped Z?

And if he did go back to the Tipped Z, would what had transpired here, between us, make any difference?

Last night, in bed with Wyatt, it had felt like a beginning. Now, as I sat alone on the bleachers surrounded by a massive crowd of strangers, I wasn't so sure.

The thought of returning to the ranch lowered my mood another few notches. Suddenly all I could think about were the problems. I would have to give Ted's ring back. I was certain he wouldn't let me go easily. I knew he was planning something—some means of persuading me we should go on, that we were good together.

Then there was Snoopy. There would be x-rays and an official diagnosis. There would be arguments with Jay about what was best for the horse versus what was best for TruGlide.

And there would be Wyatt. Or there wouldn't be Wyatt. If he won, I couldn't see him returning to our obscure ranch where his newfound recognition would be of little use to him. If he lost, I couldn't see him returning either. He'd be restless, wanting new horizons, new colts to start, new experiences.

In short, I couldn't see how this was going to work out at all.

The realization I would never have Wyatt the way I wanted came upon me in a wave of startling clarity. It settled like a chilling fog. I sat in the bleachers, suddenly cold. Jay had booked the suite for another night but he'd also told me there was an evening flight back to Tucson. My ticket was transferrable if I didn't want to stay. When he'd mentioned this earlier today, I'd thanked him as a giddy rush of adrenaline had swirled through my veins. I'd thought of Wyatt's note. *Call me later?* I'd convinced myself I would want the suite because Wyatt would again help me make use of it.

Now, I watched the group of trainers laugh at something Wyatt said. My expectations seemed flimsy and girlish. If Wyatt won, he'd have better things to do tonight than hang out with me. If he lost, he'd be itching to hit the road.

I stood up. The muscles in my legs were tight and stiff. I paused to let them unkink.

I don't know how Wyatt saw me. I was not the only person standing in the bleachers. The crowd was waiting, with people milling around the seats. I could not have been distinct and noticeable.

But as soon as I stood, Wyatt's head turned. I saw him see me. He was smiling, but he'd been smiling before. He made a waving gesture with his hand that seemed to say, "Come here."

I sat down again. I saw Wyatt dig in his pocket for his phone. A moment later, a text arrived. "Are you done with TruGlide stuff? Will you come down? There's a place for our important people."

So I was down on ground level, standing with the parents and wives and husbands and children of the other competitors, when Wyatt's name, at last, boomed over the speakers.

I was watching him, of course. After I received his text, he'd left his place in the arena to meet me at security. Wyatt had given me a quick kiss on the forehead that left my veins buzzing with adrenaline. He'd whispered, "Thanks for coming down."

Then he'd been gone, hurrying back to his place in the arena. I'd watched him, my eyes fixed on his broad back, his firm profile.

The announcer didn't do anything gimmicky, like list the 4th place contestant first. As the arena quieted in anticipation of the announcement, he opened the envelope, paused a moment, and read. "And the winner of *Start the Horse, Connect the Heart* is Wyatt Lewis."

I saw Wyatt stiffen. His shoulders and back went rigid. His muscles seemed to freeze. Then he looked over his shoulder. His eyes searched out mine as if to say, "Is this real?"

For a single instant, our eyes held. There was a millisecond of delay as the news sank in. Then the arena erupted into cheers. One of the other competitors clapped Wyatt on the shoulder. Wyatt turned, grinning, and shook hands with those he had defeated.

I was also there, standing next to him, when he received the oversized check and the prizes and gave his brief acceptance speech. It wasn't until later this struck me as a little sad. The other competitors all had a small crowd to attend them. If I hadn't been there, Wyatt would have been alone.

In the end, Wyatt and I did return to my hotel suite. We passed a quiet night together. I watched Wyatt process his win. It stunned him. "Lea's horse," he said multiple times, "was just as settled as mine."

In the morning, Wyatt drove me to the airport. He'd be heading back to the Tipped Z the long way. He'd borrowed Rascal, my brother's flashy black bridle horse, to ride in the performances. He asked if I wanted to ride back with him.

I did want to ride back with Wyatt. But I knew I could not. Snoopy would be returning to the Tipped Z soon. I needed to be there to receive him. I needed to tell Ted we were over. I needed to stand up to Jay about Snoopy and force him to do the right thing.

So I stepped out of Wyatt's truck in the predawn chill outside the Oklahoma City airport as slow traffic drifted around us. Wyatt handed me my little suitcase. His hand was warm where it brushed against mine.

As I wrapped my fingers around the plastic handle, Wyatt encircled me in his arms. He wore a plain t-shirt, sneakers, a pair of jeans, and the old baseball cap. He hadn't shaved. I felt the scratch of his chin as he kissed my forehead.

At his touch, little bursts of adrenaline deployed all over my body. Wyatt, I was learning, was like a drug. He was addictive. The more I had him, the more I wanted him. In two days, I'd grown ridiculously accustomed to having him near me, to looking to him when I had something to say, to knowing he was nearby and I was on his mind.

What would happen now? I wanted to think we'd return to the ranch and things would be there as they were here.

But I didn't believe that.

So I stood a moment longer than I would have, soaking in the feeling of his warm arms. He spoke, murmuring the words near my ear. "I hope you have a good flight."

I took a step back, looking up into his face. No matter what happened, I told myself, I would never let the memory of this weekend turn sour. Even if we got back to the ranch and suddenly Wyatt was distant again, coming and going, never settling down—even if this thing between us turned out to be nothing but a weekend of high spirits and loneliness, I would never forget what it felt like to be the one Wyatt wanted.

"And you drive safe." I gave his arm a little punch, as if he was typically reckless while hauling horse-trailers across the country and I couldn't be assured of his good behavior without extracting this promise.

He kissed me one more time. Then I was turning, walking away, heading towards the sliding doors that led into the terminal. The wheels of my suitcase stuttered every few strides as they bumped over the seams of the sidewalk. My heart seemed to be beating too hard in my chest.

I merged with the flow of bleary-eyed, luggage-laden people moving towards the doors. Before stepping inside, I looked back. Wyatt stood by the open door of his truck, watching me. When he saw me look, he winked. Then he climbed into his cab and drove away.

Chapter 12

Erin picked me up from the airport. Landing in Arizona felt like emerging from a luminous fairytale back into the mundane reality of everyday life. Everything felt too bright and too harsh.

Erin was driving her little car and smiling at me through the windshield. I waved as she eased up to the curb. I looked at her the way the returned survivor of a shipwreck might regard old friends and family—astonished my experiences hadn't somehow left a physical impression on her.

My sister-in-law looked just the same. She hugged me after I set my suitcase in the trunk. She felt small in my arms. Her shoulders were slight in comparison to Wyatt's. Her smell was distinctly more feminine.

"How was everything?" Erin asked the question as she put her car in gear and we drifted away from the airport terminal. I wondered where Wyatt was—how far he'd gotten since he'd dropped me off that morning. It was now late afternoon. The sun was intense, spilling out of a flat, brilliant sky.

I told Erin everything. At first I intended to summarize, leaving out key details like the fact I'd slept with Wyatt. But I've never had a very good filter. With Erin, it's particularly bad. Something about the quiet, attentive way she listens, asking just the right question whenever I stall, prevents me from holding anything back.

We were in my apartment, mostly through a beer, by the time I finished my story. The drive alone had turned out not to be long enough to explain everything. We progressed from Snoopy to Ted to Wyatt, the story seeming to grow less plausible with every turn. When I told her about standing by Wyatt's side as he accepted the gigantic check of his winnings, Erin stopped me. "Wait." She looked confused. "What was this event again? He said he was going to a colt-starting. He needed a seasoned horse, so Clint loaned him Rascal. Weren't you at some reining expo?"

Gradually, I managed to explain. As my words sank in, Erin grew quieter and quieter. I got to the part where now I was home. I didn't know how things would be with Wyatt but I had to officially end things with Ted and maybe refuse to ride Snoopy anymore. With that summary of the situation, my outpouring ceased.

Silence fell. My apartment was dim and cool, most of the blinds drawn over windows. Erin picked at the label on her beer bottle, her brow furrowed. She looked up and I could see the concern in her eyes. "You really don't want to marry Ted?" The question was hesitant. "You guys have always seemed so good together."

I felt a pang at her comment. Ted and I had been good together. Right up until he'd started forcing all his strange expectations on me.

I shook my head. "We were good for a while. But I see now Ted and I don't want the same things."

Erin set her bottle aside, sitting up straighter. We were in my small sitting area. I was perched on the edge of the couch, Erin was curled up in an armchair I'd found on the street corner in my college days when I'd been living in the dorms. It had taken me and my roommate an hour to maneuver it up the stairwell, laughing helplessly the whole time.

"Do you think so? You don't think it's not all a misunderstanding? He doesn't seem like the kind of guy who would be trying to force you down a path you don't want to take."

A cold feeling began to settle over me. The elated excitement I'd been feeling as I told Erin my story began to cool. I looked at her and she met my gaze. "You don't think I should leave Ted for Wyatt." I couldn't keep a mild tone of accusation out of my voice.

Erin sighed. She looked back down at her beer bottle, rotating it with two fingers. "I think you should leave Ted because you want to leave Ted, not because you want to be with Wyatt. Wyatt ..." Erin paused, her face twisting in a little grimace. "Wyatt's not reliable, Nora."

I felt a surge of anger at her words. What did Erin know about Wyatt? She'd met him only a few months before. He'd arrived, just like he said he would, to be my brother's best man.

I sat up straighter, feeling color come into my cheeks. I was about to retort, but Erin held up her hand. "No, Nora." She sounded sad. "I didn't come to that conclusion on my own. It's what Clint says about him."

That shocked me to silence. My brother was not prone to making judgmental pronouncements. He also wasn't one for bad-mouthing his friends.

The words took the heat right out of me. I sank back against the couch cushions, remembering the train of thought I'd had as Wyatt drove away from the airport. "You're right." My whole body felt cold and stiff. "And I know that. And you're also right about Ted. But what happened with Ted and what happened with Wyatt are separate. I don't want to marry Ted. Even if Wyatt takes Rascal and flees for Canada, I still don't want that."

The words were true. I could feel their veracity as I spoke. Saying them out loud was liberating.

Whatever happened with Wyatt, Ted and I were done. I knew at least that much.

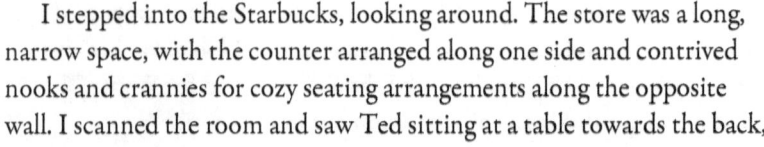

I stepped into the Starbucks, looking around. The store was a long, narrow space, with the counter arranged along one side and contrived nooks and crannies for cozy seating arrangements along the opposite wall. I scanned the room and saw Ted sitting at a table towards the back, two coffees steaming on the table before him. I was five minutes early but Ted had clearly planned to arrive well ahead of me.

Meeting for coffee had been Ted's idea. I'd tried to demur, suggesting something later in the day. He'd pressed. I'd given in. Snoopy wasn't due to arrive until later, so my morning was free.

For a moment, I stood in the doorway. Ted hadn't seen me. He was gazing off to the side, looking out a window. He looked good, sitting there. His face was kind, his clothing in style without quite being stylish. He was a fit, successful, attractive man.

And I didn't want him at all.

I made myself move forward, weaving around the back of two oddly shaped orange armchairs and approaching Ted's table, steeling myself for the conversation I knew was coming. I'd spent the morning giving myself mental pep talks. *Be kind but firm. Do not allow yourself to be persuaded to try again. Nothing he can do or say changes the fundamental fact you don't love him.*

At last, Ted saw me coming. He looked up. I expected him to rise, to kiss me, to hold my chair as I sat down.

He did none of these things.

I walked around to my chair. There was something hollow behind Ted's eyes as he watched me hang my purse on the back and settle into my seat. I began to worry. Had something happened? Was Ted secretly dying of cancer? Had he lost his job?

"Thanks for the coffee." I pulled my cup towards me, feeling the warmth on my palms.

"No problem." Ted's voice was stressed. His smile had a faded look and his face was hollow—haunted somehow.

I understood. Ted, somehow, must have found out about Wyatt.

I didn't understand how it could have happened but the signs were too clear to dismiss. I resisted the urge to start explaining, to launch into some preemptive defense. I took a sip of my coffee. It was something light and creamy and there was too much sugar in it.

"You had an easy flight?" Ted's tone was listless. I told him my flight was fine, remembering the way Wyatt had winked at me from next to his truck.

Ted drew in a long breath and sat up straighter. He set his palms on the table as if preparing to push himself to his feet. He looked at my hand, my bare finger. He seemed to speak without meaning to. "Was he there when you called me? Listening? Did you break it off with me to make yourself feel a little better about climbing into bed with another man?"

It was such a bitter, harsh question. I sat a moment in stunned surprise. Ted's face had morphed into an expression I'd never seen before—a twisted, jealous snarl.

I considered my options. Ted couldn't know, whatever he'd heard, that I'd slept with Wyatt. He was guessing. Jay must have said something to him. After all, the desk attendant who had unlocked my suite would have known there was a man with me. She must have told the manager, who would have told Jay. Jay would also have noted my rumpled appearance and oversleeping the next morning.

Still, it was pure conjecture. No one had any evidence.

For a moment, indignation flowed through me. That Ted would accuse me this way was outrageous. It was insulting.

I almost snapped back at him. But I checked myself in time. Ted, I reminded myself, was looking for reason in something that seemed senseless.

I reached into my purse and drew out the box he'd given me at his house that night. The ring was inside, nestled in its little creased velvet pillow. I pushed the ring towards him on the table. "I called off the engagement because I wasn't happy. Our relationship hasn't felt right to me for months."

Ted stared at the box. His eyes had gone red around the rims. His mouth was a hard, bitter line. "Since Wyatt arrived? Is that about when things started going wrong?"

"Since you manipulated me into taking this shitty job." I couldn't help it. The words snapped out as I felt my cool evaporate. "Wyatt has nothing to do with this, Ted. The problems between us are about you, and me, and you trying to make me into something I'm not. I've never felt so cheapened and objectified. And you don't see it. Hell, you like it. You and Jay are like my little puppeteer team, turning me into something more fake and more vapid by the week."

I forced myself to stop. I was breathing harder than usual. I could feel a torrent of words all dammed up, bursting to be released. I wanted to say mean things to Ted, to make him feel some of the humiliation I had felt when I had to go out in public wearing a little black cape festooned with fake sparkly stones.

But I held back. Lashing out would make things worse.

To divert myself, I sipped my overly sweet coffee and waited for Ted's response. He was staring at me with an expression of disbelief that seemed to suggest I'd slapped him. "Jay and I have been helping you." He spoke in a tone of outraged indignation. "We've been working to advance your career."

I pushed the mug away. This was pointless. We were never going to be able to have a civil conversation. Still, I couldn't seem to help myself. "Did it never occur to you I might not want the kind of help you've been forcing on me? That your idea of a career for me is insulting and demeaning? Would you be happy, Ted, being a glorified underwear model with one or two stage tricks and a whole team of stylists?"

Ted had been looking angrier and angrier. But my question seemed to stop him short. He blinked as if I'd dumped cold water on his head.

I pressed my advantage. "The very implication you think this role is a great opportunity shows how little you respect me, how little potential you think I have."

Ted, suddenly, looked defeated. He closed his eyes and rubbed his temples, his shoulders sagging. This was actually one of the things I'd always liked about Ted. He wasn't the type of man to defend a point past reason. He could concede when he was wrong.

I waited. Around us, the coffee shop hummed with the hiss of espresso machines, the clink of cutlery, and the low murmur of conversation. I wondered how often things like this happened here. How many small, significant moments played out at these cozy tables?

Ted drew in a deep breath. "You're right." He cupped his hands around his coffee, tone hollow. He was looking at the ring box rather than me. "I never saw it before. I thought you wanted to be a performer. I thought this would be a more active role for you. But that isn't how it's worked out."

We sat in silence. I waited for the inevitable shift, the suggestion he could help me find a new career, we could start fresh.

But Ted didn't suggest that. He sighed, reached out, and picked up the ring box. He stowed it in the pocket of his jeans. I noticed his mug was empty. "But you did sleep with Wyatt this weekend?" His tone was dull and mild, not angry or accusatory.

"When I broke things off with you, I didn't even know Wyatt would be there. It was a surprise the next day when I found out he was in the competition."

Ted looked up, unimpressed. "But you slept with him."

I didn't answer. Which was its own admission.

Ted nodded. He stood up. With a sense of shock, I realized he wasn't going to try to get me back. For one ridiculous moment, I felt offended.

He stood there, looking down at me, his hand on the back of his chair. His eyes were full of pain and resignation but he was taking it about as gracefully as could be expected.

I looked up at him, feeling guilty. I almost apologized. But I stopped myself. I had nothing to apologize for. This was life. It sucked sometimes.

Ted stood a moment longer, his glasses winking as he turned his head. "I wish things had worked out differently."

I decided I could be generous enough to give him this one lie. "Me too."

I watched Esperanza's gleaming haunches flex and coil as the filly trotted up the hill. Erin sat on her back, looking relaxed and confident. I pushed Sally into a trot to keep up.

We reached the top of the ridge and Erin stopped. Esperanza was a little sweaty but showed no signs of stress. The filly sighed and cocked her hip as soon as Erin offered her a rest.

It was Sunday—nearly a week since I'd returned from my trip to Oklahoma. It had been a busy week. While I'd been gone, I discovered, my brother had convinced Erin that Esperanza was ready to leave the arena. They'd ridden out together several times. Clint had complimented the filly's behavior. This had launched Erin into an elated state of pride and confidence and made me slightly jealous. After all, I'd been the one to help Erin through all the preparation. And then my brother swooped in at the last minute and stole the prize?

I didn't really mind, though. It was enough to see Erin now, sitting on her filly and looking happy. Of course, they were nowhere near the end of the road. Esperanza was very young. Young horses were never entirely predictable. Still, we had enough to do around the ranch we kept our horses pretty busy, which meant they had less opportunity to get into trouble.

Erin and I were on our way back from replacing the hinge on a gate that had gone rusty and stiff. It had been the kind of job that required more riding than work: my favorite type.

Now, the sun was falling. The heat of the day was still thick around us. But I didn't mind. It felt good to be back on the ranch. It felt good to be away from the clang and echo of the cavernous performance arena, to be out under the sun.

Still, life wasn't all flowers and bubblegum. I was adjusting to the strange reality that I was single. Whatever had happened with Wyatt had clearly turned out to be temporary, because (surprise, surprise) he was not here. He'd returned Rascal some time in the middle of the night two days ago and driven off again without speaking to anyone. I tried not to let this fact tie my stomach into kinks and make me sweat bullets. I wasn't always successful. I kept hearing Erin's words. *He's not reliable.*

Wyatt wasn't reliable. It was such a damning indictment because it was true. Clint hadn't said his old friend wasn't trustworthy or he was a womanizer or he wasn't fiscally responsible. He'd laid out the simple, bare truth.

Wyatt wasn't reliable. He wasn't there when you needed him.

I sighed, shifting in my saddle and trying to turn my mind to other things. But Erin glanced at me and I could see the sympathy in her eyes. It didn't take someone nearly as perceptive and observant as Erin to guess how I was feeling. When Rascal had reappeared without Wyatt, even Clint had seemed stunned. He'd been in a bad mood for the rest of the week. The hand he'd hired hadn't worked out, so the ranch was short-staffed again.

The only good news all week seemed to be my father. The day before, I'd seen him ride out with the reins in his left hand. No one made any remark. But the sight had filled me with a kind of giddy relief. Later that day, he'd tossed a shot at a difficult angle, dallied with perfect timing, and laid down a calf like he'd taught us to. "If you take off any skin," he'd told us when we were kids, "you go to bed without supper."

I don't recall my father ever sending us to bed hungry—but we took his point. A cowboy cared for his animals. You had to rope livestock sometimes but you didn't have to do it in a way that hurt them.

Erin reached down and gave Esperanza some slow, firm rubs on the neck. In the distance a string of cattle appeared, trailing their slow way across the horizon. Erin's filly perked up, her head popping higher to track the movement.

"Sometimes," Erin said in a careful tone, "I think certain things happen to give us clarity on other things."

I released a small snort of a laugh. I knew what she was trying to do. It wasn't going to work. "So I had to sleep with Wyatt so I could use that as a reason to break up with Ted, only to realize Wyatt doesn't want me after all?"

Erin gave me a sympathetic look. The cattle disappeared into a gully. Esperanza's head dropped back down. "I don't think it's that Wyatt doesn't want you. I think Wyatt wants freedom to the detriment of everything else. But at least you know that now. It's a clean break. No more Ted. No more Wyatt. A fresh start."

I considered her words. I wasn't sure Wyatt did want freedom. His wandering had always seemed unhappy to me—the pacing of a frustrated predator who finds itself confined to an environment that doesn't meet its basic evolutionary needs. "Now if I could just figure out a way to quit my job," I said, "I could sell all my belongings and flee to India and you could write one of those self-discovery novels about my amazing journey of change."

Erin grimaced. I knew she was trying to help. The problem was, there wasn't much anyone could say that would make me feel better. The fact of Wyatt's disappearance was like a knife to the gut—a messy, painful wound that would take a long time to kill.

Behind us, the sun dropped behind the mountains. I straightened in my saddle. "We'd better get back."

Erin nodded and moved out again. Esperanza was tired but the filly moved willingly enough. As we crossed the ridge and picked our way down the other side, the trail split. One way led back to the Tipped Z. The other, which was overgrown and faded to merely a faint hint of the trail that used to be there, led directly to a distant fence.

As we moved past the fork, Erin turned to look at me. "Where did that trail used to go? I always mean to ask Clint but we don't go this way often."

I looked beyond the fence. We were at the edge of the Tipped Z's land. The fence bisected a valley that ended in a low range of foothills. On the other side of the foothills was a subdivision. I felt a sad twist in my stomach. "It used to be the Rocking J. That was the ranch Wyatt's family owned. His father refused to help when the ranch was in trouble and Wyatt's grandfather had to sell it to a developer. We could have houses all the way up to the fence someday, I guess."

Erin faced forward again. "That's so depressing."

I considered the path for a moment. It was faint and overgrown but the sand was turned up here and there, as if someone had recently ridden across it.

Erin was right. It was depressing and there wasn't much else to say. The sun was sinking. Our horses were tired. We walked for another minute or two, then Erin pushed Esperanza into a trot, heading home.

I opened Snoopy's stall door and watched him amble out the aisle and into his pen. His stride was short and inhibited. Although I hadn't ridden him since we'd returned from the show, it was evident he hadn't recovered from all the time in the trailer. It was looking increasingly likely he never would.

Our vet had come out to do the x-rays. He'd turned up what we'd feared. Snoopy had bone spavin and had likely been receiving hock injections for some time. He also had arthritis and tissue degeneration around the joint in both legs. In short, it was only a matter of time before the horse was completely lame.

I followed Snoopy into his pen and swung the gate shut. He walked to his pile of hay and sniffed at it, then raised his head to watch a herd of horses moving in the distance. It was a fine, cool morning. We'd had a monsoon the night before. The air and sky had a clean, scrubbed feel to them. Although it was technically against the terms of our boarding agreement with the TruGlide Corporation, I'd removed Snoopy's fly sheet. He stood in the pale light, practically glowing. His remarkable silver coat shone. I wondered with a sad twist of the gut what would have become of this horse if he hadn't been such a looker. Would he have had a better life?

Maybe. But then again, maybe not. The same thing that had happened to Snoopy was done to plenty of unremarkably colored two-year-olds every year.

I didn't know what was going to happen with Snoopy. The knowledge his fate was out of my hands made me melancholy. He was performance bred, he was half lame, and he'd arrived here a total basket-case. He would never be a useful horse. Yet, somehow, I'd gotten attached to him. He'd come around. He was no longer the spastic, unpredictable creature that had come off the trailer. He was content, standing there in his pen, watching the horizon.

I was about to turn, to get started with my day's work, when I heard the thud of boot heels in the hay room. For a moment, I felt a stir of hope and anticipation. But it wasn't Wyatt. Wyatt was not here. I glanced behind me to see my brother's lean form materializing out of the early morning shadows that clung to the interior of the barn.

I stayed where I was. Something about Clint's stride suggested he was on his way in my direction. But he detoured. For a moment, I thought I'd been mistaken. Then I heard the shift of his footsteps as he left the dirt floor of the hay room and stepped onto the concrete of the stall aisle.

A moment later, my brother was standing next to me. After spending more time around Wyatt, I had almost forgotten how tall and lanky Clint was. He came to a stop next to me, following my gaze to Snoopy. Then I heard a snuffle. I turned to see Clint was carrying a puppy.

Lop was the last of Peach's litter. The rest had been placed in homes over the course of the last few weeks. My brother was protective of his bloodlines, picky about who he sold to. He also kept the pups much longer than most breeders did. Lop was a gangly thing these days, nearly four months old.

As I turned towards Clint, my brother dumped the puppy into my arms. Lop, delighted, squirmed up in an attempt to lick my face. He was a warm, fuzzy bundle of wiry hair and soft skin. I laughed and blocked his advances, rubbing his ears in consolation.

I had always thought Lop the pick of the litter. That he was the last of the puppies to go seemed to indicate Clint agreed with me. I was wondering if Clint intended to keep the dog himself. But as I stooped to set the puppy down, Clint spoke. "He's yours if you'll take him."

I stopped in surprise. Lop wiggled up and managed to score a lick on my chin with his soft, warm tongue.

I found myself with nothing to say. Clint's offer made no sense. I'd never had a dog. My father always emphasized dogs were tools. Those of us who were not around enough to keep one trained and useful were not authorized to keep them on the premises. I couldn't have a dog in my apartment. Any dog of mine would have to live here.

I set Lop down. The puppy collapsed at my feet in a heap, rolling onto his back and waving his oversized paws in the air. I rubbed his belly.

Clint watched us with a gentle expression. "He's a good dog. Too good to sell. But I've got Dots and dad is ..." he paused, searching for a way to say it. "Dad is getting older."

I straightened. Lop scrambled up, mottled coat now full of small bits of hay and clinging dust. He sneezed, walked closer, and sat down on my foot.

I closed my eyes for a moment. I knew what Clint was doing. This was one more piece in his plot to bind me to the ranch. If I had a puppy here, that puppy would need training. No promising get of Peach's line would be allowed to become a pet. "I wouldn't know where to start with training him."

Clint was gazing out at Snoopy. "I'll help." His voice was deep and certain. "And Erin can, too. It will be a good chance to learn, for both of you."

I regarded my brother's profile. I seemed to see a younger Clint—my teenaged brother—within this handsome rancher. I knew what Clint looked like when he fell off a horse and sat up in the arena, palms bleeding. I'd seen him cry. I'd seen him hurt. I'd seen him so angry he couldn't speak.

Now, I thought I was seeing something else. There was a tension in his shoulders, a set to his jaw.

My brother, I realized, was afraid.

He turned, at last, to look at me. His intense gaze seemed to bore into mine. When he spoke, his voice was choked and a little pleading. "I can't run this place alone, Nora. What happened with Dad ..."

He trailed off. I stood, feeling frozen, feeling trapped. I looked away from my brother, out at the horizon, and felt that complicated jangle of emotions that always came with thoughts of the ranch and my place here. I understood my brother was asking me for help. But I still didn't know if I could be the one to give it.

Off in the distance, we heard the quiet purr of a motor. We both turned as an unfamiliar car nosed its way past the electric gate and rolled towards the barn.

Clint and I both stared, dumbfounded, at the car approaching on the dirt drive. It was a sleek, gleaming thing with chrome wheels and slim tires that seemed offended by the very fact some roads in this world were not paved.

In the hay room, Chet, Fuzzface, Peach, and Dots all came to life and stirred themselves to alertness. The four dogs moved in stiff unison, heading towards the vehicle. Lop stood up as if to join them but I scooped him back into my arms. "Oh no you don't," I murmured. He squirmed for a moment but subsided.

Clint had gone as stiff as the dogs. He bent and stepped through the gate into Snoopy's pen then just as quickly stepped through the fence so he was in the parking area. He strode towards the approaching vehicle with the same sort of tense, alert watchfulness the dogs were displaying. I almost laughed. We were used to trucks around here, not gleaming Beamers with tinted windows.

Encumbered by Lop, I decided to go the long way around. I walked back down the barn aisle, through the hay room, and out the small door that led to the parking area. The car had drifted to an uncertain halt beside my massive, ancient Dodge. I couldn't see who was behind the wheel.

I suppose it shouldn't have surprised me when the door opened and Jay appeared, stepping out and blinking in the morning sun. He looked at the dogs and my brother and seemed to shrink, not moving out from behind the car door. He spoke. The voice I had heard sounding intimidating and firm so many times now seemed weak and quavering. "I'm Jay Hazen, head of marketing, TruGlide Corporation." When this elicited no response from my brother, he looked more worried. "That," he said, pointing at Snoopy, "is my horse."

I stepped around the hood of my truck, moving into view. Jay saw me and a look of relief crossed his pale face. "Nora." He stepped out from behind the door at last, as if only my presence had convinced him my brother and the pack of dogs would not fall on him and rip him to pieces. "Is this the welcome you give all your boarders?"

He said it with a small smile, as if he was joking, but I could see he was annoyed.

My brother spoke a word. The dogs dispersed, disappearing back into the barn. I set Lop down as well. The puppy bounded towards Jay as if they were long-lost-friends. Jay stared down at the puppy as if he was a disease-carrying mutt. "Lop," I said, "here." The puppy froze. Clint had been teaching him basic obedience practically since birth. But still, I could see the resistance in the young animal as he turned and came back to me. "Sit," I said. He sat on my foot. I stooped down to pet his ears.

Jay looked from me to Clint and back again. I realized he was waiting for a response. Clint spoke, seeming to connect the dots. "I'm sorry, Mr. Hazen. We didn't know to expect you." He stepped forward and offered Jay his hand.

Jay let the car door fall closed and stepped forward as well. They met between my truck and Jay's gleaming rental. Jay wore fine slacks and a rich shirt open at the throat. His hair was gelled and arranged to perfection. My brother wore old jeans, worn chinks, and well-heeled boots.

The two men shook.

"I came to see the horse." Jay squinted towards Snoopy, letting his hand fall back to his side. "I showed the x-rays to two more vets. They both go on as if the animal shouldn't even be able to walk. I saw him at the most recent event and he looked fine. Of course, I understand he was drugged then. I may not be a horse expert but I do need to make a decision on behalf of my company. If the animal has become a liability, we need to take steps to minimize the damage to our bottom line."

I stared at Jay as he spoke. Lop shifted so his wiry body was slouched against my leg. I shouldn't let him lean on me, I knew, but I found the warm weight comforting. The words Jay was choosing, his tone and posture, all seemed to suggest he was talking about a piece of equipment, or perhaps a building. Not a living, breathing animal.

Jay stopped talking. Clint looked in my direction. I gave him my best pleading look. Somehow, I knew, Jay wouldn't listen to me. I'd already told him what I thought about Snoopy's condition. When Jay looked at me, he saw the glitzy, vapid creature he hired people to take photographs of. Not a human with a functional brain.

My brother's eyes flicked down to Lop, then back to me. I gave the faintest of nods.

And just like that, Clint and I struck our bargain. I'd take on Lop if he would get Jay to see that Snoopy could no longer perform.

Clint's mode shifted. He straightened and loosened at the same time. When he spoke, his tone was relaxed and friendly. I had seen my brother in this mode before, of course. But it was one he assumed rarely around friends and family. It was his horse salesman mode.

He turned and moved towards the corral, forcing Jay to drift after him. "The thing about hock injuries," he said smoothly, "is they can be hard to spot at first. Maybe the horse seems a little stiff now and then, but it goes away as he warms up. What Snoopy has, bone spavin, is degenerative. So while he's not in a lot of pain right now, hard riding will make him a lot worse, very quickly."

I hung back. My brother and Jay reached the fence. I'd told Erin all about Snoopy, his condition, my fears for what Jay would decide to do with him, as well as my personal plan for how I thought he could still serve the TruGlide Corporation despite his lameness. I knew she'd relayed it all to Clint.

Now, my brother neatly summed it all up as Jay listened, moving as smoothly through the facts as if he and I had just had a long conversation about this ourselves.

It surprised me, a little. I'd thought Clint uninterested in Snoopy. I'd thought Clint too preoccupied with the goings-on around the ranch to pay particular attention to the details of my life.

I looked down at Lop as my brother and my boss continued to converse. The pup looked up at me. He had one tiny fleck of blue in his left eye, only visible when his head was cocked at certain angles. "I guess I have a dog." He yawned, grinning. I sighed, then stepped forward to join the conversation.

"I'm pretty sure it's against some Tipped Z code of ethics to be wrangled into a last-minute job without any explanation."

I spoke from astride Sally. We were riding away from the ranch house, following Erin as the rode Duke along the little single track.

Erin looked over her shoulder, grinning. "Just a little farther." She reached back to pat Duke's dappled rump as she spoke. I didn't know why she was riding the steady old gelding instead of Esperanza. So far, Erin had offered me no explanation whatsoever about where we were going, or why. She'd found me as I'd been ready to head home, entertaining thoughts of a warm bath and maybe some Chinese food.

It had been a long day. Between the training I was doing with Lop and the two new colts Clint had convinced me to start, it had been a week of long days.

We rode in silence for a time. The trail wound around the base of a small hill. Erin stopped there in the shade of a large mesquite.

I let Sally drift up and stop next to Duke. Erin was gazing out at the blank horizon. I looked in the same direction with confusion. It was late in the day on Thursday. The day Jay had shown up at the Tipped Z, he and Clint had discussed the matter of Snoopy at some length. As far as I knew, no decisions had been made. Jay hadn't said as much, but I got the feeling my entire job hinged on what happened with the silvery horse. I'd become slowly aware there was nothing on my calendar. Jay hadn't booked me for a single event, appearance, or even photoshoot since we'd been to *Start the Horse, Connect the Heart*. This realization had been growing to feel increasingly ominous as the days dragged by.

Between all that and Wyatt's continued absence, I was feeling a little less patient than usual. "Erin," I said in my best plaintive tone. "What are we *doing* out here?"

Erin gave a small smirk but said nothing. Duke sighed and cocked a hip. I pulled my hat brim a little lower to shade my eyes against the late sun. I gave Sally a conciliatory pat on the neck, as if she was the one who was missing out on a bath and an easy dinner.

We sat there. As the moments dragged by, it became clear we were waiting for something. We didn't speak. But I watched Erin. She seemed smug at first. Then the smugness faded to restless worry. She'd devolved to fiddling with her reins and checking her phone every ten seconds when I finally spotted the plume of dust on the horizon.

It was coming from the northeast—the direction Erin and I had gone the day we took Esperanza out to fix the gate.

Erin saw it too. She perked up. The two horses also shifted their attention, straightening up, ears swiveling forward.

A speck appeared at the base of the dust plume, and the speck materialized into a man. The man was familiar in a way that made my heart seize, then start pounding.

I recognized that set of the shoulders, the easy way he rode the horse's long trot.

It was Wyatt.

I turned to Erin, disbelief making all the words I might have spoken jumble in my throat and get stuck. She winked.

"What?" I managed to say. "Wait? How? I thought you didn't approve of Wyatt. I thought he was unreliable."

Across the scrubby plain, Wyatt's horse was closing the distance fast. Erin's eyes went serious. She glanced away from me. "I did think that." She looked at Wyatt, expression speculative. "I have more information now."

Erin turned her horse, stirring the big gelding into a brisk trot of his own. "He wants to talk to you." And without further explanation, she was riding away.

So Sally and I were sitting beneath the gnarled tree as Wyatt rode up. I hadn't seen him in nearly three weeks but that didn't stop my body from coming alive at the sight of him. A flood of things I'd been trying not to think about poured into my mind—Wyatt on the balcony, sipping the mediocre glass of wine, Wyatt in the hallway, letting the door to the stairwell swing shut so he could wrap his arms around me while I kissed him, Wyatt in the sprawling white bed, sleepy, after we'd kept each other up for most of the night.

I felt a flood of overwhelming emotion. Desire and longing mixed with pain and uncertainty. I glanced after Erin, as if she could somehow explain, but she and Duke were already far away. She'd opened him up into a canter and was letting him rocket back towards the ranch.

So I sat there, waiting. Erin rode away from me as Wyatt approached.

At last, he was there. His horse's hooves thudded as he topped the rise and slowed. He stopped a few feet away. The horse was one I'd never seen before—a red dun with good bone and square, correct conformation. I noted the light sweat all over the horse's body and the fact he still moved with plenty of energy. They hadn't come far. Where on earth had they started?

Wyatt was looking at me. I realized I'd been avoiding looking at him. I raised my eyes to his face. I had expected to find a smirk there, or maybe a smug smile. Instead, I saw something far more complicated. Fear? Longing? I couldn't tell. But whatever was in Wyatt's face, it was intense.

"Nora." He let his reins droop as his horse settled to a stop. "Will you ride with me?"

Chapter 13

We didn't talk as we rode. As soon as I agreed to go with him, Wyatt turned his horse and trotted back the way he'd come. His horse moved out with a lively gait. Again, I wondered where they could have come from. There was nothing out here except scrub desert, mountains, and the ridgeline with a subdivision on the other side.

I followed Wyatt. There was distinct tension in the set of his shoulders. I knew him well enough to see whatever was going on was important to him. So I followed, biting back all the things I might have said about his disappearance and his failure to respond to the text I'd sent him a few days after I came back to Tucson.

We were trotting along single file, not talking, when my phone rang. I was wearing my chinks with pockets on the thighs. I reached in and pulled out my phone.

The photo of Jay in the folding chair occupied my screen as Wyatt slowed his horse to a walk and looked over his shoulder. "Sorry," I said. "I should take this."

Wyatt nodded and faced forward again. I eased Sally to a walk and answered the call.

"Nora," Jay's voice came through the phone, crisp and businesslike. "I'm not good at the thing where I let people down easily so I'm going to tell it to you straight. The TruGlide Corporation has decided not to renew your contract."

I felt my stomach give a strange dip and lurch. I blinked, staring at Wyatt's broad back and the landscape beyond him. I felt suddenly and deeply offended. Of course, I had already decided I wasn't going to continue in my role as the TruGlide Girl. But I had expected them to offer to hire me in a more permanent capacity. I felt the sting of rejection, though Jay was only responding to what I had known all along. I didn't want to be the TruGlide Girl.

I swallowed, pushing my wounded feelings to the side. My father had always taught me the things we do when our pride is stung are the things we most often regret. He meant that in reference to working with horses but I found it applied pretty well to life as a whole.

I took in a slow breath. "What about Snoopy?"

Ahead of me, Wyatt had his head cocked, as if he wanted to stop and listen but knew he should not.

Jay's answer came in that same firm, clipped tone. "After reviewing the recommendations of three vets, we have decided he's not fit to continue in his current position."

My heart seized as Jay spoke. Was this good news? Or bad? What would they do with Snoopy if he couldn't perform the way Jay had intended him to? "We were hoping," Jay went on, "you would keep him at the Tipped Z as you offered and continue to work on his training so that he can appear at TruGlide events in a non-riding capacity. We feel Snoopy will make a good brand ambassador outside the performance arena. His presence at the booth in *Start the Horse, Connect the Heart* was a very effective draw. We've discussed possibly offering pony rides to children, or other light work, if and when we all agree he's ready for that kind of task."

I closed my eyes for a brief moment, relief coursing through me in a warm flood. Jay was not going to throw Snoopy to the wolves. He was taking my advice, relayed to him through Clint. Which was to take advantage of Snoopy's looks and make him into a gorgeous horse that was safe and approachable.

Sure, he wasn't quite there yet. Snoopy's ground manners were good when his handler was competent but could devolve into pushiness around less experienced people. Still, it sounded like Jay had listened to everything my brother had told him, including the idea the horse would need to stay in regular training to make and keep his manners impeccable.

I opened my eyes again. Wyatt was still there, his horse moving along at a steady walk. "Thank you, Jay." I said the words quietly.

Jay's response was predictable. "The horse represents a considerable investment for the TruGlide Corporation. Our market assessment indicates we couldn't sell him for a fraction of what he cost to acquire. We are doing what we can to make the most of a bad situation."

I listened to Jay's explanation. Was he really that heartless? Or was it all part of the persona? I 'd never seen Jay when he wasn't wearing one mask or other. Right now he was the marketer, the agent to whom the only valid reason for making a decision came down to the bottom line.

"Well," I said, "you can make his story public and put a nice altruistic spin on it all. That will be good for the company image, I'm sure."

Jay paused. There was a silence. It was so long, I wondered if the call had dropped. Reception wasn't reliable out here in the middle of nowhere. I pulled my phone away from my face to glance at it, but the line was still connected.

I put the phone back to my ear and waited. When Jay spoke again, his voice was both more personal and more strained. "I was sorry to hear about you and Ted," he said. "And I hope it's not too much of a disappointment your contract won't be renewed. I hope we can still work together without friction as far as Snoopy is concerned."

I found myself suddenly holding back the urge to laugh. The reality was sinking in. I didn't have to quit being the TruGlide Girl because Jay had relieved me of that responsibility. And I didn't have to worry about what would become of Snoopy anymore because he was going to remain in my care. The ranch wouldn't even lose the $2000 a month board deal.

"Jay," I said, "I was going to quit."

When Jay spoke again, I thought I heard a smile in his voice. "I know, Nora." Then he added, "I gotta run. We'll be in touch."

Wyatt turned around as I slid my phone back into my chinks pocket. He tipped an eyebrow at me. "Anything wrong?"

I laughed, unable to help myself. "I lost my job." Saying the words out loud made me so happy, I found myself grinning.

An answering grin lit Wyatt's face. He looked ahead. "I must admit, I'm glad." I remembered the way he'd had the TruGlide website open on the tack room computer, his words that day. *They do you an injustice.*

I hadn't been able to fully admit to myself at the time what Wyatt had been trying to say. But as he pushed his horse back into a long trot and Sally and I moved out to follow him, I looked around. Riding here, though the scrub mesquites and sage, it was impossible to miss his meaning.

I wasn't cut out for bling, for crowds, for sliding stops. My strength was in the land, in the horse that moved beneath me, healthy and sound because she'd been started in a way that would give her a long, useful life of working cattle and covering open country.

We trotted on. Wyatt was following the trail Erin and I had ridden a few days before. We moved steadily closer to the edge of the Tipped Z's land. After a while, I couldn't hold the silence. "Whose horse?"

Wyatt glanced over his shoulder. I could see a look of shy pride on his face. "Mine." He reached down to pet the creamy red neck. "My grandfather bred him. I started him when he was three. He's five now. This is his first time leaving Prescott."

I blinked in surprise. I knew Wyatt's grandfather had a little land in Prescott but hadn't realized Wyatt kept horses there.

"He looks good."

It was true. The horse was moving with good energy, his stride long and balanced, his manner alert but not edgy.

Wyatt said nothing but I could see the pleasure in the set of his shoulders. "It's the first time I ever really kept one, tried to keep bringing him along, you know?"

I did know. Wyatt was about beginnings. Following through had never been his strong suit.

We lapsed back into silence. Soon the path meandered upwards. We reached the place where the ghost of the trail Erin had asked me about headed away towards the fence and the empty land beyond. Wyatt headed down that trail.

Mystified, I followed. We walked along single file. Again I noted the signs of recent traffic. More and more, I couldn't understand what was going on here.

We followed the trail as it headed down the slope. The fence came into view. I saw a shiny new gate set into the old wire.

Wyatt's nerves were back now. I could see the tension in his shoulders, the set of his jaw. But there was also a growing excitement in his body-language. He stepped his horse up to the gate, which had a horse-friendly latch, and swung it open, stepping his horse in a neat side-pass to open the way. I rode Sally through. Wyatt shut the gate behind me.

We were no longer on the Tipped Z's land. This stretch of desert had once belonged to the Rocking J—the ranch that had belonged to Wyatt's family. But it had been sold. As far as I knew, we were now trespassing.

"Wyatt?" I said, glancing around in nervous confusion.

But Wyatt moved his horse back into a trot. "Just a little way now." He glanced back, expression pleading.

There was nothing else for it. I followed.

The trail was now so faint as to be nearly nonexistent. It dipped through a wash and up the other side, then looped around a cluster of ancient boulders. In the distance I saw the low ridge that had the subdivision on the other side.

We rounded the boulders. If I had been walking, I would have stopped short in surprise. As it was, Sally felt my body go tense. There was a brief hitch in her trot. I forced my seat to relax. She moved out again.

There was a driveway here—freshly grooved into the desert, winding to pass over the terrain and avoid the mesquites. And the driveway led to a low adobe structure that had been hidden by the boulders.

The house was old. The adobe had that rounded look of masonry that's seen a lot of weather. But the main structure was surrounded by things that were not old. There was a pipe corral, new paint glittering in the sun. There was what looked to me like a new patio and a covered parking arena under which sat Wyatt's truck and a battered two-horse trailer. The yard had a raw, unrefined look to it. There was a heap of old windowpanes stacked next to a garbage can and some rusted out objects that were too far decayed to be identifiable.

Wyatt rode onto the driveway and stopped his horse. I brought Sally to halt beside him. I was too surprised, too confused, to understand. "What is this place?"

Wyatt reached down to rub his horse's neck. His horse was showing the faintest hint of a restless desire to get back to the corral, where a fresh pile of hay sat waiting. "When my grandfather had to sell the ranch, this was all he could save. It was his house when he was young. He lived here before the family moved closer down towards the main roads and built the house I grew up in. He parceled the land and kept twenty acres and the house. He gave them to me when I turned 18."

I stared at the little house. The windows glittered in the sun. They looked brand new.

Wyatt was still talking. "The only thing he couldn't get was an easement. The developers wouldn't negotiate because they didn't want their plans for the subdivision to be dictated by someone else's road. My grandfather figured I could come in from the Tipped Z side."

I looked at Wyatt as the pieces of the puzzle clicked into place. He held my gaze, speaking as if he was trying to convince me of an important truth. "And your father would have let me punch in a driveway, sure. But I didn't want that. I didn't want to have to drive across another man's land to get to my own home."

I nodded. It might have seemed silly to someone else, but I understood.

"Besides," Wyatt continued, backing his horse up a few steps then walking him forward and stopping again so the young gelding settled, "by the time it came to me, no one had lived here for decades. The place was a shell. I didn't have the means or the opportunity to make it livable."

I looked at all the signs of recent progress and remembered the giant check Wyatt had received when he'd won *Start the Horse, Connect the*

Heart. I'd been standing there next to him when the event sponsor had written his name on the "to" line.

"Your winnings."

I stared at the little house. It had a cozy look. Though the subdivision wasn't far, the ridge blocked those houses from view, giving the place a secluded feel.

"That's right." Wyatt was grinning now. "I bought a right-of-way from the developer and punched in the driveway. I've been here, fixing it up, ever since."

Wyatt's last comment made something turn a little cold and hard inside of me. I stared at the house, feeling lonely in a way I never had before. Wyatt and I had always shared a certain sense of displacement. The Tipped Z was my brother's domain. Wyatt had lost his dream of one day taking over the Rocking J. But now it turned out Wyatt had had a place all along. He'd just never told me.

I looked down, gazing at the hard, scraped dirt beneath Wyatt's horse's hooves. "I guess you've been too busy spending your new cash to answer text messages."

The comment popped out before I could stop myself. Wyatt turned. Some of the tension had left his shoulders but it came back now. He looked at me, hurt in his eyes. He dismounted, setting a hand on the gelding's neck. "I wanted to show you," he said. "I thought if you could see, if you could ride here straight from the Tipped Z and take in this place with your own eyes, then maybe ..."

He trailed off. I sat on Sally, not ready to step down.

Maybe what?

I waited. Wyatt didn't continue. I looked from him to the house and back again. "I don't understand," I said. "Wyatt, why did you bring me here?" The words came out sounding cold and hard. That always seemed to happen when I was confused.

Wyatt seemed to deflate. He looped his reins over his saddle horn and pulled his get-down out of his belt. His gelding sighed. When Wyatt spoke, his voice sounded crushed. "When you wouldn't ride back with me," he said, "I knew it was going to happen all over again. I tried to convince myself this time was different. But I guess I should have known better. I thought if I had something real to offer you, something solid, it might make a difference."

I stared at Wyatt as if he'd grown a second head. What was he talking about? "This time?" I echoed. "What was going to happen all over again?"

Wyatt looked up. There was something dark and maybe a little angry in his eyes. There was also that intensity. I felt a surge of energy snake through my body as our gazes connected.

"Are you serious?" Wyatt's voice carried a hardness that startled me. "Are you really going to sit there and pretend you don't know what I'm saying? I'm talking about *us*, Nora. I'm talking about this thing that happens. I'm talking about the way I come back, thinking maybe this time you'll give me a chance. And then its weeks of you going cold and stiff every time I walk into a room. And then, gradually, of something changing. It's that look you give me sometimes, little hints, little things that make me hope. But then, every time, right when I think we're getting somewhere, you pull the rug out from under me."

I blinked, furiously trying to figure out what he meant.

Me pulling the rug out from under him?

"Wait." I put a hand to my head. I felt dizzy. It was if the world had tilted and now everything was on the wrong axis. "I pull the rug out from under you? How can you say that when you're the one who's always leaving?"

Wyatt looked as if I'd slapped him across the face. The woozy feeling increased. I decided I should get off Sally before I fell.

As I stepped down, Wyatt stared. "Nora," he said, "every time I've left it's because you've all but told me to go."

I looped my reins up and walked around Sally so only a few feet of new driveway separated me and Wyatt. I was beyond confused. I was also too tired for this. I rubbed my forehead. "What are you talking about?"

Wyatt held up one finger. "First, there was the time you said you'd never date a cowboy."

I blinked. I remembered the night he was referring to. It had been a long, long time ago. I'd just turned 18. Wyatt had only recently begun his wandering ways. He'd headed up to the Babbitt Ranch for the summer to start some colts there. When he'd come back, I had felt, for the first time, that Wyatt might be looking at me in a different way. The tension had built between us, day after day. Then, one night, he'd come out of the barn as I'd pulled in after a night out with friends. He'd asked me if I'd had fun. I'd bragged about the college crowd I'd started to run with. I remembered telling him about all the intelligent guys I'd been meeting.

And he was right. I could remember the giddy rush of speaking those words. "One thing I know now is I'll never date a cowboy." I'd been trying to make myself seem sexy and important, trying to imply I ran in desirable circles.

I'd been trying to make him want me more.

But apparently, I'd gone too far. Wyatt had been gone the next morning, turning down the job my father offered him.

As I stood in stunned silence, Wyatt listed other times. There was the time I pretended not to see him when he'd come into a bar and I'd been out with my friends. (I'd been embarrassed about the friends, actually, and afraid they'd all fall in love with him.) There was the way I'd pick up the phone and call for Clint before Wyatt even had a chance to say hello. There was time after time I had pushed Wyatt away without meaning to.

"And most recently," Wyatt said, "there was the insignificant matter of your engagement to another man."

I stood next to Sally, the world feeling more tilted than ever. When he laid it all out like that, it did sound pretty awful. But I had done everything I'd done to defend myself because Wyatt had always rejected me first. Hadn't he?

There was a long silence. Next to me, Sally blew out a long breath and cocked her hip. The sun was beginning to set. Wyatt was looking at me. The anger had faded. Now he seemed full of a dull disappointment. "I know you've never felt the same way about me as I've always felt about you. It's why I can never stay. It hurts me too much to be near you." He spoke in a quiet monotone. "I thought things changed in Oklahoma. I guess I was wrong."

I looked again at the adobe house. As the light faded, I saw the windows were glowing with a faint, dancing light. Had Wyatt lit candles in there? It seemed like a fire hazard to leave them unattended for so long.

I shook myself, trying to focus, trying to process what Wyatt was saying.

Was this real? Had Wyatt just said he left because it hurt to be near me?

"No," I said, fumbling towards understanding as the sun began to spill golden light onto the distant mountains. Wyatt's shoulders sank further. "No," I said again. "I mean, no, this is all wrong. You're the one who isn't interested in me. You're the one who's always hurting my feelings, always crushing my hopes. I'm the one in love with you, hopelessly, against the odds. I'm the one who's always trying to convince myself you care, only to be disappointed."

Wyatt straightened, turning to look at me with a sudden spark in his eyes. Feeling giddy, I recited my own litany. The way he would disappear every time it seemed things between us might have turned real. The way he always avoided me to instead seek out my brother's company. And most importantly, how he never, ever stayed.

When I finished, Wyatt was staring at me as if I'd just walked past a burning bush carrying a stack of stone tablets. He blinked several times and let out a long, low groan. For a moment, he closed his eyes.

When he opened them again, there was a light in them. Wyatt said, "Nora, will you come inside?"

They were candles, but they were electric. They were clever mimics of real candles, with flame-shaped bulbs that flickered and dimmed in a remarkable imitation of firelight. They were set out in a ring around a tablecloth on a freshly laid wood floor. At the center of the cloth was a basket.

It was nearly dark outside. We'd untacked the horses and turned them out in the corral, placing our saddles in a little shed with old walls and a new roof. We'd tended to the horses without speaking. But the silence between us had been one of harmony. At last, I'd followed Wyatt across the scruffy yard. He'd pushed open the door.

The interior of the house was unfinished. The floor and windows were new and complete but there were no baseboards, no switch-plates, and no furniture of any kind. The place smelled of sawdust and paint.

Our boots echoed on the floor as Wyatt led me into the large, empty expanse of the living room. A kitchen stood at one end, new appliances glittering in the low light. "I've been saving for a long time," Wyatt said. His voice was low. "I didn't want to start here until I could finish. My winnings made it all possible. Now it's down to the finishing touches. And furniture." He gave a low, self-conscious laugh.

We started across the floor together. When we reached the blanket, he settled down to sit cross-legged, producing a bottle of wine and two mismatched ceramic mugs from behind the basket. He gave me a rueful smile. "I don't have much by way of dishes, either."

I sat as well. I felt I was in some strange, suspended reality. The candles threw a soft, dancing light across the walls and floor. The room felt large and pure. It was a nice house—modest and practical. I tried to picture Wyatt here, hanging up his hat after a long day. It worked.

Wyatt handed me a mug of wine. We clinked rims but neither of us identified what we were toasting. My hand was shaky as I raised the mug to my lips. Wyatt reached into the basket and pulled out a simple meal—cold chicken, a tossed salad, and fresh rolls. He set this out and loaded a plate for me.

I watched in silence, trying to come to terms with everything he'd said in the yard. As he finished preparing the plates, I couldn't help but ask. "Was it true, what you said out there?"

He looked up, setting the food aside. In the dim light, our eyes caught and held. He seemed to consider the question, mulling it over as if it was a trick. At last, he took a sip of wine and spoke. "Do you remember the day your brother hit me?"

I thought back, trying to recall. It sounded familiar, but I couldn't call up a specific memory.

"We were fifteen, I think," Wyatt said. "You had a group of girls over. You were all getting ready to go to a little dance or something, up at the school. Me and Clint were by the barn, coming in from a ride. We saw you all come out and climb into the car. You'd all tried so hard to make yourselves look nice. Without even thinking, I said, 'Nora sure is the prettiest.' I didn't mean how you looked then, in your dress and make-up and heels. I was thinking of you on a horse, or throwing a rope, or squinting into the sun."

Wyatt paused, a grim smile forming on his mouth. "Your brother misunderstood, I guess. He hit me. Twice. Once here, once here." He tapped his jaw on one side of his head, his temple on the other. "He hit me hard. I'd never been hit like that, never by someone who really meant it. I went down, stunned, and your brother stood there and looked at me lying in the dirt. He said, 'Don't you think of my sister that way.' Then he walked off."

I stared at Wyatt in stunned silence. I remembered the day now, remembered the excitement of getting ready. I also remembered how I'd been distracted through the entire afternoon with my friends, knowing Wyatt was out riding with Clint and there was a chance he might see me before I left. I also remembered my mother backing the car out, turning, and gasping when she saw Wyatt on his knees in the driveway, my brother standing over him like a furious scarecrow.

My mother rolled down the window. "Boys," she snapped. "What's going on?"

My brother walked off as if he hadn't heard her. A moment later, Wyatt had struggled back to his feet, waved at my mother, and jogged off after Clint.

My mother sighed, rolled up the window, and said, "Teenagers." As if it was perfectly normal for her son to deck his best friend in an inexplicable show of violent temper.

Now, Wyatt let out a long, slow sigh. "After that," he said, "you were another thing I couldn't have—like the Rocking J or a father who wasn't always trying to change me into something else. But like those other things, I never got over the wanting."

For a moment, the sheer ridiculousness of it washed over me. It was a farce. How many years had we wasted, never being honest with each other? I rubbed a hand across my face, embarrassed to have been so wrong for so long. "We're such idiots."

Wyatt laughed. When I dropped my hand, he had moved. All of a sudden, he was close. He spoke in a low, urgent tone. "We're the same, Nora," he said. "We both want to ride, we want to ranch, we feel loyalty to this land, we want to help your brother, we want to be here." He trailed off, gazing at me hopefully.

"But we want to do it on our own terms." I finished the thought for him.

Wyatt's face was serious in the low light. "And together," he said, "we can."

As he spoke those words, I leaned forward. "Together," I murmured.

And then he was leaning too. My lips met his. At his touch, heat flowed through my body like a slow flame. I gave a little gasp as his hand reached around the nape of my neck.

He pulled me closer. His mouth was warm and his hand was warm and I was reasonably certain I had never been so happy in my entire life.

The kiss lasted for a long time. Finally, I pulled back, unable to contain a small chuckle. "What?" I could feel Wyatt's lips curl into a smile.

"I can't believe my brother punched you for me. I never knew he was so protective."

Wyatt sighed and sat back, rubbing his jaw in mock remembrance. "I could hardly talk for a week."

We both laughed. I felt the happiness peak and bloom inside me. I wanted Wyatt and Wyatt wanted me. It was like seeing color after decades of living in a black and white world.

Wyatt rose to his feet, stooping to pick up his wine and offering me his other hand. "I find myself less hungry for dinner than expected." His voice was a little lower than usual. "Would you like to see what I've done with the master suite?"

Wyatt set his hand on my knee, placing it there with a kind of casual familiarity that made my heart skitter and bounce with adrenaline. Across the coffee table, Erin was staring at us with that suspended look she got on her face right before she exploded with a contained emotion. Clint stood behind Erin's chair, his face as unreadable as a blank page.

"So," Wyatt continued, "in short, I'd like to take you up on your offer of employment and a stake in the ranch." He paused, adding, "If it's still on the table, that is."

Wyatt and I were at my brother's house. It was the morning following our living room picnic. After our night on the double air mattress Wyatt had set up on the floor of the otherwise empty bedroom, I was more than a little tired. But my lost sleep hadn't had anything to do with the bed. Wyatt and I had been up nearly the whole night, alternating between discussing plans for the future and ... well ... doing other things.

This morning, we'd saddled up our horses and ridden over to the Tipped Z. I filled Clint in on my lost job and what was to become of Snoopy. Next, Wyatt explained about his little house and his acreage that separated the Tipped Z from the subdivision. We'd also presented ourselves as a couple.

I'd spent the whole morning feeling utterly giddy. Now, as I watched my brother's face, I felt some of my elation fade. Clint did not look happy. The more we talked, the more he seemed the opposite of happy.

At last, Wyatt stopped. I watched my brother, feeling my high hopes sink. What if it was too late? What if Clint had done something drastic, like lease land to another rancher or sell it off entirely? I knew things had been tight around here financially in recent months. I'd always thought Clint would tell me before he resorted to extreme measures.

I thought of what Erin had told me—my brother's description of his best friend. *Wyatt isn't reliable.*

"But," Wyatt continued, "I don't want to work here full time. I'm going to keep starting colts. I'll do it here, though, without traveling. I'll bring them to my place, and use them on the ranch. I can help get your backlog going under saddle as well."

Something in my brother's face seemed to loosen as Wyatt spoke. He gave a small nod. "Half time," he said. "And you sign a three-year contract, stake in the ranch pending your uninterrupted presence here at the Tipped Z."

I looked at Wyatt, certain he'd be offended. But, to my surprise, Wyatt was smiling. He stood up and stepped forward. He and my brother shook. "I know you think I can't stay in one place," Wyatt said as their hands separated. "I'm going to prove you wrong."

Then, shockingly, Clint smiled as well. Something in his face seemed to break open. He smiled like I hadn't seen in months—not since his wedding, perhaps. He sank into a chair as if the strength had gone out of him. If I'd ever seen someone so clearly relieved, I couldn't remember when.

A little curl of guilt washed through me at the sight.

It was my turn.

"I'm not going back to Old Pueblo, either." I said. "I've got Snoopy to look after and I'll be here every day to help in whatever other ways I can."

Clint looked up at me. As our eyes met, the gratitude I saw there was almost overwhelming. "You have to help me train my dog, though," I said. "I don't know the first thing about getting him hooked onto cattle."

Clint gave another small nod as Erin shifted, sitting a little forward in her seat. "We're glad to hear this." Some little tremor in her voice made me look up at her. She was looking at her husband and her face had taken on a questioning look.

I saw something strange come into my brother's face—an expression I'd never seen there before. One of warmth and love but also something I couldn't identify. Terror, maybe?

"We have some news for you, too," he said. Then my brother resumed his characteristic silence.

Erin was the one who explained, looking at me with huge, excited eyes. "We're expecting," she said. "So I'm not going to be as much help around here before too long." Then she gave a small, disbelieving laugh.

I jumped up. Erin rose as well. I wrapped my arms around my sister-in-law and twirled her around the room. Wyatt laughed. Even Clint gave a chuckle. "Thank heavens," I said. "It's about time someone around here started thinking about the next generation of Tipped Z caretakers."

I set Erin down. Wyatt came over to shake Clint's hand again. Then he came to me. He slipped an arm around my shoulders. He pressed a kiss to my forehead.

I looked at these three people—my brother, his best friend, his wife. I'd spent so long trying to separate myself from the ranch, trying to establish my independence. What I hadn't realized was there are two ways to be a part of something.

There was the way I'd been part of the TruGlide Corporation. I'd been a tool, a device, a face with no brain behind it. I'd resisted committing to the ranch for so long because I was afraid I would feel trapped.

But there was another way to be part of something. You could choose to be there, to fill a role that fits you, that was made for you, that has been waiting for you to step up and fill it since the day you were born.

We stood that way for a few minutes, the four of us feeling our individual variations of the same emotions. Outside, a cactus wren cackled and a covey of quail scuttled from the shadow of one mesquite to another. For nearly a whole minute, we were silent.

Then Clint said, "So, Wyatt. About those colts."

Exclusive Short Story

This is the end of Nora and Wyatt's love story. Although they appear as characters in later books in the series, they're no longer in the spotlight.

There is a 30-page short story you might enjoy, though! It exists in the form of a story called *Thrown* which reveals a secret link between the first book in this series, *A Man Who Rides* and this book, *A Man Who Starts*.

Thrown is available only to members of my mailing list!

If you want to check it out, please visit:
stefaniwilder.com/clintanderin

About the Author

Growing up in Tucson, Arizona, Stefani always hoped to marry a cowboy. She did not. (Instead she married a man who turned into a cowboy, but that's a story for another day.) She has always loved to write stories and ride horses, and now frequently writes stories about riding horses (and falling in love.)

Stefani Wilder is a pen name for Robin Stephen.

Please visit one of her websites for more details:

- stefaniwilder.com
- robinstephen.com

A Man Who Heals

Tipped Z: Book #3

Stefani Wilder

Though she spent most of the rare happy moments of her childhood at a ranch camp, Jordan never thought there was space for horses (or cowboys) in her adult life.

Jordan thinks she's doing pretty well. She survived childhood with an abusive mother. Now she's holding down a job and getting herself through the day-to-day slog of modern living. But her only social outlet is an online game where her partner is a horse named after the one she lost as a kid.

Jordan is well aware racking up so many hours in a fantasy world isn't exactly healthy; her brother is constantly hounding her to get out more. When another player in the game starts making friendly overtures, she can even concede this might be a bad sign. So when an ad pops up in her work queue about a ranch offering riding lessons, she decides she needs a new outlet. She heads to the Tipped Z, where she meets her instructor, Erin, and a ranch hand named Grant.

Grant proves to be interesting, and not just because he seems potentially interested in her. Though he's clearly a cowboy, he mysteriously refuses to get on a horse. When Jordan sets out to figure out why, she realizes she's going to have to deal with some of her own unaddressed trauma if she wants things with Grant to evolve.